like always

like always

a novel

Robert Elmer

WATERBROOK
PRESS

LIKE ALWAYS
PUBLISHED BY WATERBROOK PRESS
12265 Oracle Boulevard, Suite 200
Colorado Springs, Colorado 80921
A division of Random House Inc.

Most Scripture quotations are taken from the Holy Bible, King James Version.

Some Scripture quotations are taken from the Holy Bible, New International Version®.
NIV®. Copyright © 1973, 1978, 1984 by International Bible Society. Used by permission of Zondervan Publishing House. All rights reserved.

The characters and events in this book are fictional, and any resemblance to actual persons or events is coincidental.

ISBN 978-1-4000-7165-4

Library of Congress Cataloging-in-Publication Data
Elmer, Robert.
  Like always / Robert Elmer. — 1st ed.
    p. cm.
  ISBN 978-1-4000-7165-4
  1. Middle age—Fiction. I. Title.
  PS3555.L44L55 2007
  813'.54—dc22

                              2007001524

Printed in the United States of America
2007—First Edition

9 8 7 6 5 4 3 2 1

Til min Mor

one

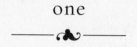

*I know God will not give me anything I can't handle. I just
wish that He didn't trust me so much.*

MOTHER TERESA

Sorry!"

Merit Sullivan pressed the accelerator to the floor and held her breath as
her minivan shot through the tail end of a yellow light. *Okay, red,* she admitted it.

Colored lights flashed in her rearview mirror, and a police officer on a
motorcycle materialized behind her.

"Perfect."

Her cheeks flushed crimson and her mouth went dry as she maneuvered
to the shoulder of Oak Grove Road, the motorcycle cop pulling up behind
her. The light had turned red a half second before she flashed into the intersection, but it had to help that she'd never received a ticket before. The piercing blue lights sliced their way into her head, and Merit felt the twinge of a
budding headache. She closed her eyes and tried to breathe slowly.

"Driver's license and registration, please?"

Merit jumped and looked at the helmeted officer stooped by her window. She fumbled through her purse, prospecting for her wallet. By the time
she found it, she'd built a small pile of lipsticks, her checkbook, expired grocery coupons, mints, and tissues on the passenger seat, none of which would
interest the waiting policeman. Meanwhile, her tongue had cemented itself
to the roof of her mouth.

Finally she was able to hand over her California driver's license. Thank
the Lord it wouldn't expire until her forty-fifth birthday next year.

"Your registration?"

"Oh yes. Of course." She pulled at the visor above her head, and an envelope from the insurance company fluttered to her lap. "My husband, Will, usually takes care of that kind of thing. I'm sure it's here, though." She handed him the envelope.

"Yes ma'am." He glared at her from behind the traditional cop sunglasses and fished out the little certificate he needed. Well, that was good. "Do you know why I stopped you?"

"I think so."

She pressed her lips together so they wouldn't quiver and fought back the sudden urge to cry. She slid down in her seat, in case someone she knew drove by.

By this time the policeman had retreated to his motorcycle, perhaps to see if she had stolen her minivan or if she was wanted for murder. Merit popped a mint into her mouth to calm herself and prayed for mercy, knowing she didn't deserve it for a minute—except that she'd never... Well, she'd already covered that excuse.

Still his glacier-blue lights encircled her poor car, needling her eyes every time the lights glanced off the rearview mirror. Couldn't he turn them off now? She shivered and choked down the mint, waiting for her sentence and trying to ignore the cool March wind whenever it found its way inside her car. Maybe it would rain again before Easter. Or maybe the officer would make her wait on the side of the road until the Fourth of July.

Finally she heard the squawk of his police radio as he stepped toward the minivan and passed her license and registration back through her open window.

"I probably shouldn't do this," he began, "but I'm going to let you go with a warning this time, Mrs. Sullivan."

Please feel free, she thought, sagging back against her seat. *That's quite all right.*

"Thank you," she managed, "I—"

"Only let's not be in such a hurry, okay? Wherever you're going, you're not going to get there faster by causing an accident."

"Yes sir."

She nodded stiffly, willing him away, but he paused a moment before peering over his sunglasses.

"And tell Will hello for me."

Merit thought she saw the slightest hint of a grin on his lips. Without making it look too obvious, she tried to read the man's little silver name badge, but he turned away before she could make out his name and walked back to his waiting motorcycle.

Who was he? Will knew him, obviously. A friend from Rotary, maybe. Someone he'd met at work. Not anyone from church, since the policeman would have known her too. But then again, it would be easy to miss the couple who only managed to show up for the late service once a month.

She started her vehicle, clicked her seat belt in place, and checked the side mirror like a careful driver. Then she hit her left turn signal and waited for a hole to open in traffic. How long had she been sitting on the side of the road? Ten minutes? An hour? Will had to be wondering what had happened to her, but why hadn't he—

Her cell phone's voice mail alert beeped, announcing that someone *had* tried to call—probably in the middle of all the excitement. Keeping an eye on her rearview mirror and holding her speed ten miles under the posted limit, Merit punched in the voice mail code before hitting the Speakerphone option.

"Hey, honey." Her husband's husky voice sounded nearly out of breath. "It's four fifteen and I'm just passing Lafayette. Sales meeting went long. Bruce started making a big stink about quotas again, and I couldn't get out of there the way I'd hoped. Typical. Just tell Fred to hang on, and I'll be there before you know it. Love you."

Merit slowed as she approached the next intersection, her foot hovering over the brake pedal, anticipating a yellow light. Will might arrive the same time she did. Even later, perhaps. And judging by the lineup of red lights stretching down the avenue in front of her, that wouldn't be any time soon.

"This has to be some kind of sign," she said to herself. But she was afraid to check with the Lord, considering what they were about to do. Where she came from, red lights meant "stop and wait."

She stopped and waited six times before pulling into the parking lot at Fred Gribbon & Associates. As she found an open space, she scanned the parking lot for Will's forest green Land Rover, but there was no sign of it.

What else could she do but gather and replace the contents of her purse, check the mirror to see how badly her makeup had smudged, and head for the office? She even thought of a nice way to apologize to Fred—an explanation that neatly left out any mention of her scrape with the law, blazing blue lights, or husbands who hated their jobs.

As it turned out, though, she needn't have worried. Belinda, the office receptionist, looked up from filing her nails and flashed a well-rehearsed smile as Merit stepped inside.

"Mr. Gribbon called to say he'd be here by four thirty," Belinda said. The clock on the wall behind her desk showed ten minutes shy of that time. "You can wait for him in the conference room, if you like. Can I get you some coffee?"

Merit declined with thanks and a wave. She was far beyond the reach of coffee. This day called for a nice, hot bath topped by a layer of bubbles to hide beneath until her skin pruned. But that would have to wait.

In the meantime, she found a place in the firm's old-fashioned, walnut-paneled conference room, the brown vinyl chair wheezing comfortably under her trim frame. She gazed at the framed scenic photos of Mount Diablo which, judging by how faded they looked, had probably been taken about the same time Fred Gribbon moved into this office more than twenty years ago.

She winced and closed her eyes. That headache again.

A few minutes later, Will's quiet chuckle and the nasal sound of Fred Gribbon's laugh told her that her husband and his uncle had arrived.

"Oh, *there* she is!" Uncle Fred gave her a warm, toothy smile as he breezed in with an armload of folders and a fistful of pink While You Were Out slips. The man probably still used the vintage tan IBM Selectric perched on a corner of his desk. "I hope we didn't make you wait too long."

Entering on his uncle's heels, Will shrugged helplessly and mouthed the words *I'm sorry.*

"Not long at all," Merit replied honestly. She winked at her husband to let him know she was okay. For the most part.

Fred tossed his folders in front of them and deposited himself at the head of the table, then wiped his forehead with a white handkerchief. Who carried handkerchiefs anymore, Merit wondered. He folded it into quarters and replaced it in a shirt pocket before narrowing his eyes and looking from Will to Merit.

"How long have you known me, Merit?"

Merit smiled politely and tossed back the obvious answer. "Twenty-four years this summer, Uncle Fred. You came to our wedding, remember?"

"That's right. And I knew this guy here when he was still a towhead in diapers." Fred clapped Will on the shoulder.

Where was this going? Merit fidgeted in her chair, and Uncle Fred held up a finger for patience.

"All I'm saying, kids…"

Merit held back a smile. Funny how he could call two adults in their midforties "kids" and get away with it.

He took a breath and went on. "All I'm saying is that you've known me a long time, and I've never lied to you or let you down, right?"

Merit nodded, wishing Uncle Fred would get to the point so they could sign the papers and be done with it.

"So as your agent and your friend, I'm advising you not to do this."

She blinked and looked across the table at Will. He returned her gaze for a moment before speaking.

"I appreciate your advice, Fred," he said, leaving off the *uncle,* Merit noticed. "But Merit and I are both agreed on this."

"You prayed about it, I assume."

Will squirmed, the good Lutheran nephew sitting in his Pentecostal uncle's office, the office with a big velvet Jesus portrait adorning the wall by the window.

"Well, sure," Will said. "We always do."

Which was mostly true, Merit thought, if one assumed that the Lord's Prayer recited over breakfast covered this sort of thing.

"And even after you've seen the place," Uncle Fred pushed, "you want to go ahead with this?"

Merit jumped to defend her husband. "Remember, my sister lives there. And Will's wanted to do this kind of thing for…for a long time."

"Just Will?"

Uncle Fred's question hit closer than Merit was willing to admit. Of course, in a do-over she would substitute *we* for *Will,* but they weren't going to get into Will's miserable stress cooker of a sales job right now or his boss who gave him ulcers and called on Sunday nights to chew him out.

"A man's gotta do whatever it takes to keep his family together, right?" Will could defend himself too. Uncle Fred just squinted and studied his nephew.

"You're big kids." Uncle Fred finally smiled. "I just thought I'd ask you one more time before we charge ahead with this whole deal. Kind of my duty."

"Which is why we pay you the big bucks," said Will. "To ask all the right questions."

Uncle Fred chuckled and held up a sheet of paper with a lot of hand-written notes on it.

"All right, then," he told them with a sigh. "The good news is that your offer is way less than what the estate is asking."

That was the good news? He slipped on a pair of half-moon reading glasses, licked his thumb, and riffled through a stack of papers. Merit wondered how many colds were passed from office worker to office worker by people salivating on paperwork.

"So there's a good chance," he continued, pausing to lick his thumb again, "that the executor of that estate is going to laugh this off as a joke."

"If that's the good news, what's the bad news?" Merit allowed herself a modest smile and tried not to worry about germs.

"The bad news? Ha!" By now, Uncle Fred had caught his stride, pulling out forms and stacking them in a neat pile on the table, ready for the ballpoint attack. Belinda had dutifully decorated each one with cheery little pink arrow stickers, so even Merit couldn't mistake where to sign.

"Yeah." Will grinned, picking up a plum-colored "Gribbon & Associades" pen, the word *Associates* misspelled. "What's the bad news?"

The bad news, Merit thought, would be giving up her job working with special-needs kids at the school, even if it was part-time. The bad news would be leaving her friends at the book club. The bad news would be leaving the house she loved, with neighbors she loved even more. The bad news would be...

"The bad news is that even with this ridiculously low offer on a horribly run-down resort in the Middle of Nowhere, Idaho...well, your offer's probably way higher than what it's actually worth."

Some comfort. Merit ignored the pile of pens on the table, fished her own pen out of her purse, and sighed. Really, what other choice did she have at this point?

Oh, what we do for love, she thought.

two

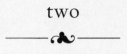

In war, there are no unwounded soldiers.

José Narosky

Airman First Class Michael Sullivan watched out the tiny entry-door window of the plane, waiting for toy buildings to grow and Matchbox cars to morph into snarled freeway traffic. Over the past year he hadn't missed *that* part of the good old USA.

His ears popped, a little tardy this time, as he returned to his seat and the Air Force C-141 transport found its way through fading daylight toward Andrews Air Force Base for a refueling stop. They would need it after their long hop across the Atlantic.

"Coming home, Airman?"

Michael looked over at the man sitting next to him, a master sergeant with several stripes on his shoulder and a regulation crew cut of gray hair. His black name tag read "Gustafson." The guy had snored for nearly the entire flight, chatting with a civilian woman across the aisle when he was awake, ignoring Michael the whole time. With just a few minutes left in the flight, why was he asking the question now?

"Almost, Master Sergeant," Michael answered. He just had to survive another cross-country transport ride to Travis Air Force Base, and then he could probably hitch a ride back to Walnut Creek from there. Simple. Even this close to the end of his journey, Michael would follow military protocol and maintain a polite distance from the officer. From the look of his raised eyebrows, though, the guy wanted the whole story.

"I still have a few more hours before I make it to Travis, actually," Michael continued.

"So you're stationed in California."

"Was once. Now it's my last stop." Michael stifled a yawn. He could count on one hand how many hours he'd slept in the past twenty-four. "My enlistment's up."

As soon as he said it, Michael realized his mistake. He should have kept the last comment to himself.

"You're not reenlisting with the rest of your squad?" The career Air Force officer frowned at him, then looked pointedly at several of the other passengers, all from Michael's squadron. After all, if you weren't a lifer, you weren't much. Not according to this guy.

Michael shrugged. "Thought about it, but…"

But that was no excuse, and Gustafson's dour expression said as much. Even so, Michael had heard it all before, back in Iraq, and it hadn't changed his mind then, either. But the master sergeant seemed to have his own theory on Michael's desertion.

"Let me guess: there's a girl waiting back home." He glanced down at the hand in Michael's lap, looking for a ring.

"Well…" What could he say? "We've been keeping in touch, sort of, while I was stationed over there."

No surprise there. Every airman claimed some kind of love interest, so maybe that would lighten the conversation a bit. And yes, the master sergeant sort of chuckled, like he'd heard that story before, but no, Michael wasn't going to get into a long story about Jessica. Not with a stranger and not when the plane was about to land.

Jessica had as much to do with his decision to come home as anyone did. And he had friends back home, plenty of them. Then there was the strange letter from Will about making his own place in the world, and how you never know how things could change, and that they were thinking about maybe doing something new.

Right. His parents do something new? They'd lived in the same house in

Walnut Creek since before he was born. They would change locations when he became president.

"So what took you overseas?" Gustafson asked, interrupting Michael's thoughts once again as the plane hit a patch of turbulence over a cloud bank and dipped lower.

It was Michael's turn to frown. How did someone who had always wanted to fly end up maintaining trucks and Humvees in Iraq before he…

"732nd Logistic Support Squadron." He gave his official answer. "They sent a bunch of us specialists to a garage at Forward Operating Base Speicher, outside of Tikrit."

There. That kind of combat pedigree finally impressed the other man, whose eyebrows lifted at the mention of the Iraqi hot spot in the heart of a lingering conflict. Michael suppressed a grin at the reaction and decided to milk it a bit more for the story.

"Guess the Army guys needed a little help keeping their Humvees running," he went on, "with all that sand and the IEDs."

"Right." The guy nodded and took it in for a moment. And no, an IED was not some kind of birth control.

"Improvised exploding devices," Michael explained, shaking his head. "Homemade bombs are kind of an everyday thing over there. You learn to deal with it."

"So you *did* like your duty over there. Lots of excitement," Gustafson remarked.

He would have expected the master sergeant to say something like that.

"Not that part. I liked fixing things that were broke. Putting them back in action. I was thinking, when I got back, I could maybe open my own shop, someday…"

Michael let the thought dangle. *Forget it.* The master sergeant didn't really care about his plans, just his war stories.

"So…you saw a lot of those IEDs?" asked Gustafson.

"A few. I don't know. They told us to expect them, especially when they got the bright idea—I mean, when someone decided that they would put Air Force guys like me in as convoy security."

"Security? You're kidding." Now the master sergeant was hooked, and Michael was sure the guy had been stuck behind a desk too long. "I'd heard of that. Wasn't sure they went through with it."

Michael nodded. "Oh yeah. Gave us each a brand-new M-4 rifle, body armor, the works. The Army was hard up for warm bodies who could point a gun, so who do they call?"

That was as much bravado as Michael was prepared to summon. The master sergeant, duly impressed, snapped his jaw shut and seemed to regain his composure as their plane finally touched down, bumped once, and taxied forward.

"So…," Master Sergeant Gustafson ventured, "you ever have to use it?"

Michael knew the guy was just curious. Probably he flew a desk, the kind of noncom who'd never touched a weapon outside the shooting range and who went home to a wife and kids in the Washington suburbs every night. In his place, Michael would have asked the same question, probably. But that didn't make answering it any easier, since he'd stupidly let himself wade into a place he hadn't intended to go.

"Er…use what?" Michael stalled, wishing he knew how to ignore the questions of a master sergeant. It was too late to close his eyes and pretend he was asleep.

"The M-4."

Michael bit his lip and turned his gaze to the window. A drizzle painted sideways streaks across the glass, and he wished to heaven that it didn't suddenly remind him of the private tears he had shed in the quiet of the barracks the night after that first disastrous convoy duty. But the emotions exploded within him, just like the hidden IEDs they'd cursed for the past year and with just as much force. He winced at the pain.

"Some of us had to," he finally mumbled, and that would have to satisfy the curious master sergeant, *sir.*

The plane lurched to a halt and the cabin lights snapped on. Michael breathed a quiet sigh of relief and promised himself to never volunteer that kind of story again.

But the master sergeant paused before standing to get his bag.

"Nice talking to you, Airman," he said. "Good luck going home. That's where you're going, right?"

Michael nodded. "That's right, sir. Wherever that is."

Who did he think he was talking to? The base chaplain? He hadn't meant to say that. It had just slipped out, giving the master sergeant fodder for one last comment.

"One good thing about reenlisting." The master sergeant shrugged into his night-blue official issue coat. "The way I look at it, you don't have to worry about trying to reinvent yourself or waste a lot of time deciding your future every year, 'cause that's somebody else's job."

"I suppose that's true, sir." Michael shook the man's hand and nodded the way he had for the past few years whenever a superior said something that sounded dumb to him.

The worst part was that the master sergeant was probably right.

"And if you never had much family," said Gustafson, "the way I never did, you always have a home in the Air Force."

"Right."

"You think about it, huh? There's always time to change your mind."

Michael actually did think about it. Seriously, even. The part about someone else deciding his future for him? Strangely compelling. And having a family there that always accepted you, understood you, didn't pester you for every little thing? Even better.

He must have looked as if he was really mulling it over, because the master sergeant gave him a smile and a pat on the back. And that was the master sergeant's mistake, since it reminded Michael of the recruiting officer in Walnut Creek who had first signed him up, back when he and Josh Peters had decided they were going to fly airplanes and wear blue uniforms. You bet, said the recruiter. Sign here.

Yeah, and they could give him the next fifty years to change his mind; it wouldn't matter. He stood there as Master Sergeant Gustafson and the rest of the passengers filed off—most of them smiling and chatting, glad to be getting off the airplane for a break. If they weren't in his squadron, maybe they were reporting for duty here in the States after an overseas assignment. Or maybe they had wives or husbands waiting here at Andrews. Good for them.

Michael closed his eyes and leaned against the bulkhead, imagining who might be waiting for *him* back home. He imagined staying well away from sand and dust for a long time to come. Never picking up a gun again, if he could help it. And never again having to point it at a small child with large, frightened eyes in a broken country where…

"We're clearing out the aircraft here, Airman. Wake up and smell the coffee."

Michael opened his eyes as a mechanic hustled through the cabin, toolbox in hand.

"I'm going." He gathered his things: an American news magazine he'd bought at the commissary back at Ramstein Air Base before boarding the plane, his coat, and an unfinished package of Skittles. To tell the truth, coffee didn't sound like a bad idea.

And just to say he'd considered all the angles, he gave a parting thought to what his life would be like if he changed his mind and reenlisted. Did they still want someone who could replace a Humvee engine, ride shotgun on a supply convoy, chew gum, and tote an M-4—all at the same time? If so, they would probably have all the paperwork drawn up and signed before he found a seat on the next westbound flight out of Maryland. Funny how quickly the military could move for that kind of thing.

He looked down at his watch. Almost there. No offense to Master Sergeant Gustafson, but he would go home, or he would find what was left of it. Maybe that was the only way to forget what he had lived through.

three

Deep down in me I knowed it was a lie, and he knowed it. You can't pray a lie—I found that out.
MARK TWAIN, in *The Adventures of Huckleberry Finn*

D o you think he'll look different than when he left?" Merit wondered aloud as they slalomed through traffic on the interstate heading north. Will had that NASCAR-guy look on his face as he weaved into the fast lane, and they headed over the Martinez-Benicia Bridge. Below their wheels, San Francisco Bay mingled with the muddy waters of the Sacramento River Delta, looking a bit too much like yesterday's cappuccino.

"I think we can pretty well count on it." Will gripped the wheel and glanced over the bridge railing toward the river. "Guys don't come back from that kind of duty the same."

Merit wasn't sure what that meant exactly, except that the mother in her wished it weren't so. She checked the backseat to make sure both girls were still sleeping, then slipped her hand over to take hold of the steering wheel, the way she always did on this bridge. Just in case.

Sure enough, she caught them beginning to drift as Will's gaze followed the ships below. She knew how he loved to watch the ships on their way upriver to Sacramento, but this was the impressive Mothball Fleet, dozens of retired old warships and cargo ships, gray destroyers and rusty tankers—a ready reserve fleet awaiting recall or the scrap heap.

"Keep your eye on the road," Merit warned, and Will snapped his attention back to the traffic ahead of them as if he'd been surprised by the sight.

"Sure are some nice old ships out there." He caught one more glance. "Kind of a shame they're just sitting."

"I'm glad they are." She pulled her finger back from the wheel; they'd crossed the bridge. The way she saw it, if those ships were tied up here, they weren't being used for a war, filled with boys like Michael.

They followed the freeway as it veered northeast, leaving miles behind them without another word. Travis Air Force Base lay just ahead, the welcoming ceremony due to start in an hour and a half. Their car radio sputtered stray notes from a classical station nearly out of range, but neither made a move to turn it off or change the setting. Instead, Merit pondered how to welcome home the boy who had become a man. Still her son, but perhaps a stranger now.

His letters over the past year had been few, brief, and to the point. First about the training, the presumed but unwritten destination, then about the machines he fixed, hints about something more dangerous and much darker. Something they'd hear about on the news until she stopped listening.

He'd mentioned a chaplain once in a while, so hopefully he hadn't pulled away completely from his faith, even though he'd never mentioned anything spiritual.

At least he'd never asked about his old girlfriend Jessica, since Merit would have been afraid to answer truthfully. It was better for Michael to find out what she was really like sooner in life rather than later, but not too soon. She'd heard what some boys did over there. Poor, young boys whose girlfriends had broken their hearts with those awful "Dear John" letters.

So much for the Air Force being a "safe" decision. Those people had turned their adopted son into a soldier, a man, and she didn't like it.

"I'm going to ask him," Will said, breaking the silence a few minutes later. Obviously, someone else had been thinking about it too.

Merit knew what he meant. "No, please, Will. You haven't even given him a chance to get off the plane."

"Come on. I think it's the perfect way to get him back, give him a chance to get back to something normal, something with the family again. Give him something to consider, something to fall back on. And every man likes to be offered a job."

"Is that what he is now?" She shook her head, trying to shake her mental picture of little pudgy Michael in the fifth grade, taking apart his bicycle and not being able to get it back together again. He'd thrown the broken chain across the garage, breaking the window, then bawled his eyes out. And now...

On the radio, Tchaikovsky faded into a neighboring station playing the Rolling Stones. Merit reached down and snapped it off.

"I just think you should at least wait until we hear back on the offer," she told Will. A quick glance told her the girls were stirring in the backseat, so she lowered her voice a notch. "You're talking as if it's a done deal, us buying the resort. You know it's not."

Will puffed up his chest as if she'd insulted him. "You don't think anyone else is trying to buy the place, do you?" It was a rhetorical question. "Of course the owners are going to say yes. Eventually. They'd be crazy not to."

"But if they don't?"

"I'm telling you they will. One hundred percent."

"You're making it sound like some kind of...divine revelation or something."

"Divine revelation?" He wrinkled his nose at her. "That doesn't sound very Lutheran to me."

"Honey, it has nothing to do with Lutheran or not. All I'm saying is that—"

"That it's going to be good for our family. And I thought we were both agreed."

"I agreed because I hate to see you so miserable at work. I agreed because your boss is going to give you a heart attack one of these days. I—"

"And you know how much I appreciate your saying *that*."

"But I didn't agree because of..."

Her quick glance at the backseat finished the sentence for her, because of *them*. And neither Abby nor Olivia knew anything about this scheme, not yet. Merit would make sure of it, one more time.

"And you promised not to tell them," she finished.

"I told you I wouldn't, so I won't." Will held up his hand to reveal the scout's honor sign. "Even though I still don't think it's a good idea to keep it a secret. They're going to find out, you know, sooner or later."

"Not if it doesn't happen."

"Oh, thee of little faith."

His boyish grin melted her a couple of degrees, and she yelped when he squeezed her knee. He always did that, didn't he? Made her laugh when he knew he was losing an argument.

Well, she wasn't backing down about not telling the girls. Not until this wild idea had changed from a crazy offer to a firm deal—if it ever did. Until then, there was no way Merit would allow the girls—her two precious girls—to be dragged through the debris of their parents' wild-goose chase.

"Kids are flexible, Merit. You know that. They'll love it."

"Oh, they'll love going to school with all the—"

"Don't say something you'll be sorry for."

"I was going to say the bears and coyotes. Don't they have wild animals up there?"

He smiled but kept his eyes on the road.

"Only friendly ones. You know, Smokey Bear, that kind of thing."

She hit him in the side, not hard. "I'm being serious, Will."

"Mama bears are always serious. And only you can prevent forest fires."

"And about Michael, even though I still think it's going to end up a moot point, if you ask him now, he's going to say no. And even if he doesn't, we don't have the place yet."

"Okay, we're going around in circles now."

"I thought you knew the way to the base."

"Oh, so now you're the silly one." Will pulled up to the base guard post, rolling down his window as he did.

"Promise me, Will. You'll wait to ask him."

He sighed and slumped his shoulders. She hoped that was a yes.

ॐ

"Just like on TV!" Olivia clutched her little American flag and smiled from their spot on the bleachers, where several dozen families sat waiting for the big gray plane to approach. And Merit had to admit, they'd watched this scene unfold before on the six o'clock news: happy reunions as soldiers returned from duty in the Middle East. The obligatory scenes of hugs and kisses, tears and speeches—all to the music of a military brass band.

At their real-life version of the TV event, a conductor in uniform raised his little baton and launched the military band into an energetic version of the Air Force theme. Olivia, their third grader, started to sing along.

"Off we go into the wild blue yonder…"

Will turned to his younger daughter with a question on his face. "How did you know the words to that?"

She sang through the first line, dum-te-dummed a couple more, then answered, "Michael taught me before he left." She pointed her flag at an approaching plane. "He said maybe I could ride along in one of his airplanes."

"You're not going to ride in any airplanes," Abby said, not bothering to look up from the book she was reading.

"How do you know?" replied Olivia.

Merit leaned a bit closer to her younger daughter. "Michael shouldn't have been making promises he couldn't keep, dear. You understand he's not going to be in the Air Force anymore, don't you?"

"I know." Nothing—not even her crabby big sister—seemed to dampen the little girl's spirits—or her flag waving. Not on this special occasion, with

TV news cameras ready, officers in full dress uniforms standing by, and plenty of balloons and flags to decorate the homecoming of the 732nd Logistic Support Squadron. A couple of balloons escaped the grips of their owners and darted heavenward.

"And that means that—" Merit began, thinking she'd better explain a little more, but Olivia interrupted with a wise shake of her head.

"I knew it would probably never happen, Mommy." Olivia's voice fell. "Lots of things never happen."

Merit almost said "that's right," but thought better of it. Instead, she just smiled and let the wisdom of her eight-year-old stand.

Something else was obviously puzzling Olivia, however. She looked around the crowd. "Where's Jessica? I thought she would be here too."

"She's not coming," Abby monotoned, turning the page. "They're not going to be boyfriend—"

"You can read that book later, Abby." Time to give Abby a gentle prod in the side. Merit didn't want to discourage her older daughter from reading— just reading at the wrong times.

But Abby's nose didn't move. Her eyes scanned the next page as she held up a hand to fend off her mother.

"Please? It's just getting to the good part," she explained, pointing at the page. "The boy and his raccoon are in this pie-eating contest, and—"

"You're always just getting to the good part." Olivia poked her sister in the arm with the tip of her little flag.

"Just because you can't read." Abby squirmed away from her sister and stayed glued to her story.

"Very funny. You always think you're so smart, just because you're a year older than me."

"Year and a half."

"Year and three months. But I guess you never were so good at math."

"That's enough, girls." At home or in the car, Merit might have let the fight escalate so the girls could learn to resolve their own conflicts, but not here in public. This time Merit stepped in to referee and reached across to confiscate Abby's book. "You can finish this book later, Miss Abigail. I'll put it in my purse. Your brother is going to be here any minute."

"Aw, Mom," Abby whined, holding back. "The plane isn't even here yet. We're just sitting here."

"And bickering. Relax. Look around. It'll be here in just a minute." Merit meant to grab the book, a copy of the animal classic *Rascal,* but only managed to extract Abby's bookmark. It wasn't a real bookmark, but the kind of paper scrap Abby usually found to keep her place in the books she read. Something about the crumpled paper caught Merit's eye.

"Where did you get this?" Merit unfolded it carefully, and her daughter cowered as if she'd just been caught with her hand in the cookie jar. Merit recognized the printout of the real estate listing, the little photos of the lakeside resort, the note Will had scribbled to her in the margin: *Let's make an offer!*

"I'm sorry," Abby whispered. "It was in the trash, so I...I mean...but are we moving to a lake? 'Cause if we are, I want to have a pet raccoon, just like in the book. And a pet skunk, and a woodchuck, and a crow. Only in the book, the crow and the raccoon fight, sometimes so maybe that wouldn't be such a good idea."

"A *skunk?*" Olivia exclaimed, wading right in. "Are you crazy? Skunks are horrible and they *stink.* Who would ever have a skunk for a pet?"

"The boy in the book." Abby had obviously thought this through. "They're kind of like a cat, and they're pretty, and he had lots of cats too, and a big Saint Bernard dog, and he built a canoe in his living room."

Olivia the girlie-girl knew that building something in the living room was almost worse than having a pet skunk, since it would make a mess on the carpet. That, however, didn't seem to bother Abby at all. And while the girls continued their pet discussion, Merit held up the bookmark for her oblivious husband to see.

"Look familiar?" She made a face at him, silently asking, *What are we going to do about this?*

Will squinted as he fingered the wrinkled paper, then looked over at Abby as the light finally came to his eyes. "You mean she...?"

Merit nodded, and a grin spread slowly across his face. Had he even been listening? Was he going to say "I told you so"?

"Abby told me last night we're going to move to a lake in the wildness and have a pet skunk, Mom." Olivia crossed her arms and stuck out her lip, the way she did when her older sister tried to convince her that Nancy Drew was a real person or that the back of their closet really did open up into another world. "I didn't believe her, as usual."

Merit couldn't blame Olivia for being skeptical.

"But are we?" Olivia tried once more.

"No!" Merit finally snagged Abby's book and stuffed it into her purse. "I mean, no one is getting a pet skunk, or a raccoon, or a crow! And no one..."

She wasn't sure how to finish her declaration, but she wanted her husband to hear this, loud and clear.

"And no one," she went on, "no one has decided anything about moving yet. So you don't need to worry about a thing."

Will raised his eyebrows at her and tipped his head slightly, which was sign language for *"Are you sure you want to say it that way?"*

"So what's all this about the place at the lake?" Abby pointed at the real estate ad still dangling from her father's hand. "I think it would be cool to live there."

"I don't," Olivia said firmly. "I would miss all my friends. And besides, I hate skunks!"

Merit couldn't help giggling at her night-and-day daughters: Abigail, who would grow up to become a forest ranger in Montana or maybe a long-haul truck driver, and Olivia, who would probably star in a Broadway musical between appearances in makeup and shampoo television commercials.

"See?" Will looked at his wife. "They really ought to be in on this."

She looked from one face to another, sighed, and finally conceded defeat. So much for girls sticking together.

"All right." She wagged a warning finger at them. "But I have to tell you, girls, that this is not a done deal. In fact, it's not even close to being a done deal."

Again the eyebrows from her husband.

"Well…," Merit backtracked. "Let me explain what your daddy and I have been talking about."

But she didn't get a chance, as someone from the crowd pointed out the approaching gray military jet, and several of the youngest children squealed at the sight. That was the cue for the band to begin playing once more, and everyone craned their necks to see.

"Is that him?" Abby asked. After all, she hadn't seen her big brother for over a year. None of them had. Merit couldn't help bobbing with excitement, just like all the other mothers in the crowd.

Will checked his watch, looked at the crowd, and nodded. "I think it is."

four

Waiting for the fish to bite or waiting for wind to fly a kite. Or
waiting around for Friday night or waiting perhaps for their
Uncle Jake or a pot to boil or a better break or a string of pearls
or a pair of pants or a wig with curls or another chance. Every-
one is just waiting.

DR. SEUSS

No, I *can't* forget about it just for tonight. I'm not the type to just roll over and play dead when something's not right."

Will didn't mean to raise his voice. The words just came out that way. He knit his fingers around the steering wheel of their Land Rover—the one with four-wheel drive and the navigation system they'd never used and the car alarm that never seemed to work, except when they didn't want it to—and tried to think of a way to back out of the tension he'd detonated all over their date.

"I'm sorry you've had another hard week." Merit reached over to pat his knee. Ordinarily, he would have purred like a kitten at her touch. "All I meant was there's nothing we can do about it now. It's Friday evening, and all you need to do is enjoy a nice dinner with your wife."

She was right. And he *did* want to enjoy dinner with his wife. But that went with forgetting the crazy office politics at East Bay Health Supply. Forgetting Bruce, his control-freak boss. Forgetting the offer on the Idaho resort that they hadn't heard anything about in two weeks. Forgetting everything.

For now.

"Besides," she went on, "when have you ever turned down your favorite fish? Do you want the view of the bridge or a booth this time?"

They slowed as the traffic on I-80 condensed.

"What can we do in a booth that we can't do with a view?" Will asked.

She smacked him on the knee. "The fish is fresh. You don't need to be."

"You set me up. I couldn't help it." He smiled. Look how fast she'd turned his attention from worrying about their offer to halibut, fish stew, and a side order of Sicilian-style scallops. How did she do that?

"You can too help it," Merit scolded. "Especially in public."

"The booths have curtains." He thought he'd see how far he could push her.

"Hey." He stepped on the brakes and cast a worried glance in his rearview mirror at the too-fast driver behind them. Traffic, traffic, traffic. Someone laid on their horn. "Must be an accident or something."

"Good thing we're not in a hurry." Merit leaned her head against the neck rest and closed her eyes. After the usual insane day at school with two of the kids sick, and then taking care of her own girls that afternoon, Will supposed she had a right to relax. And he wasn't going to bore her with any more of his own horror stories from the office, but—

She came to life when her cell phone jingled the obnoxious Celine Dion tune he had never been able to convince her to change. She snatched the phone out of her purse and held it to her ear, smiling at the person on the other end of the line.

"Don't apologize, Michael. We know it's only until you get set up."

We do? Will wondered what Michael was asking this time. Of course he was glad their son was home, living in his own little apartment, but…

"Of course you can. We're not using it tonight. Your dad and I are headed to Santucci's for dinner. Keys are hanging on that hook in the kitchen. Just tell the baby-sitter you're taking it. And Michael?"

She paused for a moment, and her voice seemed to choke. "We're just so glad you're home, after all you went through over there. It's…I know I've said it before, but I'm your mother and I can repeat myself. Okay, dear. I'll stop now. Love you too."

She clicked the phone shut and turned to her husband. "That was—"

"Notice whose phone he called?" Will interrupted. "And I thought he was going to buy a car of his own."

"He is. In fact, I think he did. A little Japanese…something. He told me his check just has to clear."

"Hmm…" Will frowned. "I told him he needs to build up his credit. And if I were a twenty-two-year-old, I wouldn't be caught dead in my parents' minivan."

"He's almost twenty-three, and your parents never owned a minivan, Will. They weren't invented yet."

"A station wagon then. I still wouldn't—"

"And don't talk about him like that. He's just getting back on his feet, barely put away his uniform. He's been through a lot. And you know what will happen if he thinks you're pushing him too hard."

"I didn't think I was pushing." Will sighed as he felt her frown, knowing he wasn't winning this argument, either. "Okay, okay. We let him go at his own speed. I just don't want him to…you know, it's just good to move ahead. That's all. I was just thinking that—"

The chirp of his cell phone interrupted, and he snapped it out of the drink holder and looked at the caller ID.

"Hot dog." He punched the answer button, barely taking time to read "F. Gribbon" on the screen. "I've been waiting for this call all day."

"You have?" Merit asked, acting surprised. "I had no idea."

He winked at his wife, then cleared his throat. She could be sarcastic if she wanted. This phone call could be the introduction to a brand new chapter in their lives.

"Uncle Fred!" Maybe he sounded too chipper. He toned it down a notch or two. "What's the good news?"

"Returning your call, Will," came the tinny voice on the other end of the line. "I got your messages."

That was it? Uncle Fred the real estate broker sounded more like Uncle Fred the undertaker. Not good. Maybe he was joking. Uncle Fred didn't joke.

"All five of them?"

Uncle Fred managed a dry chuckle. "I'm sorry. I was in meetings all day. I know you're anxious to hear something after all this time." He took a deep breath. "Look, I followed up on your offer, I don't know, five or six times in the past two weeks. The owners are still in Costa Rica, as far as I've been able to find out."

"And what do they say from Costa Rica?"

"That's just it. Nothing. Not a yes, not a no, but…"

"So we haven't gotten through to them yet." Will could hope, couldn't he? "That's why we haven't heard back."

"No, that's just it. I'm afraid we have."

"But you just said—"

"I have all the contact information I need, and as far as I can tell, I've been leaving messages in the right places. They just haven't responded, and their listing agent won't tell me anything helpful, either."

"In other words, they're ignoring us."

"Right."

"Because our offer was too low?"

"That's the way I'm reading it. My take is they're insulted, and that fits with everything I can glean from the agent. They don't seem to be in any hurry to sell, and there's no law that says they have to answer you if they don't want to."

"There isn't?"

Traffic sped up once more. Will glanced down to see that Merit had slipped her hand over to the steering wheel the way she always did when he was getting distracted. And on the other end of the line, he thought he heard his uncle sigh.

"Look, Will, I'm really sorry about the way it's playing out. I know how you…you and Merit had your hearts set on this. There are two things we can do at this point. One, you can up the offer and resubmit. But—"

"But you know we can't do that, Uncle Fred. We don't have anything else to offer."

"Right. I hear you. The other thing to do is to just take it as a no from the Lord and let it go."

Will bit his tongue to keep from snapping at his uncle—although the comment didn't surprise him.

"You're making it sound like no answer is some kind of…divine revelation or something."

Not until the words slipped from his mouth did Will realize he'd recycled them from someone else—Merit.

"Look, Will," said Uncle Fred. "I'm not trying to tell you what to do. And you know I'll keep following this as far as we can. But truth is, it just doesn't look good right now, and at some point you're going to have to accept that."

Will felt the muscles in his neck tighten and tried to ungrit his teeth. "The only thing I'm accepting right now, Uncle Fred, is that we still don't know for sure, and you still haven't found out for sure. Okay?"

He bit his tongue as soon as the words were out of his mouth, not so much for what he had said, but for how he'd said it. His uncle didn't answer right away, and out of the corner of his eye, Will could see Merit waving him down. *Down, boy.*

"I'm sorry, Uncle Fred," Will finally managed. "I know you're doing the best you can. It's not your fault."

Uncle Fred's garbled reply stuttered through the connection.

"Hello?" Will asked as they drove past the shelter of a hill. They were getting close to the water. "I think I'm losing your signal. Hello? Can you hear me?"

His uncle may or may not have heard his apology, but Will listened for a couple seconds more in case the call hadn't quite dropped.

"Thanks anyway, Uncle Fred." He snapped the phone shut and tossed it into the cup holder.

"Will," Merit said.

What could she say to make him feel better about this? It wasn't her fault, not Fred's fault, not anybody's, except—

"They could at least have given us the courtesy of a reply. I can deal with a 'yes,' and I can deal with a 'no.' But to be ignored like this…it absolutely makes me crazy."

"But that doesn't mean—"

"I mean, come on! You have a place for sale, someone makes you an offer, and you tell them yes or no. You don't just ignore them."

"I know, but look—" She leaned a little closer as the freeway finally emerged from the hills and they caught sight of the Carquinez Bridge dead ahead. "Oh, turn here!"

He made the off ramp just in time, grateful they hadn't been followed by a Highway Patrol car. He followed the road down to the bayside town of Crockett—well, people called it a town, but with San Francisco only a few miles away, it qualified as a suburb that had once been a town—and their favorite little waterfront seafood restaurant.

"Good thing both of us are driving," he mumbled, knowing it was true.

Five minutes later, Merit looked at him over the top of the car as they stepped out into the breeze. Here at the straits, river water from the Sacramento and San Joaquin rivers mingled freely with salt water from the bay, and Will granted his lungs a full breath of pungent air. A freighter trundled slowly by, displaying green and white lights in the dusk of early evening.

He pointed to the older sedan they had parked next to at the edge of the little lot, as if the car could heed his warning. "You ding my Land Rover, fella, and—"

"Can we just…" Merit began, her eyes big. "Can we just enjoy the dinner? Forget about job stress for a couple of hours, and the offer, and your Uncle Fred? Just be together and have fun?"

Will lowered his wagging finger, looked at her, and considered her invitation, one he could not turn down. "Like always, huh?" He could do that.

He remembered to open the restaurant door for her, and once they had been shown to a booth, he remembered to switch off his cell phone and watched his wife hold the menu up close to read. They tried to remember the last time they had come to Santucci's and what they had ordered then. He couldn't remember but thought maybe it had been the crab.

She looked up at him and rested her menu back on the table.

"I hate to say this, dear." She smiled sweetly, and Will instantly recognized the "would you do something for me?" tone. "But I took out my contacts, and I think I left my glasses in the car. Could you—?"

He slipped outside and was just about to pull the driver-side door open when he noticed something glittered the wrong way, a reflection from a distant streetlight on something in the front seat he didn't remember leaving there. In the distance, a dark figure ran out of the parking lot and into a dark patch of bushes, causing Will's heart to leap.

It didn't take long to discover the broken glass that now covered the passenger seat and the gaping hole that used to be a side window. He groaned. Inside, their nearly new, four-hundred-dollar stereo system had been rudely yanked from its moorings and trundled away—likely by the runner Will had seen a moment earlier.

"I can't believe it." For a minute he just stared at the crime scene while a dull ache gripped the pit of his stomach, replacing the fear from just moments before. He squeezed his fists together to fight off the feeling of being violated and yelled into the darkness.

"Hey! You!" He fished a CD out of the glass littering the seat and floor. "You forgot one!"

The artist on the CD cover smiled up at him, a contemporary gospel artist Merit liked to listen to on her way to work. Without thinking, Will flung it into the shadows, Frisbee style. It fluttered like a bat against midnight blue until it finally clattered into the bushes on the far side of the parking lot.

"You need to hear that more than we do!" he hollered, then stubbed his toe as he kicked at the glass that had fallen out onto the asphalt. "Jerk!"

Didn't anyone around here keep an eye out for this kind of thing? Whatever happened to security guards? He jammed his hand into his pocket, pulled out his cell phone, and started to punch 911 before he realized the phone wasn't on. Then he thought better of it. Is this the sort of thing people were supposed to call 911 for? Here in the Bay Area, break-ins happened all the time. With three million plus people, what did he expect, anyway?

For murders, press one. If your home was broken into by a masked gunman, press two. If you locked the keys in your Lexus, have a nice day.

He snapped the cell phone shut and limped back to the restaurant. Now his finger was bleeding from the broken glass. Wasn't that a badge of honor? And he'd totally forgotten what Merit had sent him out there to fetch in the first place. Good thing it wasn't...

He paused for a moment in front of the entrance to the restaurant and held out his hand to feel the first drops of rain. He imagined what it would take to duct tape a garbage bag in place over the window to keep the inside of the car from getting soaked.

"Perfect," he mumbled. "Just perfect."

five

I can't say as ever I was lost, but I was bewildered once for three days.

DANIEL BOONE

Strange, the snow.

Not so strange for the Idaho panhandle, just strange for April. Even yellow-and-black-striped Townsend's warblers, the males normally twittering this time of year, just huddled in the budding aspen branches and stared quietly at the blanket of wet white as it continued to fall.

The snow was good for birdwatchers like Stephanie, who crouched behind an old fir and adjusted the eyepieces on her field binoculars. She focused on the closest *Dendroica townsendi,* the first of the season. She imagined the chilly little creature thinking perhaps it had taken the wrong turn on its way back from wintering in Mexico. Was this the right lake? the right state? Or maybe he was questioning his internal calendar.

"No, little guy," she whispered, "you're in the right place."

The warbler puffed up his feathers, shook his shoulders, and eyed her suspiciously.

Easy for her to say, with her toasty Land's End parka and gloves and a view of the southern lake that never failed to quicken her pulse, no matter how many times she saw it. Across the water, Bernard Peak burst from the rocky east shore and jutted another thousand feet into dusky, low-lying clouds laden with the unexpected snow. If the birds weren't inclined to sing a praise song, perhaps she would—or the rocks might.

The nice part about the snow, though, was how it muffled sound in the woods and made Stephanie feel like the only person alive for miles. After all,

Kokanee Cove, population 501 in the off-season, lay at the head of the inlet, perhaps a mile behind her, still dozing on a Saturday morning under a comfy blanket of wood smoke. Few campers would have shown up yet at the adjacent state park this year, and no one else was silly enough to be out in the woods tramping around in a late spring blizzard.

"Well, no one's ever called me sensible," she told the warbler.

And just to prove it, she cinched up the hood of her parka and turned her head up toward the slate-gray sky, opening her mouth wide and catching the biggest flakes on her tongue. In the process, she bumped into a low-hanging fir branch, which dumped a load of wet snow on her head.

"Ack! Enough of that." She shook out her long, dark hair and kept walking. Good thing no one but the birds was watching, and perhaps the occasional deer if she was patient enough to wait for them to show. Following their tracks through the brush brought her to a hint of crumbling asphalt covered with a layer of moss and meadow grass—all that was left of the old Navy training base that had occupied this remote, unlikely site back in the 1940s.

Well, not quite all. She passed the foundation of what had once been an officer's home and tried to imagine the men and women who might have lived here. Kids playing in the yard, surrounded by hundreds of acres of north Idaho woods and tens of thousands of boot camp recruits. In the distance, the kids would hear the cadence of young men, shouting as they marched, preparing for combat duty on both oceans, some unknowingly living the last months of their young lives.

"Whoa. That's a morbid thought," Stephanie said out loud. She looked up at a skinny crow eyeing her from its perch on a dead alder, keeping his own noisy cadence with unseen pals. She'd already seen plenty of crows on her walk this morning, dutifully checking *Corvus brachyrhynchos* off her Kootenai County Bird List. "But you wouldn't know anything about morbid, would you? And please don't say 'nevermore,' even if you aren't a raven."

The crow shook its head obligingly and flew off toward another chorus of squawks.

For the first time on her morning walk, Stephanie shivered. Why did she always walk down this crumbled trail from the state park and down to the crumbled Kokanee Cove resort? Just to feel more depressed?

Who me? Depressed? She did her best to avoid the thought dogging her with each step. And though she slowed as the trail wound down the hill to the lake, she still lost her footing and sat down—hard—in the slush.

"Oh!" This wasn't supposed to be a sledding hill, though she made it one as she slid several feet. Finally, she found enough traction on a granite out-cropping that she could stand back up. And once again, she was glad no one was watching.

Except You, Lord, she prayed, brushing off the slush and taking in the sight of the little resort below. Ex-resort, actually. The store and snack bar, where she had worked summers as a teenager, balanced off-kilter on its foun-dation of floating logs. It could use a coat of paint, for starters. The icy lake waters had not yet claimed it, but that would change before long if someone didn't do something.

Adjoining docks had shed half their planking, which seemed to suit a pair of *Bucephala clangula* just fine. Stephanie liked the cute little Goldeneye ducks, with their high foreheads and white breasts. When she got too close, though, they skittered off across the mirror-gray waters of Kokanee Cove, then flapped their wings and took off. They flew low across the fjord-like inlet, keeping a close but informal formation as they looped north for a fly-by of north-shore vacation cabins, then corrected back toward the blurred but still jagged outline of Bernard Peak.

The old resort hadn't looked like much when she'd worked there a few years back, but it had looked better than it did now. The boathouse at the far end of the floating docks looked almost as bad as the little log caretaker's cabin just up on shore. She crossed her arms and sighed.

It had been nice, once. Everyone had their own version of the story, but no one had ever really explained to her why it had sat empty for the past cou-ple of years or how the previous owners had run out of money. Mr. Mooney at the Kokanee Cove Mercantile said they got sick and moved to Central America to stay warm. Stephanie thought they should have just tried Tucson like all the other snowbirds around here. Better to sit in a trailer park in the middle of the desert and play cards all day. She didn't mean to grump on the snowbirds. There was nothing wrong with heading south in November. Her warblers did it every year too.

Looking at this old resort was a lot like standing at the hospital bedside of a person you cared about, praying they might get better. Not that she had any personal experience in hospital ministry. The closest she could come was when her grandma Betty died when Stephanie was twelve, after they went to see her in the rest home. But she could imagine how it might feel. She imagined a lot of things she hadn't actually experienced.

But what did she expect? Kids from Kokanee Cove didn't get out much, except the ones who graduated from nearby Timberlake High and left the next day to join the Navy. And then there were the girls who got married when they were eighteen, had babies a few months later, and spent their lives in mobile homes, changing diapers. *Wonderful.*

Sorry. She hadn't meant that last snide remark, even if she'd only thought it.

But really, what did she expect? Here she was, barely twenty, home-schooled her whole life, even before it was cool to be homeschooled. She'd never made many friends around Kokanee Cove, except perhaps some of the older people. Few ever had a chance to get to know the bookish little girl who told people she wanted to be an ornithologist and who had grown into the bookish young woman who didn't tell people much of anything. She still remembered the guy who kept a cabin cruiser at the resort, though, the one who first called her Bird Girl.

"Bird Girl!" She said it out loud for the benefit of a *Turdus migratorius* perched on the windowsill of the resort cabin, staring menacingly at his own reflection. "You hear that, robin?"

The robin didn't care, just pecked at the window as the tears ran down Stephanie's cheeks. She swiped at them with her glove. What had brought this on? Her parents were happy enough that the Bird Girl still lived at home with a house full of books and Sandra, her mother's parakeet.

Of *course* she loved her parents, even with all their…well, everyone had quirks. It was just that…

"I give up," she told God, but it was only a formality. He knew and she knew she'd given up a long time ago. If Kokanee Cove were big enough to support a newspaper, she could just imagine how the headline might read: LOCAL GIRL STAYS HOME, STILL WATCHING BIRDS.

Still home, here in this achingly beautiful, hauntingly quiet, lovely, lonely place, where she could live the rest of her life like the old buildings of the resort, perched by the lake she loved and hated at the same time, crumbling and decayed.

This isn't all you have for me, is it, God?

She waited for the answer but only heard the breeze off the lake whistling through the tops of the firs and a loose shingle flapping on the roof of the boathouse below. She didn't think that was the "still, small voice." Actually, she wasn't sure she even wanted to hear the answer, though she still dared to ask the question.

Dad would have an opinion about still, small voices, but that was his job as the pastor of Kokanee Cove Bible Chapel, where he'd preached for the past twenty years—as long as she could remember. Pastor Bud. He'd already given her all the answers he knew. Most ended with a Scripture verse, but what was wrong with that?

Nothing.

But still she listened, until her ears picked out a faint fluttering, a whimpering cry.

What?

She thought it might be coming from the owl's nest behind the cabin, but it didn't sound like an owl. She started slowly toward the noise, now louder, now more of a chirping sound—not an owl, but close. She spied movement behind the cabin in the shadow of a fir tree, weak and desperate in a pile of branches and needles, probably a nestling out for its first flight, maybe hurt.

"Look at that."

The young kestrel fluttered about on its side, its blue gray wing feathers askew and a few clusters of down still clinging to its brand-new feathers. *Falco sparverius,* with a wingspan of fifty-one to sixty-one centimeters, only something was clearly wrong with this fellow's wingspan. This runt of the litter had fallen or tried to fly out of the nest and had been left to die.

"You're hurt," she told it. "Don't move."

The young bird looked up long enough to panic. It tried to flutter away but only managed to turn in awkward circles with its one good wing. If she was going to do something, it would have to be fast—and now.

"Stop!" she commanded. The bird took that as encouragement to flutter its wing even more desperately, though it hardly worked as it should.

Meanwhile, the bird's would-be rescuer stripped off her parka and gave pursuit.

"You can't do this!" she told the bird, but he could, and he did. He flopped around like the bird her father had hit years ago on Highway 54, plastering feathers all over the front grille of their Explorer and reducing Stephanie and her mother to tears. But this little bird would not end up as road kill.

Stephanie dove with the parka stretched out in front of her like a net and missed. While she regrouped, the young kestrel fluttered down the hill toward the old resort's gravel beach, screeching the whole way.

Kree-kree-kree!

"I'm not going to hurt you," she whispered, advancing more slowly this time and crouching nearly down to her knees. The injured kestrel eyed her warily, his little chest heaving in fright. She would have to get this over with quickly. "Just…sit…still!"

This time her aim was better and a moment later, her parka came alive, dancing across the beach, draped over the animated young bird. Stephanie caught up to the animal and scooped him up in her arms.

"Settle down," she cooed in her best mother kestrel imitation. Under her firm grip, the bird had little choice and settled down for the double-time hike back to town and the Mercantile. Stephanie breathed a quick word of thanks that the kestrel wasn't very big, the way a red-tailed hawk or an osprey might have been, and forty minutes later she backed through the Mercantile's door, bird bundle in hand. The door's jingle bells nearly jangled off the string.

"Mr. Mooney!" Stephanie called when she didn't see anyone behind the counter.

No one answered.

"Hello?"

She checked down the aisle with the fishing lures, canned soups, and local maps. No Mr. Mooney, which meant he was probably out back with the animals. She hurried through the compact store past the milk and soda pop cooler and pushed past the back door marked Kokanee Cove Animal Rescue.

It wasn't much by city standards. Two rows of small cages against one wall, like a pet store, and a couple of larger pens in the back. A tiny bald man crouched at the far cage, refilling a water dish for a raccoon with a bandaged head.

"Got something for you, Mr. Mooney," Stephanie called.

"Huh?" The little man looked up at her with wide eyes, then smiled and dipped his shoulders. "Steph! I didn't hear you."

"Sorry." She explained how she'd found the young bird.

"Kestrel, eh?" Mr. Mooney took a look as they carefully unwrapped the bird. Stephanie held the head as he felt the bird's wings and talons. "Wing's broken, probably. We'll give him some time here, see if we can get him healed up, then set him loose before he gets too used to us. Where'd you say you found him?"

He nodded as she explained.

"The resort, huh? Heard an out-of-town developer is going to buy the place, turn it into some condos with a casino."

"Where'd you hear that?" Stephanie looked around the back room. A little coyote pup peeked out at her from one of the cages.

"You know, people coming in the store. The Kokanee Cove grapevine."

"Right." She groaned. That was the main mode of communication around here. No newspaper and no radio, except for out-of-town stations. She'd grown up around the grapevine.

"Anyway, good thing you found him." Mr. Mooney gave her a wink as he hoisted their newest patient into a holding cage.

"Even though officially I'm not the one with the federal raptor permit?"

"If you want to get technical about it. But from the look of this guy, I don't think he would've lasted too long out there in the snow. You did good, Miss Bird Woman."

Bird Woman. Stephanie nodded. Better than Bird Girl, for sure. And coming from Foster Mooney, it didn't sound half bad.

But…a casino?

six

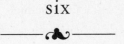

And in the end, it's not the years in your life that count. It's the life in your years.

ABRAHAM LINCOLN

O ne, two..."
    Michael counted lug nuts as he replaced another customer's tires. This rig carried four of WallyTire Tire Center's most expensive all-season rubber, which put a little more ka-ching in Wally's cash drawer. No problem with that, and Michael didn't mind the work so much. It sure beat working on Humvees in...

Don't go there. He cut off the memory before it had a chance to splash mud on his day.

Just put your head down and work, he ordered himself. *Don't look back, and don't think back. Tighten another wheel down, go on to the next. Tighten one more...*

"Sullivan!" Marilyn the cashier's voice echoed through the door. "Phone call for you!"

"Got it." Michael wiped his hands on a rag and trotted over to the wall phone. A moment later his mother apologized for calling him at work.

"Not a problem, Mom. Really. What's up?"

Her voice sounded different, like she'd been crying or something, but he wasn't going to embarrass her by mentioning it.

"I just wanted to give you a heads-up. Your father is probably going to be calling you, and—"

"Oh yeah? What about?"

She paused, sort of catching her breath. "Actually I promised I'd let him be the first to tell you."

"Oh. Sounds like a big secret or something."

"No, no. Nothing like that. I just want you to have an open mind when he talks to you. You know what I mean?"

"You mean 'open mind,' like I should say 'great idea' no matter what he lays on me? You sure you can't tell me what this is all about?"

Another pause. "It's just that…well, okay. Your father and I got a call today, and—"

Good thing Michael looked around the work bay just then.

"Gotta go!" he interrupted. "Jason's about to…"

…dump a whole stack of bright green plastic antifreeze jugs, piled carefully into a seven-foot pyramid. Michael hung up the phone and dove for the nearest corner, just in time to keep the whole display from tumbling to the floor.

"Whoa." Jason's eyes widened as he stepped back from the near disaster. "Good catch, dude."

"You take them from the top." Michael straightened up and demonstrated. "Like this, see?"

"I knew that." Jason was about Michael's age, graduated from the same high school, but maybe not the brightest bulb on the Christmas tree. "You built this thing, huh?"

Michael nodded as he straightened everything back up. No harm done. Nothing to do but return to tightening lug nuts on the tire he'd been working on.

"Hey, Mike!"

Michael sighed and glanced over his shoulder. Please, no more dumb questions about what it was like over there, and did he shoot anybody, or did he meet any Iraqi women.

"Did Wally ever tell you we get a fifteen-minute break every two hours?" Jason asked.

"He told me." Michael nodded and moved to grab the next wheel—the one Jason had leaned his foot on.

"So how come you never take it? Dude, you've only been here two weeks, and you're already making me look bad."

"Three. And I'm not trying to make anybody look bad. Just trying to do my job."

"Yeah, I can tell. You're, like, some kind of working fool. Running out to the cars, building displays. Is this what they made you do in boot camp? Go, go, go?"

"Boot camp was nothing compared to—"

Again, he cut his thought off midsentence. Jason didn't seem to notice, but then, Jason hardly noticed when his own shoe was untied or his shirttail was untucked.

"Well, I think Wally hired you for the PR too. You know, like, 'Motherhood, apple pie, God bless America, and come on in and meet our local war hero.' Right?"

"You wouldn't say that if you'd been there." Michael shook his head and sighed. "I don't know about God blessing anything."

"Whoa. Didn't know that was such a hot button. Guess heroes are touchy like that."

"Would you cool it with the hero stuff? Wally can say whatever he wants, but I'm nobody's hero. The only thing—"

"You're just trying to be cool about it." Jason waved him off. "I think we should have you autograph tires for customers, like with a white pen? Maybe we could charge a few bucks extra."

Jason launched into a high-pitched laugh at his own joke. Unfortunately, he was right about the way their boss looked at the whole hero thing. And Michael tried not to look at the poster Wally had made of Michael's official Air Force photo—the one with him in full uniform. Wally had posted it prominently on the wall, next to the Snap-on tool kits and the American flag, just above the display for their premium all-seasons. Other tire centers had calendars or pictures of girls in bikinis standing next to the latest model cars or holding batteries. Here they had a picture of a war hero.

Or in his case, a war survivor.

Except he wasn't sure the name fit. Survivors, after all, came home to a big kiss from their waiting girlfriends. And survivors got on with their lives without constant nightmares about...

"Hey, I don't mean anything by it." Jason pointed his thumb at the homemade poster. "I just think you ought to feel honored. People would probably come up and salute you, still."

"That's just it." Michael turned back to his work. "It creeps me out."

"Hmm. See, that's what I don't get."

Since Michael didn't explain, Jason went on.

"Well, maybe I'll just paste my own face up there then, so all the girls who come in here will ooh and ahh at Jason Warner, war hero. If we can't get you to sign tires, at least I should be able to get some dates out of this, huh?"

"Knock yourself out."

That invited a strange look from Jason, who stepped around the car and narrowed his eyes at Michael. "Hey, you're not, uh..." Jason searched for words. "You know. 'Cause if you are, I mean, I'm not hydrophobic or nothing, and it really doesn't bother me one way or the other. Just maybe it would be nice to know, know what I mean? No offense."

Michael turned the air gun on his co-worker and pulled the trigger. It spun the ratchet with a loud whirr. Jason flinched.

"Would you knock it off? I'm not a hero, and I'm not gay, if that's what you're getting at. But I am trying to get this car finished, okay?"

"Whoa. Sure thing, dude." Jason held up greasy hands in surrender, then flashed a grin of what must have been relief. "Just making sure. You never know when somebody's, you know, different. Or a born-again, something off the wall like that. But I still think you really ought to use that war hero stuff for a little extra advantage, you know? Not every guy has that kind of leverage. Don't you think?"

Or a born-again?

Michael caught his breath, about to say something, then decided to just ignore Jason and turned back to his tires. He had nothing left to say, not after that wimpy objection to being a hero. He'd known some heroes. Seen guys who risked their lives for all the right reasons. Some guys who came home in a pine box. Only he wasn't one of them, and that's what Wally and Jason and his parents and his little sisters and everybody else didn't get. Hero? No. So what was he supposed to say?

Yeah, I was scared out of my wits over there most of the time. Sick-to-my-stomach scared.

Some hero.

And yeah, I blamed God most of the time for being silent when everything was blowing up around me, including some of my best friends.

Some Christian.

He spit on the floor and attacked his tires until he heard the mechanical beep of a customer pushing open the front door. Jason had already disappeared, and Wally was helping another customer from behind the front desk. His boss turned and whistled toward the shop.

"Sullivan!"

Michael didn't waste any time trotting up to help the customer, a young mother with three little ones in tow. He tried not to look at them, but the little boy—about four or five—pointed his little plastic rifle at everything in the store, from racks of tires to pictures on the wall. His mom didn't notice, but she needed a new set of tires, she thought. Could he show her what they had on sale?

Michael escorted them around the displays, starting with the all-seasons Wally always wanted him to sell. He couldn't help but feel the stare of the little boy.

"Not now, dear." The woman brushed off her son as she studied a price list by the first display. The boy kept tugging her shirt.

"The rest rooms are over there," she said, pointing to the door. "Your sister can take you."

He shook his head and aimed his toy gun at Michael's face. Michael wanted to introduce him to a little firearm etiquette but didn't have a chance.

"I don't *have* to go!" announced the little guy. He whispered something into his mother's ear and pointed at the We Support Our Troops poster. His mother looked at the poster, then at Michael, then back to the poster.

"I think you're…" She looked at Michael with a question in her eyes. "Are you?"

"Everybody asks that." Michael sighed. "But I have no idea who that is."

"Are you famous?" asked the little boy, holding his gun up to Michael. He wasn't fooled. "Could you sign my gun?"

If Michael closed his eyes, he knew he would see another little boy, not much older than this one, kicking a soccer ball and hiding behind the burned-out skeleton of an Iraqi car, half a world away. Only the other boy…

"I'm sorry." The mother grabbed the gun away from the boy and stuffed it in her purse. "He didn't mean anything by it."

She couldn't have known, but Michael sighed with relief when she hustled her children outside a minute later, thanking him for the information, and saying something about passing it along to her husband.

That was fine with him. Half an hour later, it was also fine with him that he was left to close up the store after Wally and Jason and Marilyn had left.

"You're just a working fool!" Jason waved at him as he hurried out.

"Yeah, that's me." Michael locked the door from inside and turned the Open sign to Closed. "Or maybe just a fool, period."

With Wally finally gone and no one else to ask questions, he could pull a ladder up from the tire racks and position it under the poster. And if anyone asked, well, of course they still supported the troops. Just not this particular one.

Before he had time to think about what he was doing, he climbed up and reached for the poster. Then the phone rang.

"We're closed," he addressed the phone, but it continued to ring. He would have let the answering machine pick up, but he had clipped one of the cordless extensions on his belt. And if Wally was calling…

He punched the button to answer. "WallyTire. Michael speaking."

"Hey, there's a familiar voice. Are you guys still open?"

"Oh! Yeah. I mean, no, Dad. Mom said you—I mean, I'm just…" He grabbed the poster and tore it down with a satisfying rip. He wondered how he was going to get rid of it without leaving evidence. He would just have to take it with him. Although how obvious was it going to look now? "I'm just closing up tonight."

"That means you haven't had dinner yet?"

"Uh…" Michael glanced down at plan A: the popcorn machine in the waiting area and an abandoned slice of pie Jason's mom had brought by yesterday.

"I guess that's a no." Michael's dad sighed, but his voice still bubbled. It almost didn't sound like him. "Well look, then I'm glad I caught you, because there's something I want to talk to you about. It's pretty exciting, and we just heard this afternoon."

"Huh? Heard what?"

"I can meet you at a Denny's or something."

"You can't tell me over the phone?"

"You're turning down dinner?"

Michael only paused for a moment.

"Which Denny's?"

seven

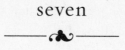

Wherever you are—be all there.

JIM ELLIOT

From the corner booth, Will saw his son step into the diner and look around. He caught Michael's eye with a wave.

"Glad you could join me." Will flinched. He sounded like he was greeting a potential client. "I mean—your mother and I have hardly seen you since you got back."

"Yeah." Michael slipped into the booth and fingered a menu. "Guess I've been busy at this job. Busier than I thought I'd be."

He didn't look anything like the Michael who had left for boot camp four years ago, and it wasn't just the lack of pimples or the broader, square shoulders hardened by combat duty. Something else had hardened as well.

"So you're not tired of the work yet?" Will asked.

"Tired? Naw," Michael said, missing the pun attempt, weak as it was. "It's only been a few weeks. Wally's way out of focus, but he's okay."

"Not as bad as your commanding officers?" Will thought he might as well try to fish for a little more of the story, whatever the story was. But the question didn't get much of a reaction—just a noncommittal shrug.

"I only ran into one guy over there who was a real piece of work, and he was on his way back to the States in a couple of weeks."

"Transferred?"

"Killed."

That ended the interrogation. Michael slumped into his side of the booth and hoisted a menu to his face. Will considered pushing for more details but decided against it. Michael would talk about his tour of duty when he was ready. Or he wouldn't.

"Hungry?" Will couldn't remember a time when Michael hadn't been hungry, but maybe that had changed too.

"Getting there."

Could the conversation get any more awkward?

Michael studied his options while they traded grunts about fascinating topics like the weather (hot, huh) and the Giants winning the pennant (cool, huh). Moving on to more challenging discourse, they commented on how much the price of gas had gone up again (lame, huh).

Will nodded at the back of Michael's menu, the contents of which his son had likely memorized by this time. *At this rate, we're going to run out of small talk in a big hurry,* Will thought. The young waitress with the Bozo-red hair hadn't even taken their orders yet.

When she finally arrived, Will ordered a bacon mushroom burger, since Merit wasn't there to remind him about cholesterol. Michael ordered an omelet with extra cheese, since he didn't need to worry about cholesterol in the first place.

"Oh," Will added, "and a cup of coffee. Black."

Michael ordered the same.

Will grinned at his adopted son as they passed their menus to the waitress. "I forgot how you always liked to eat breakfast at dinner," he said. "A bowl of cereal for a bedtime snack, right? How did they feed you? I mean, did you eat okay…over there?"

Food would be a safe topic. Even military food on the battlefield.

"Sure." Michael nodded and finally seemed to relax a little. "You can have anything you want in an MRE."

Meal, ready to eat. Will had heard horror stories about the military version of the instant breakfast, lunch, and dinner. As they waited for their food, Michael explained what they were like, and Will hoped he would finally ease up and tell him what had happened in Iraq. Five minutes later, though, the conversation lagged once more.

"Been going to church anywhere?" Will asked, trying a more roundabout approach. Not that he was one to ask himself, but—

Michael apparently found the label on the bottle of ketchup fascinating. "You know Wally's been scheduling me to work on Sundays. I haven't had a chance yet."

Will nodded. *Now what?*

They sat in silence for a few minutes, Will trying to find a way out of their conversational dead end. Before he could, the waitress brought their orders.

"No, actually, *he* gets the omelet." Will pointed to his son, and the waitress switched their plates. They situated their food and unwrapped their utensils from napkins.

Will paused, and he and Michael glanced at each other. Will would have prayed for the family once, when Michael was little and Merit was along. But now? Michael fingered his fork, waiting.

Finally, Will bowed his head and closed his eyes. He silently counted to ten backward, popped his eyes back open, and dug into the meal.

Michael followed his lead, dousing the omelet with ketchup.

"Whoa, Mikey! Where'd you learn to eat eggs like that?"

Michael pointed to his full mouth instead of answering.

"Forget it." Will returned to his burger, catching the dribble down his chin with a napkin. Now they had an excuse for not saying anything, as they quietly inhaled their meals. Michael was the first to finish.

"So," Michael swabbed the rest of his ketchup with his little finger, parked his knife and fork on the cleared plate, and looked up. "I'm still waiting for your big news. You said you wanted to talk to me about something."

Will had to give the kid credit for being the first to bring it up. He would have, but he was still working on his last few fries. First things first.

"Actually, yeah. I did." He knew he had one chance to ask this, and at this point, he had to admit Merit was right. Michael wasn't going to accept any offers from his dad. Not a chance in the world.

Michael raised his eyes to target him directly. "Holy smokes, Dad. Were you this way when you asked Mom to marry you?"

Will held up his hands, pretended he had no idea what the kid was talking about.

"Look. Your mom and I have been doing a lot of thinking lately. To tell you the truth, things haven't been so good at work."

"When have they ever been? You've always hated your job and that nut case boss of yours. What's his name, Brian?"

"Bruce. Yeah." Out of habit he glanced down at his cell phone, clipped to his belt. "I'm surprised he hasn't called to yell at me while we've been here."

"So what's new and exciting about that?"

Will hadn't expected a plain fact like that to hit him so hard, but it helped make his point.

"See, that's what I'm saying. I've always wanted to do something I enjoyed, something that would bring our family together."

"You mean like that nighttime janitor job you used to drag me to when I was little? That was the worst." Michael made a face.

"What do you mean, the worst? I thought you liked that job. It taught you how to work."

"I trapped spiders and fell asleep under the desks. It was the worst, Dad. Believe me."

"Oh. Well, anyway, it's not going to be like that. But listen." Will leaned forward, as if telling a secret. "Your mom and I just put an offer on a little resort in Idaho. It's by Lake—"

Michael straightened. "A resort? Are you kidding? What kind of resort?"

"Let me finish. It's on Lake Pend Oreille. Kokanee Cove."

"Oh, you mean where Aunt Overdose lives."

Will tried to look stern, but Michael's nickname for his aunt was more than appropriate. "Aunt Sydney does live there, yes. I think that's part of the reason your mother agreed to this whole thing. We'd be closer to family."

Michael finally smiled. "Family you haven't talked to in twenty years."

"Not that long."

"Okay, fifteen. What was I, six years old when we went to visit, and she went ballistic because Mom wouldn't let her smoke pot in front of me? Said we needed to open our minds?"

"You remember that?"

"Vividly. I was totally intimidated by her hairdo too. She looked like a pharaoh with all that blue makeup on her eyes and that big braided thing in back. And those claws she had for fingernails? Could have scratched my eyes out."

"I think you let your imagination get away with you, there. Sydney never had fingernails. She was more into vegetarianism and compost piles."

"I'm confused. I always thought she and Mom hated each other."

"No, it's not quite like that. Even though they've hardly spoken to each other since that…marijuana incident."

"But it's not all better now, is it?"

"Not yet. Sydney never apologized, and your mom thought she was protecting you and the girls by keeping you away. It's going to take some time to heal, but moving there will be a big step. I think a lot of things are going to change."

"Hmm. Well, I still think this is totally weird, Dad. You're really going to sell your place and move away from the Bay Area? give up your job and everything? your 401(k) contribution? your health plan? You can't be serious."

"Listen, we'll still have a health plan," Will told him.

Well, they would, pretty much. But Michael still looked skeptical, so Will decided to try the idealistic angle.

"Okay. Sometimes all that stuff doesn't really measure up. Sometimes you have to just go for something because, well, it's the chance of a lifetime, and you'd regret not trying it."

The irony of the conversation was not lost on Will, as his son suddenly reminded him of Uncle Fred. Where had this come from?

"Oh!" Michael snapped his fingers. "That's it. This is some kind of midlife crisis. Maybe you should just buy a Corvette instead."

Will paused as the waitress arrived to refill his coffee cup. Michael took another cup too. When had he started drinking coffee?

"It's not a crisis," Will said when the waitress left, "unless you count the ongoing crisis at my office. But look, for the past three weeks we've had this offer on the place, way low. It's contingent on us selling the house, but that should be no problem in this market."

"Mm-hmm." Michael nodded, his eyes glassing over slightly. "Let me guess: a fixer-upper."

"Well, it needs a little work, is all. It'll give me a chance to work with my hands."

"Dad." Michael gave Will a look, a little sideways glance. "Are you kidding?"

"What? I've always liked to do stuff like that. I just haven't had the chance."

"One word, Dad: birdhouse."

"Okay, rub it in, Mr. Fix-It Professional. Just because that project didn't turn out so well—"

Michael cupped a hand in front of his mouth so he wouldn't spray coffee all over the table by laughing. Will should have known it would go like this.

"Look, don't get me wrong," said Michael, after he'd caught his breath. "I think it's cool you want to try something new. But do you think maybe you ought to start out slow? take a class or something?"

"I've been checking out home improvement books from the library. You'd be impressed."

"Right." Michael nodded. He didn't look convinced.

"Anyway, the owners were in Costa Rica, and we thought they were ignoring us, but it turns out they were working at rebuilding this clinic way out in the sticks where there wasn't a phone. It just took them longer to get back to us than we thought it would."

"Speaking of the sticks, this place is really out there, isn't it?"

"There's a little store in Kokanee Cove. A post office. And there's that Navy research station on the lake."

"Oh yeah, I remember that now."

"But here's the deal. The resort has its own little floating store—at least, it used to be a store. And there's the docks, a workshop, and a couple of cottages. Like I said, it needs a little work, but, you know..."

"Guess I don't know." Michael took a sip of his coffee before adding another packet of sugar. "Did you really talk Mom into leaving her house? her job?"

"It's going to happen, as soon as we can get the place sold and everything packed up." Will paused. "But the other part is that, well, the owner before us did some outboard motor repair, and they ran a fuel dock by the store." He checked to make sure his son was still following. "I'm gearing up for the handiwork—painting, basic carpentry, that kind of thing. And your mom will help with what she can, maybe run the store and handle the books. But obviously neither of us are mechanics, and..."

"Oh." Michael closed his eyes. He got it.

"And that's why I want you to consider coming up and working with us. I couldn't pay you much, but we could work out some kind of part-ownership deal. You know, sweat equity."

"Sweat equity, huh?"

For a long moment Michael looked as if he might be considering the offer. But then his nod turned into a slow shaking of his head.

Will gave it one more shot. "I'm sure we could figure out something fair."

"Yeah, no. I mean, it's really nice of you to offer, Dad. I just don't think I can do it."

"Oh, come on. A good mechanic like you? You can figure out those outboards in a second. Didn't you fix all kinds of vehicles over there?"

"That's not it, Dad."

"Oh, this isn't about Jessica, is it, because—"

"It is *not* about Jessica." Michael's eyes flashed, and Will leaned back. "She's got other…I mean, we're not…" Michael sighed.

"I didn't mean to pry," Will said.

"You're not prying. Jessica's just…we're still friends, but…I don't know. I guess she just wasn't into waiting around for years. You know how it is."

"I'm sorry."

"It's all right. But I don't really want to talk about it."

Another awkward silence fell, and Will stared into his coffee cup and tried to regroup.

"Okay, so if it's not Jessica, then what's holding you back?" He didn't mean to sound pushy, but he knew he did.

"You really want to know?" Michael set down his coffee cup. "Me working for you would be a disaster. We always argue."

"Argue? What are you talking about? Give me an example."

"How about right now? And when I was sixteen, you didn't want me to get a motorcycle, so I went out and bought the biggest, baddest Kawasaki I could find. Which if I still owned it, by the way, I wouldn't have to borrow your van so much."

"Your mom doesn't mind."

"Yeah, I know, but I'm trying to tell you that I always look for a way to contradict you. You wanted me to go to college, so I joined the Air Force. You wanted me to stay in the States, so I volunteered for duty in the Middle East. You voted Republican, so I voted Democrat."

"You voted Democrat? You're kidding. I didn't know that."

"Yeah. Absentee." Michael shook his head. "We just don't see things the same way. It's like we're this classic case of opposites they talk about on radio shows. And you really want me to work for you?"

"I don't think we're that opposite. In fact, I think maybe the problem is that we're too much alike."

Michael rubbed a hand across his chin and groaned.

"In fact," Will went on, "my dad and I were just like this. We were great buddies when I was young. He was my scoutmaster, coached my Little League team, the whole bit. I thought he was perfect, until I went off to school. Suddenly he couldn't do anything right."

"You thought that about Grandpa?" Michael asked, sitting up a little straighter. "What happened?"

"I turned twenty-one, twenty-two. Got out of college and into the real world. Suddenly he got smarter again."

Michael didn't answer, just stirred his coffee and added more sugar. Pretty soon the spoon would be able to stand on its own.

"I wish you could have known him better before he died," Will added.

"Yeah."

Well, that was something they could agree on. Will was right about them being alike, and his son had to know it.

"So what about my proposition?" he asked.

Michael's expression clouded over. Maybe Will should have stuck to the grandpa stories.

"I'm sorry, Dad. I don't want to hurt your feelings, but you asked."

"You're not hurting my feelings," Will lied. "But you didn't even think about it. Maybe you could—"

"No, Dad. Thanks, really. But no. I have a good job now and—"

"You call that a good job? After everything you learned in the service, you're going to fix tires? I call it a giant step backward."

"Well, I call moving to Nowhere, Idaho, an even bigger giant step backward."

Will chewed on his coffee mug to keep from saying something more he'd regret.

His son went on. "The point is, I still have lots of friends here in Walnut

Creek, and I don't think I could take living out in Idaho, anyway. What do people do there on the weekends?"

It was a rhetorical question. Will just fingered the check and nodded. What an absolutely, totally stupid idea. Why had he thought Michael would say anything different? And why had he wanted him to?

That's when Will realized he couldn't buy back the past from a real estate agent. That had been his mistake, thinking he could.

"Like I said," Michael finished, "it's totally cool for you and Mom, but…"

"Yeah," Will said, "we're gonna go sit in our trailer, drink beer, and listen to country music. That's what people do in north Idaho."

"You don't have to get sarcastic on me."

"Sarcastic? Who's being sarcastic? Barn dances too. Take up quilting. Grow a mullet. Get a shotgun. Milk my own cows. We're moving out to the sticks, you know."

"Okay, you made your point."

"So did you."

Stalemate.

Will looked up at his son and sighed. "I guess your mom was right."

Michael didn't answer. At that point in the conversation, he didn't need to.

eight

Life is always walking up to us and saying, "Come on in, the living's fine," and what do we do? Back off and take its picture.
RUSSELL BAKER

Y ou're shaking, Will."
Merit reached over to calm her husband as he turned the rental car onto the gravel driveway. Behind them, their little car kicked up a parade of gravel and a cloud of dust. Ahead, she could barely make out the faded lettering on a crooked little sign.

"Kokanee Cove Resort." Will read it for both of them, and she reassured him with a little smile she forced to her lips. "Bait, tackle, boots for hire. I mean boats."

It had been her husband's dream, idea, and initiative, but since they'd signed the papers the other day, Merit knew she had to stop crying and buy into it as well.

No second thoughts, girl, she reminded herself, squeezing her hands so they wouldn't shake. *You're in this together.* Easier said than done.

She gasped with wonder, though, when they rounded the last curve and crunched to a halt in front of the docks.

"I'd forgotten how incredible the view is," she whispered.

Steep mountains bracketed the bay on either side, making it look like a Norwegian fjord. Even in the last week of April, patches of sparkling snow still clung to the heights. Not far to the left, the little town of Kokanee Cove seemed to guard that end of the lake. And off in the other direction, frothy whitecaps studded the bluest waters Merit had ever seen, from a brilliant azure around the wooded edges to a deeper cobalt and ultramarine in the middle. Like an ocean, the lake stretched north, on and on into a blue haze, wandering more than forty miles into the Selkirk Mountain wilderness.

They stared at the vista, letting the dust settle around them, until Will turned the ignition off.

"Welcome home, Mrs. Sullivan," he said.

Merit swallowed hard but kept her eyes on the view. Better to concentrate on the beauty beyond than on the sorry sight much closer. She'd already cried enough back home.

"Do we really own this place?" she asked.

Will nodded. "And we came all this way to see what we bought, so let's see!"

He jumped out of the car like a child on Christmas morning, and Merit followed. After all, they were partners in this venture, and now that the deal was going through, they needed to take stock before they moved.

"All right," she said as they walked toward the docks. "You want me to start the to-do list?"

"This old dock probably just needs a few more logs." Will extended his hand to help her down the short gangplank to the floating store. Well, *floating* might have been a charitable term.

"Are you sure we won't sink?" Merit asked, stepping gingerly from one broken board to the next. A family of turtles splashed into the lake from their sunning spot on the end—a spot that had obviously been shared by more than a few water birds over the years.

"Looks pretty solid to me." Will stomped on a board to make his point, and his leg disappeared to the knee through a sudden new hole.

"Will!" Merit cried, jumping forward to catch him. "You're going to break your leg!"

"Nah," he said, playing the tough guy, but Merit could tell he had ripped his jeans and scraped his knee as his foot went into the water. "Board just needs replacing."

"That and a whole lot more. You really think you can fix all this? And that water's got to be ice cold."

He couldn't argue as they inspected their new purchase. Merit tried to remember what it had looked like before. Maybe it had been the dark and the charming carpet of snow, but it hadn't seemed quite this...

Will forced open the store's front door. One of the hinges popped off in the process.

"Oh dear," she said.

"Well, we knew it was going to take some elbow grease."

"It's not elbow grease I'm worried about." She followed him inside, nearly tripping over a couple of oil cans in the shadows.

"Doesn't it remind you of Mount Hermon, just a little?" he asked.

As her eyes adjusted to the dim light streaming in through the dirt-streaked windows, she tried to compare this place to the Bible camp back in California where she and her husband had first met. She had been a counselor; he part of the housekeeping staff. Here, though, she had to look past the knee-deep rubbish, the boxes, and the rusty outboard motors.

She sneezed.

"Not really what I had in mind, but I guess..." At least she could use her imagination. "Here's where we could put our little lending library."

Will squinted as she pointed to a shelf behind the counter. "Library?"

"You know. Good books for people to borrow. Summer reading. I'm going to have the girls from the Bookworm Society back home help me out."

Will nodded, but by that time, he had made his own discovery.

"Look! It's just like one of those old soda shops." He stepped over a pile of fishing poles, and true enough, a half dozen swivel stools framed an old-fashioned, red-speckled linoleum counter. The nearest stool squealed when he gave it a spin, setting off a rustling sound from somewhere in the far corner.

Merit retreated to the doorway. "Will, there's something alive in here."

He made his way over to investigate, but didn't have to go far.

"Whoa!" he yelped, jumping back.

Merit flinched and screamed as something brushed by her head on its way out. The next moment, she was locked on to her husband out on the dock, trying to catch her breath.

"What was that?" she finally asked. The funny part, if there was one, was that Will had yelled even louder than she had.

"Um...um..." Will looked around but still held on to her as tightly as she clung to him. "Bats, I think. I think we woke them up from their nap."

That's when it hit Merit, standing on half-sunken docks next to a derelict floathouse that had once been a store in the middle of a beautiful nowhere. Without letting go of her husband, she looked into his eyes and couldn't help...giggling.

"What's so funny?" He returned her look, more puzzled than amused.

"You should have seen yourself," she managed between giggles. "You nearly went through the roof!"

He smiled. "Well, I wasn't sure at first..."

Her giggle grew into a full-scale laugh and infected Will. They laughed until they cried, long and hard, like they hadn't laughed in months—no, years.

"I'm going to make sure you walk a few steps ahead of me for the rest of this tour, Mr. Sullivan," Merit finally ordered.

"Yes ma'am." He led the way back up to shore, clapping his hands, stomping his feet, and saying "shoo-shoo" all the way up the gravel path to the caretaker's cabin.

"That's enough, Will."

He looked over his shoulder with a grin. "Never know if there's a family of raccoons living up here. Or maybe a bear."

"Stop. You've already forgotten how the silly little bats spooked you."

"Spooked *me*? You were the one who made all the noise."

"Oh, now, wait a minute. You're not going to deny you screamed like a girl back there, are you?"

"To my dying breath."

She laughed again as Will grabbed their bags from the car, and they mounted the steps to the front porch. She had to admit, it looked like a Thomas Kinkade painting—the one little log cabin nestled by a lake, smoke curling out the chimney, and a canoe pulled up on the shore. Only in this case, the canoes looked full of holes, and she wasn't sure if the little front porch roof would stand up to the next storm.

Will thumped on the side of the house with his fist, dislodging flecks of green paint from the trim.

"Solid," he told her. "Just needs a fresh coat of stain, some weeding, a couple of new windows, maybe a new roof…"

"Is that all?"

"That's not a nice way to talk about our new home."

"Sorry," she said. "You lead the way inside."

He dropped the bags, crossed his arms, and frowned. "Ladies first."

She shook her head. If there were any more bats in this place, she wasn't going to be the first to discover them.

"You're the man," she told him.

He took that news well. Too well. He bent down and tried to scoop her up in his arms.

"Will, no!" she objected, not very firmly. "You're going to hurt yourself."

"You're the one who said I was the man." He tugged and struggled with her as they backed toward the front door. "Well, this man is going to carry you across the threshold."

She couldn't stop laughing again. "You didn't even do this on our honeymoon."

"Better twenty-four years late than never."

"Will!" she cried. "Watch out!"

They fell in a heap on the porch, a tangle of arms, legs, and laughs.

"You're crazy," Merit said.

"Oh, come on. That's not what you said on our honeymoon."

"Did I let you carry me on our honeymoon?" She reached up to turn the doorknob, hoping it wasn't locked.

"How soon you forget." Will got back to his feet and helped her up. Together they shoved open the door.

"Welcome to Sullivan's Kokanee Cove Resort, Mrs. Sullivan. How do you like your castle?"

Merit locked her arms around Will's neck, pulling him closer as they twirled in the entry of her castle by the lake. The inside smelled a little musty, but not as bad as she'd feared. They could dress up the plain wood floor with a few area rugs. The pink porcelain fixtures in the bathroom would clean up. And the kitchen—well, she'd been camping before. If Will swept out all the spider webs, she could figure out how to cook over a wood stove.

"No raccoons and no bears," Will announced with a wave of his hand, once they'd finished their quick inspection tour. They'd discovered only one piece of furniture: an overstuffed plaid couch huddled at the far side of the living room, left behind by the previous owners.

"And hopefully none of our bat friends." Merit was afraid to look in the rafters. The old-fashioned vaulted ceilings added a touch of class if you ignored the little bird's nest tucked above one of the beams.

Will followed her gaze. "Some people pay a lot of money to keep exotic birds," he said. "Ours come free with the house."

His expression reminded her of the time Michael came home from first grade, so proud of the picture he'd painted, begging for her approval. How could she keep her heart from melting at those big brown eyes? She slipped her arms around Will's waist.

"I think as long as you're in it with me," she told him, "this castle is going to suit us just fine."

"You think so?" He smiled and turned to face her, and she met him with a warm kiss, an unexpected invitation.

"Over there," she whispered, nibbling at the lobe of his ear. "The couch."

"What?"

If he didn't understand her intentions, another kiss or two helped. She motioned with her chin and did her best to steer him toward the only piece of furniture the former owners had left behind.

"It looks like there's room for two," she said.

"Are you kidding?" But he had to recognize the flavor of her hints. "What will the neighbors think?"

"You mean the raccoons?" She grinned, grabbing a beach towel from her bag. "I'm sure they won't mind a couple of old people cuddling in their own house."

❧

Merit was right—no one minded.

When they finally emerged from their castle later that afternoon, she straightened her hair as best she could and surveyed her new kingdom.

"Where's my royal barge?" she asked, but Will seemed to have anticipated her question. He'd already run ahead to the boathouse and was dragging out one of their rental canoes, a weather-worn, all-aluminum model with "Kokanee Cove" stenciled on the side.

"There's two more in there," he reported, "just like this one."

A moment later, he had the canoe in the water and stood with his hands on his hips, a silly grin on his face. That little boy look again.

"Oh, Will, I was just kidding." She stopped at the end of the dock. "It's still too cold."

"Just for a spin. We need a picture of the place from the water. And we can't say we've been here if we haven't been out on the lake."

"I can."

"Chicken."

She sighed at the challenge. "Well…don't we need paddles or something?"

"Right. Paddles. Excellent idea."

He ran to the boathouse while she held the canoe next to the dock, still wondering about all this. But a minute later he returned with paddles under his arms and helped her climb aboard.

"Uh, honey." Merit pointed at the trickle coming from one of the seams as Will stepped into the back end of the canoe. "You might want to take a look at this leak."

"Hmm…" He squinted at it and tossed a couple of old orange life preservers in the canoe. "I wouldn't worry about it. Hop in and we'll take a quick ride."

Merit tentatively placed a foot in the boat, looking for a graceful way to embark. Unfortunately, the silly canoe started rocking all on its own, and the next thing Merit knew, she was lying in the bottom of the boat, looking up at her husband, who was laughing his head off.

"It's not funny." She swatted at him as best she could, nearly tipping them over. It would serve him right if she had. "Don't laugh."

"I'm sorry. You okay?"

"I could have been hurt."

"But you're not." He pulled a stroke with his oar, sending them away from the dock. "So are you going to help me paddle or just lie there with your feet in the air?"

He couldn't seem to stop laughing as she gingerly maneuvered to a sitting position. She picked up her paddle from the canoe floor.

"Don't forget I earned a Girl Scout merit badge in canoeing, Mr. Sullivan."

"No, I didn't forget. But you could've fooled me."

She reached forward as if to pull a long stroke, then pulled back and lifted the paddle just so, sending a wall of water—

"Hey!" he sputtered. "No fair!"

"Life isn't fair."

This time it was her turn to laugh as a giggly, immature water fight broke out. Good thing no one was watching.

Except a girl on the shore, standing in a grove of fir trees near the caretaker's cabin. At this distance it was hard to tell, but she might have been laughing along.

"Will!" Merit whispered over her shoulder. He splashed her one last time. "Someone's up there."

"Oh." Will straightened and looked around.

The girl on shore must have realized they had noticed her and drew back into the early evening shadows with a halfhearted wave, as if embarrassed to be caught staring at the strange people in the canoe.

"Well, we certainly made a great impression on the natives," Merit mumbled.

"Yeah, good thing she didn't stop by about an hour ago, huh?"

"Will!"

Merit blushed, amazed that her husband of twenty-four years could still do that to her.

An odd chirping sound made her stop paddling, and she looked for some exotic bird or more spies in the woods.

"Oh, hey!" Will brightened. "It's actually ringing. They told me back at the store, I mean the Mercantile—whatever they call it—anyway, they said there wasn't any cell coverage out here."

Now she remembered him changing his ring tone in the car on the way here, a new ring tone for a new phase of their life. She hoped she hadn't doused the phone in their water war. Will located a dry spot on his shirt, wiped the phone clean, and flipped it open.

The people at the store had been mostly right. Will paused for a moment, repeated his "hello?" and frowned. "Sorry, Michael, you're in and out. Say that again?"

He scrunched up his face as if that would help bring in the distant signal, and he must have caught enough words to make sense of the message. "Oh. Listen, it's okay. Really. You had every right to question our decision. It was sort of drastic, I'll give you that. And besides, I asked for your opinion, right?"

Another pause.

"Say what?"

Another strained expression, then a nod. "Really, you don't have to apologize. I'm just glad you can…"

Will cocked his head to the side like a puppy dog, then said "hello" a couple more times.

"Here." Merit reached for the phone. "Let me talk to him."

Will shrugged and handed it over. He pulled out his camera to take a few shots of the resort, and she talked to dead air for several seconds before realizing the call had dropped. She handed the phone back to her husband.

"Well, at least he got through," she told him. "What did he say to you?"

Will snapped a couple more angles before replacing the camera in his pocket.

"He told me we should get back to Walnut Creek as soon as we can."

"You mean the girls are being a handful?"

"No, I don't think so. He's just not used to babysitting for a whole weekend."

"Anything else?"

"He hopes we have fun fixing the place up."

"Ha! Easy for him to say." Merit pointed down at the water in the bottom of the canoe, which had started to lap around their ankles. She shivered. "We'd better get back to the dock in a hurry, or the only place we're going is to the bottom of the lake."

Will looked down and lifted his feet.

"Uh-oh." He shifted back to paddle mode and took a long stroke. "Forget the torpedoes! Full speed ahead!"

nine

Why can't we get all the people together in the world that we really like and then just stay together? I guess that wouldn't work. Someone would leave. Someone always leaves. Then we would have to say good-byes. I hate good-byes. I know what I need. I need more hellos.

CHARLES M. SCHULZ

K eep your eyes closed." Merit's best friend, Cheryl Miller, held her hands over Merit's eyes so Merit couldn't cheat.

"They're closed, they're closed." Merit held out her hands in a futile attempt to avoid running into anything as they walked through the back rooms of the Walnut Creek Public Library. She brushed against a book cart and knocked a few books onto the floor. "And you don't need to bother with your hands. This blindfold is going to cut off the circulation in my head as it is."

Already, she could feel a faint throbbing under the folded silk scarf. If it didn't come off soon, the throbbing was sure to grow into a major pain.

"Just want to be sure, girl." Cheryl knew what she wanted to do, and nobody would convince her otherwise. "We're almost there."

They'd better be. Merit heard a giggle off to her right. She pointed toward the sound.

"It's not funny, whoever that is. And don't try this at home."

"Sorry, Mrs. Sullivan," said Juneau Likely, one of the high school kids who worked afternoons reshelving books. The sweet, little, dark-eyed girl with the very unlikely name. Of course, with a name like Merit, she had no room to talk.

"If you were really sorry, Juneau, you'd tell me where my kidnappers were taking me!"

Though by this time, Merit knew. If this was the back room of the library, the meeting room where the Bookworm Society met every month was just down the hallway. Cheryl wasn't helping navigate much, though, just stumbling along Merit's side, stepping on her shoes every few feet.

"Are you going to be happy when I fall flat on my face, Cheryl? I thought you were my friend."

Cheryl just laughed.

"I'll call 911," replied Juneau, now from behind Merit and Cheryl. Someone else joined in the giggling, probably one of Juneau's friends. Merit stumbled at the edge of a carpet but caught herself.

"You do that!" she called back. "Tell them to bring in the SWAT team!"

They finally stopped—probably at the meeting room door, if Merit had judged correctly. This would be the revealing moment when Cheryl pulled off the embarrassing, constricting blindfold. She heard shuffling in front of her, a collective gasp, and finally the "SURPRISE!" she'd suspected and even hoped for in a small way. Off came the blindfold—finally—and Merit couldn't help blinking at the bright overhead lights.

The ladies from her book club were all there, circled around a U-shaped arrangement of folding tables covered with bright orange paper tablecloths left over from the previous year's Halloween party. They surged toward Merit for a group hug.

Merit forgot her headache and the embarrassing hike through the library. They really shouldn't have done this. She thanked God for her friends and their hugs.

Suddenly, her legs went weak and wooziness spun her head and churned her stomach.

She gripped Angela Cooper extra hard. "Angie, I need to sit down for a second."

Angela, an older woman in her late sixties, held Merit by the shoulders and cocked her head in question. "Are you all right?"

"Of course, I'm all right." Merit laughed it off as she lowered herself into a chair by the table. "It's all Cheryl's fault. She put that blindfold on so tight, it cut off the circulation in my cranium. You know who to blame if I start talking stupid."

That brought a laugh and a bit of well-deserved, good-natured scolding from the group for her best friend. Merit's head started to clear as soon as she sat down, and the headache even began draining away. No harm done.

"This is really sweet of you all," Merit managed to choke past the sudden thickness in her throat. "Unnecessary, but sweet."

"What do you mean, unnecessary?" Cheryl demanded. "When the president of the Bookworm Society is about to move away, what are we supposed to do?"

President twice, former secretary, treasurer emeritus, and book selection coordinator. She'd founded the club too, with help and support from Cheryl, not to mention establishing the scholarship fund and bringing in new funding for private school libraries. The only thing she'd never done? Snack coordinator. No one had yet survived any of Merit's attempts to produce edible brownies or other baked goods. As Will could testify, she was still working on nonlethal recipes.

"And besides," added Angie, "we couldn't eat all these goodies by ourselves."

Merit looked at the tables piled high with chips and salty snacks she didn't need, carrots and celery sticks with blue cheese dip, and a steaming plate of little meatballs swimming in aromatic sauce. On a facing table crowned with a punch bowl and cups, they'd arranged cheddar and Gruyère cheese bites speared by festive red and blue toothpicks, mounds of buffalo wings, a platter of nicely arranged Ritz crackers topped with smoked salmon and herbs, and several dozen oversized, homemade chocolate chip cookies.

Then there was the mound of decadent brownies next to the large, white Costco cake, upon which the decorator had written We'll Miss You, Merit in sky blue frosting.

It looked like more than enough to feed everyone in the room—at least fifty women—many times over. Why did they always bring so much food? No one would want to fix anything for dinner tonight.

"Sorry about the banner." Cheryl pointed to the back wall as she plopped down next to Merit. In large blue letters, someone had printed Bon Voyage!

"You ladies do know Will and I are not going on a cruise, right?" Merit whispered back.

"Kind of a last-minute idea. We went to the card store, and it was either that or Congratulations, which we thought was even less appropriate. Christie really wanted to get you a banner, though, so we got that one."

It didn't matter. Nothing mattered except the genuine well-wishes of the ladies Merit had spent every month with for the past seven or eight years. When they started telling her how much they were going to miss her, or how much their kids would miss seeing Mrs. Sullivan at school, or what a difference she'd made in their lives, Merit knew she was going to need an extra package of tissues.

Marjorie Wilson said she'd only read trashy novels until Merit invited her to the group. And look at her now!

Annie Trent said she'd brought one of Merit's book picks home and laid it on the bedside stand, and her husband had started reading it, even though he'd never read a book for fun in his entire life, and was that a miracle or what?

And Susan DePui reminded her how her little girl—who had Down Syndrome—always came home happy and energized after Mrs. Sullivan read to her during library hour at school. Susan fanned at her face before turning away.

Merit tried to keep smiling. Did everyone have to make her feel like Mother Teresa?

"Oh dear," Merit said to Angie, who scooped up a generous slice of brownies to go with a pile of corn chips. "I get all red and puffy faced when I cry."

"We all do, Merit."

The receiving line paused long enough for Merit to enjoy one of Susan's emotionally satisfying fudge brownies, the kind with real sour cream that would have to be offset by running several miles tomorrow on the Iron Horse Trail. And when she ran out of good responses, another brownie served as a convenient mouth stopper, an excuse to chew when she should have been saying "Thanks, I'm going to miss you too" or "That's so sweet of you to say."

Finally, Bernice Carruthers, the oldest woman in the group by far, tottered up and took Merit's hands in her own. Merit could feel the wrinkles. The other woman didn't let go.

"I just wanted you to know I've been praying for you every day, Merit."

That was particularly sweet, and Merit told her so. But Bernice had something more on her mind.

"No, it's not like that, dear." She shook her head, obviously agitated. "I don't sleep much, but I've been waking nights to pray. The Holy Spirit wakes me up out of a sound sleep and says, 'Bernice, you pray for that young Merit Sullivan!' So that's what I do."

The *young* was relative, but Merit counted it anyway.

"I see." Merit cleared her throat. They didn't talk much about their faith at the Bookworm Society, except for Bernice, who everyone knew was a fiery believer. Lutherans like Merit didn't pray like that much, though Merit certainly wouldn't admit it now. "I appreciate—"

"Are you and that man of yours doing all right?"

Is that why Bernice thought she was being prompted to pray at odd hours of the night? The faltering marriage of Will and Merit Sullivan?

"He's very excited about taking on the resort. I mean, so am I, but…"

Bernice smiled knowingly at the evasive answer, but kindly didn't force her to say how much she was going to miss her job at the school, the special-needs kids, her house, all her friends.

"My Tom was like that," Bernice said. "Always chasing after rainbows, building things in his shop. He had big ideas." Her face dropped. She'd been a widow for as long as Merit could remember, easily twenty years. "But you're not so sure, are you?"

Merit choked on a corn chip. Did it show that much? Why did she have to be so painfully transparent?

"Uh…no, actually," Merit stammered. "It's very beautiful up by the lake. Very peaceful. And I think once I get used to the idea, it's going to be very nice. It sort of reminds me of the camp where I met Will."

The hunched old woman obviously wasn't fooled by her cheery tone. She crossed her arms and leveled a stern stare at Merit. Cheryl leaned over and slipped an arm around Merit's shoulder, coming to her rescue.

"We're going to miss her like crazy," Cheryl said.

"Of course, we are," agreed Bernice. "But I'm not going to stop praying for you two. Maybe this is what you need to get plugged back into a good, Bible-believing church. They have some of those up in Idaho, don't they?"

Implication: Will and Merit didn't attend a "good" church. Merit turned to her friend for help. More than anyone else in the room, Cheryl would understand.

"I don't think you need to worry about them, Bernice." Cheryl said it loudly enough to smooth out the awkward exchange. "I'm sure Merit and Will are going to get settled just fine."

Merit looked for another brownie as Bernice finally smiled and drifted off. Merit appreciated the older woman's concern—who couldn't use a little prayer now and then?—but with Bernice, things could easily get dramatic. Merit's pastor, Jerry, probably would have called her "one of those crazy fundamentalists." Merit didn't know whether she was or not, but she did know she breathed a little easier when Bernice left.

"Thanks for the backup," she whispered to Cheryl. "Can you tell I'm running out of pleasant?"

"You're not running out of anything, Merit." Cheryl patted her hand. "All you have to do is be yourself when they ask you to..."

Her voice trailed off. There was more to this going-away party than Merit realized.

"What?" she asked. "When they ask me to do what?"

Cheryl didn't have to answer.

Marcia Cobb had set up a podium just behind the cake and clinked politely on a punch glass with a ballpoint pen. The real meeting came to order. She leaned into the microphone and tapped it for good measure.

"Am I on?"

Doris Hodges let her know she was with a vigorous windmill wave. In other words, *get on with it.*

"Okay, then," Marcia continued. "Let's settle down, everybody."

Marcia had once been crowned Miss Contra Costa County back in the early 1950s, and even today she still held herself with that straight-backed aplomb beauty pageant contestants learn early—the balancing-books-on-her-head look.

"We all know why we're here," Marcia began, projecting over their little crowd. She didn't need the sound system. "And you know we're all going to miss our Merit terribly when she and Will leave for the wilds of Idaho."

The wilds. Merit supposed she wasn't too far off.

"But before they leave this weekend, we wanted to present her with a small token of our affection."

Bernice Carruthers presented Merit with a lovely floral arrangement and a gift basket of new release paperbacks (mostly cheesy romance books), a coffee mug with the Walnut Creek Bookworm Society logo (that cute little worm with a big book and glasses), packets of fancy chai tea (which they knew she loved and probably believed she would never be able to get in Idaho), and small squares of Ghirardelli chocolate. They knew all her cravings. After so many years of monthly book club meetings, how could they not?

Marcia went on with her very nice introduction for the next few minutes, and all the ladies clapped at Miss Contra Costa County's cordial comments, but that only meant they would expect Merit to say something clever and inspirational as well.

There was no escaping the lump that swelled in her throat as she dutifully took her place behind the microphone.

"I, ah…" She blinked her eyes for a moment, took a deep breath, and somehow found the words to continue. "I told myself I wasn't going to start bawling, but since everybody else is, what else can I do?"

While they laughed, she took another deep breath and dabbed at her mascara. Butterflies fluttered in her stomach, unwelcome and persistent, and quickly more than just a flutter. But there was no time to think of tummy troubles just now. She pushed it aside and continued.

"First of all, I just have to thank all you ladies for, for…," she waved her hand at the tables, "for all this wonderful food, for making me feel special, for being here. However—"

The unwelcome butterflies fluttered even more furiously. What had she eaten to bring this on?

"However, if one more person mentions how brave they think I am… well, I'm just going to scream! I am not in the least bit brave. Nothing like that. It's just an adventure that Will has wanted for…well, ever since we've been married, he's talked about doing something like this. And since we're a package deal, off we go!"

That brought a small round of applause, though she hadn't been looking for it. She waited for the clapping to die down before going on.

"We're excited to fix up the place, and I even talked Will into letting me have a corner of the resort store for a little lending library. So if you have any donations to the cause…"

Nods from the crowd told her she wouldn't have a problem getting a few books together.

"Good. And I have to tell you that even though Will and I are moving away, I'm counting on you all to come visit us at the resort. You have to promise me that. Your whole families. No charge to anyone in this room. In fact…"

She had an idea. Silly, perhaps, but what would it hurt?

"Here's what I want you to do. I want you all to raise your right hand in the air and repeat after me."

Like a court clerk, Merit raised her right hand and waited for everyone else to do the same. A few of the ladies looked at each other like they weren't quite sure what was going on, but peer pressure finally got the best of them.

Merit led them in a pledge.

"I solemnly promise…" She waited for them all to repeat the words. "…that I will come to visit Merit and Will."

"…and Will."

"No matter what."

"No matter what."

She looked out at the collection of faces—some wrinkled and worn, others wearing puzzled expressions. She wondered if they would keep their vows, however induced.

An undeniable storm gathered in her stomach, but she wasn't done yet.

"And that everything is going to be…"

She paused once again to wipe away the tears, and Cheryl gripped her hand as she finished.

"…like it always was."

If only she believed her own words.

And if only she could shake off the feeling that…

"Merit, honey?" Cheryl whispered in her ear. "Are you sure you're feeling okay? Your hand is clammy, and your face is white as a sheet."

Merit's stomach managed a complete somersault.

"I'm sorry, Cheryl." She barely managed the words, pressing her lips together to hold back a wave of nausea. She calculated the quickest route to the rest room. "But I think I'm going to be sick."

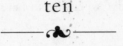

ten

Felix Unger: The man puts his ketchup on his salad.
Oscar Madison: So? I like ketchup. It's like tomato wine.
from *The Odd Couple* (1970–75)

Are you going to barf again, Mommy?" Olivia looked up at Merit as they unpacked kitchen boxes. Will stomped the fir needles from his shoes and set one last load down in a pile on the cabin floor.

"That's not a very nice question to ask your mother, Olivia." Will mopped the sweat from his forehead with the sleeve of his shirt. "She's done a lot of work in the couple of weeks since school got out, getting us moved. It's not easy for us old people."

"Speak for yourself, Mr. Sullivan!" Merit laughed from the kitchen, a little L-shaped counter with a nice view of the docks and bay. "You're the old man around here."

"Yeah, I'm ancient, all right." Will bent over at the waist and did his best old man imitation. "Three whole months older than my wife."

"And don't you forget it."

Merit leaned against their little dumpling refrigerator, as though catching her breath. The ashen look on her face made him wonder.

"I didn't ask if Mom was old," said Olivia. "I already knew that. I was just wondering if she was going to be sick again."

"Olivia—" Abby began to scold her sister too. But her mom didn't seem to mind.

"Not right away, honey. All that pizza and leftover going-away cake made my stomach a little weird. I think I just need to lie down for a minute, if you'll let me."

Olivia shook her head. "A person can never have too much pizza and cake," she replied.

For a moment, Will thought his daughter might have been right to ask. That pale look on Merit's face as she closed her eyes…

"She's tired," he whispered to Olivia with a wink. "That's all."

"It's okay, Will," Merit defended. "She was just asking."

Merit looked far too comfortable stretched out on the couch. Will hoped he wouldn't have to move it again from its spot on the inside wall. Twice was quite enough.

"You need anything, honey?" he asked, not expecting an answer.

"Actually…" Merit's voice thickened to hazy. "I was thinking we should try moving the couch over to another wall, where the light won't…"

She dropped off. Will looked at the girls with a little smile.

Outside, a jay of some kind chattered in the low-hanging branches of a maple tree, as if to welcome them—or scold them for moving into its territory. Beyond that, the sound of an outboard motor droned on the lake, a fisherman returning from an early morning outing. The sound reminded Will of the horrendous load of work he still needed to tackle out on the docks just to make them safe. Moving their stuff into the cabin was just the beginning.

He had plenty of other things to do: check out the fuse box, scrub the laundry room floor, fix the loose steps on the back porch, tighten the railing on the ramp down to the docks, repaint the two floating buildings—the boathouse and the store, haul away years of accumulated trash and junk. The list went on.

Merit must have schlepped one too many boxes of kitchen utensils and living room furnishings, and it showed on her face. They'd moved everything in now, though where they'd put it was another question. Still, he shouldn't have let her carry so much, like some kind of Sherpa.

"Tell you what, girls." He turned to Abby and Olivia, who were pulling pillows out of a large box. "Let's leave your mom here to take a nap while we go visit Aunt Sydney. She might be wondering why we haven't said hi to her yet."

They stopped what they were doing and looked from their dad to their mom, even though by this time Merit was breathing deeply, fast asleep. For a moment, he considered waking her, reminding her how she needed to face her older sister again, but thought better of it.

"Do we have to?" Abby's voice sounded small and just a little desperate. "We were going to go exploring, and besides, Michael says she's…"

"Michael says she's what?" Will crossed his arms, and Abby cowered just a little. Her voice softened even more.

"He said she's batty."

Baby-sitters these days. And big brothers. One never knew what kind of influence they might have on impressionable young minds. Unfortunately, Michael was closer to the truth than Will cared to admit in front of the girls.

"Batty, huh? Well, then maybe we should see if we can find an ice-cream cone at the Mercantile after visiting Aunt Batty—I mean, Aunt Sydney. Would that make it a little better?"

Olivia giggled.

"Ice cream?" Abby's high-pitched voice would wake anyone out of a sound sleep, let alone a mother. Merit's eyelids fluttered, and Will put a finger to his lips before gesturing for the girls to follow him outside.

"We moved here so we could mend fences and be hospitable," he told them as they headed for the Land Rover. "So how about we start today?" Of course, then he had to explain what he meant by fences.

Five minutes later, they drove up a dirt driveway outside town in the state park, over a hill, and down a rutted gravel path.

"Is this really where Aunt Sydney lives?" asked Olivia.

Will couldn't blame her for sliding a little lower in her seat. He nodded as he wondered what he was getting his daughters into. Or himself.

"Yeah, this is the place. I think."

The trailer was one of those 1950s Airstreams, all aluminum and none too even on its foundation, like someone had dumped it there forty years ago and had never bothered to level it up. A six-foot chain-link fence circled the perimeter. The message was clear: *Leave me alone.*

That part he remembered from their visit here fifteen years ago. The trailer itself looked the same. He just didn't remember all the—

"Wow," whispered Abby. "She sure likes windmill whirligig things, huh?"

Olivia started counting. "Two, three, four…"

Several of the painted wooden spirals hung from the lowest branches of a fir tree that shaded the trailer, spinning like strands of homespun DNA.

"Five, six, seven…."

Others looked like little men chopping wood or woodpeckers working on a tree branch, springing into action when a breeze caught the propellers.

"Eight, nine…"

A couple of the wind machines featured orca whales chasing their tails, around and around. Most simply chimed and gonged in the breeze, and they could hear the symphony of notes the moment Will turned off the car.

"I think they're creepy," declared Abby.

"There's nothing creepy about lawn decorations," he told them.

There was no turning back now. They had come to say hi to Aunt Batty, so they were going to say hi. Maybe this way he wouldn't have to do it again for another fifteen years.

With no sign of life inside, Will led the way up a short set of stairs and across a deck (of sorts) that reminded him very much of the docks back at the resort. Maybe it was the trampoline effect on the soft wood.

"Careful," he warned the girls, and they tiptoed behind him.

They didn't notice the cats until they had almost reached the front door.

"A kitty!" Abby bent down to pet the first one, a small black-and-tan tabby who had slipped around the corner of the deck to greet them.

"And two more!" Olivia made the discovery under the steps, and the count began. Before Will knocked on the door, the girls had tallied at least a dozen.

"Anybody home?" Will rapped once and then a second time before a tattered curtain finally parted and a wild pair of green eyes stared out at them. Will felt his daughters line up behind him, and a long moment later, the door finally cracked open.

"It's Will, Sydney." His voice sounded shakier than he'd intended. "Your brother-in-law, Will. We've moved into the resort, so I thought we'd come by to say hi."

Either the woman had not been expecting visitors or she always dressed in an ankle-length tie-dyed dress and sandals. She'd wrapped her long hair in a pink scarf that matched her pink painted fingernails, but unruly tufts found their way out here and there, like snakes trying to escape a sack. A tiny black cat, not much bigger than a kitten, clung to her shoulder like a fur stole.

Will gave the girls a look and a shake of his head, hoping they'd get the hint and stop staring.

"Well, well," Sydney said.

Abby and Olivia squeezed his hands. They could stand on the deck and try to confirm the fact that they were indeed related, or he could break the awkward silence.

"I brought the girls by to meet you," he said. "Merit would have come too, but she wore herself out moving—"

"I heard you were buying the old resort," she interrupted, finally pulling back the door and motioning for them to come in. He had to duck to avoid bumping into one of the Native American dreamcatchers hanging just inside the door. "It's a shame you couldn't leave it in its natural state. Better energy that way."

"Uh, well, yeah. A guy from Kootenai Electric was out the other day. Got us all set up with the power feed."

She ignored his feeble joke, and Will looked around the inside of Aunt

Sydney's dark little cave and started to get the picture. On one wall hung a full-size watercolor portrait of a cougar, surrounded by several more dream-catchers and feather arrangements. A floor-to-ceiling carpeted cat-climbing tower occupied an entire corner of the trailer, and perhaps that was the source of the mild but unmistakably odd odor. If the girls had thought there were a lot of cats outside…

"Wow," said Abby, finally emerging from her father's shadow. "How many cats do you have?"

Aunt Sydney smiled for the first time, a crooked sort of upturn of the lips that didn't quite match her yellowed teeth and dark eyes.

"I lost count after Gloria Steinem had kittens," she admitted, pointing to the cat at Will's feet.

The girls didn't seem to think it strange to meet a cat named after a feminist pioneer, though of course they would not recognize the name. Gloria Steinem the cat, however, was making Will's leg itch where the creature had rubbed up against him. His jeans were no protection at all. Gloria Steinem obviously had no idea this human was allergic to cats.

"When was that?" asked Abby.

The older woman picked up another tabby and placed it on the kitchen counter, where the cat could choose from a half dozen bowls of food. Will's eyes started to water and his throat began to feel tight. They would need to get out of this trailer soon.

"Four years ago, I think," Sydney answered. "No, five."

Will stood with his daughters just inside the front door, trying to make conversation. They wouldn't be able to sit. It looked as if every chair had been taken over by feline companions and their equipment. Aunt Sydney didn't seem to notice.

"Abby says we're going to have a pet raccoon," Olivia blurted. "Just like in *Rascal.*"

"Liv," Will put in, "that's still not a practical idea."

But Olivia's announcement brought a righteous frown to Aunt Sydney's wrinkled face. "I'm sure you wouldn't want to keep a raccoon," she retorted. "They're wild creatures, and we're *all* diminished when they're caged. It's like slavery."

It was Olivia's turn to wrinkle her nose in confusion.

"Like slavery…" she began, and Aunt Sydney was only too glad to explain, pointing out the grievous sins of Mr. Mooney at the Mercantile, who held captive animals against their will. Birds and small animals had a right to be free, didn't he know?

The girls nodded their heads politely, but not even Will could follow the connection between the supposed consciousness of wild forest creatures and fluoride treatments in large cities. He considered suggesting that impeaching the president would be the only logical course of action, then thought better of it. She might not follow his sarcasm.

After several minutes of mind-numbing verbal fog, Will couldn't resist checking his watch. These cats were going to kill him. His nose had started running like a faucet, and he could feel his cheeks puffing up. He waited for Sydney to ease up on her monologue, then squeezed in a hint.

"Well, girls, I think we'd better get back home and see how your mom is doing."

Abby had already made her way to the front door. No need to talk her into anything. Olivia, however, was still listening intently, her head cocked to one side like a puppy.

"Liv?" he interrupted the lecture as gently as he could, and Aunt Sydney winked at her new young disciple.

"You come back any time you like, Olivia." Maybe this had been the first time anyone really listened to her. "We'll have coffee."

"I've never had coffee before." Olivia glanced at her dad and smiled uncertainly. "But I'd like to come back."

"Uh, she's not into caffeine," Will explained. He wondered what had possessed him to bring these two innocent little ones with him to this less-than-innocent place. He saw a computer parked on the kitchen counter, out of place. Aunt Sydney must have noticed the look.

"I have a Web site," she announced.

"Cool!" Olivia bounced on her toes at the news. "Does it have, like, games on it or lots of graphics?"

"No games. Just photographs and some writing. It's kind of a rescue mission."

"Really?" Olivia asked. "Our Sunday school class volunteered at a rescue mission last Christmas."

When Sydney frowned, Will knew he hadn't rescued his daughters quickly enough. He dragged them toward the door, but too late.

"My site is a little different, dear," explained the woman. "It's to rescue as many people as we can from the lies of the government, the lies of the multi-national corporations, and"—she leveled her gaze at Will and lowered her voice—"the lies of the church."

Where did *that* come from? Fortunately, Olivia had picked up another cat and wasn't paying attention.

"Sounds fascinating." He shepherded his girls safely toward the door, hoping they hadn't heard the last comment. "We'll have to check it out." He didn't ask for the Web address.

"Wait a minute." Aunt Sydney shuffled over to a card table set up next to her little wood stove piled high with small willow hoops, feathers, beads, yarn, and other such craft supplies. She selected a dreamcatcher that looked like a spider web and gave it to Olivia.

"You hang this up in your room over your bed," she told the girls. "The Ojibwa native peoples tell us that long ago, Asibikaashi the Spider Woman taught mothers how to make webs like this and hang them above the beds of their children."

Abby started to giggle, probably at the Asibikaashi the Spider Woman part.

"What for?" Olivia asked.

"Well, to filter out all the bad dreams and only allow good thoughts through. See that little hole in the middle?" She pointed. "That's for the good thoughts."

Abby wrinkled her nose. "Guess they have to be awfully little good thoughts to fit through, huh?"

Olivia poked her older sister with an elbow and smiled at her aunt. "I think it's pretty. Thank you."

"Yeah, that's nice of you, Sydney." Will had had enough of the legends. They really had to go. "Maybe it'll help the resort's fun-shoe...whatever."

"That would be feng shui, Will, and I don't think you understand. The goal is cosmic equilibrium of individual objects within—"

He sneezed and rubbed his poor nose. But Aunt Sydney was just getting warmed up, and she obviously wasn't going to stop until she had convinced them all to seek cosmic unity and happiness.

"Thanks again, Sydney," he interrupted, stepping backward onto the trampoline porch. "Sorry we have to run, but we really to need to get back and check on Merit. I'll tell her hi for you."

Will thought he saw the woman stiffen at his words, but she recovered quickly.

"Don't forget the town meeting tonight," she called after them. "Seven o'clock at the community center. We've got a group protesting the Osprey Point developer. Can you believe he wants to put thirty condos in the middle of an environmentally sensitive area like this?"

Will thanked her again and retreated to the car. The girls must have heard him sigh when he locked the doors.

"She's weird," said Abby. "All that cosmic stuff she was talking about. It's not in the Bible. And I don't think you should keep that...that *thing* she gave you, Olivia."

"She is *not* weird!" Olivia would defend her from now on, probably. She held up her prize and its feathers twirled in the breeze from the open window. "And there's nothing wrong with the dreamcatcher, is there, Daddy?"

"Uh…" He guessed Merit would probably flip when she saw it, like it was some kind of occult talisman. Maybe it was. "Let's talk about it some more when we get home."

"Well, I liked her." Olivia obviously wanted to make sure her older sister knew she couldn't be bossed around so easily. "And I think her cats are cool."

Will found a tissue and blew his nose, grateful he'd gotten out of there alive. He wasn't sure about the dreamcatcher, but he did know one thing: Aunt Sydney's cats were definitely *not* cool.

eleven

A family is a unit comprised not only of children but of men,
women, an occasional animal, and the common cold.
OGDEN NASH

Normally the white clapboard church housed the Kokanee Cove Bible Chapel. Tonight, however, it had been pressed into service as the community center. Almost one hundred townspeople crammed into the pews and stood along the sides, nearly falling out the windows. Will and Merit squeezed in beside two large men wearing North Idaho Trucking caps. They would be standing for this meeting, but so would a lot of other folks.

"Nice little church," observed Will, and Merit agreed. It looked like a classic New England church, even though they were nowhere near New England. Red, blue, and golden light spilled through simple stained-glass windows lining each side, and a prominent cross presided over the scene from its mount on the back wall. The worn wood floor gave the sanctuary a humble, working-class character.

Merit wouldn't mind visiting this weekend, just to see what it was like, but right now churchgoing was the furthest thing from her mind. She and Will were beginning to garner strange looks from the locals. A couple of women stopped their chatter to note Merit's arrival.

"Hi there," Merit said, trying to preempt their stares. It didn't work, so she turned her attention to the crowd. In the front row, looking like a throwback to the sixties in her peculiar yellow and violet tie-dyed dress, Sydney perched on the edge of a pew with pencil and tattered notebook in hand. She focused straight ahead, probably ready to attack.

Merit also recognized the fellow who ran the Kokanee Cove Mercantile, an odd-looking man named Mr. Mooney. She'd had to ask if that was really his name.

She recognized no one else, so she resigned herself to listening in on some of the conversations swirling around her like river rapids. The two men wearing stained trucker caps next to her spoke clearly and loudly, not at all worried about being overheard.

"I think the county commissioners have already decided, and this meeting is just a show."

"Wouldn't be surprised." The second trucker cleared his throat as if he was going to spit, then caught himself.

"Yeah, you just watch. They're going to pretend to listen and then just do what they wanted to do in the first place. Developer's got those three guys in his pocket."

"Those three guys" presided over the meeting-to-be from behind a folding table where the altar would normally have been. It didn't seem to bother anybody that the meeting was already fifteen minutes late—or at least no one asked what time it was. Everyone in the room buzzed with anticipation.

Merit glanced back at the entry, pretended not to notice the continuing stares, and wondered what people would think if she and Will left early and got back to the kids. They'd made their appearance, showed their support. They were hemmed in by a dozen or more people, though, so they were trapped here for the duration.

Will leaned closer and whispered in her ear. "The girls will be fine," he told her. "This isn't the big city, remember."

She should have known Will would realize exactly what she was worrying about. But what if Abby and Olivia had to deal with a wild animal, or what if one of them got hurt? Out here, 911 meant a call to the volunteer fire department, but who was that exactly? How long would it take them to respond? And weren't they all at the meeting anyway?

She sighed and nodded. They'd be fine? Easy for him to say.

After five more minutes of chitchat, a gray-haired gentleman at the front table finally banged a gavel to bring the meeting to order. He seemed to enjoy his gavel, because he slammed it against the table far longer than needed. The buzzing settled down.

"All right, everybody," he called, "we're going to get this meeting started, so we can be out of here by midnight."

He was kidding, right? Merit looked around, but no one was laughing.

The man went on, informing them this was simply a chamber of commerce meeting, the rest of the town had been invited as a courtesy only, and he would not tolerate any outbursts, et cetera. The people took in his warnings with crossed arms and stony expressions, seemingly determined to have their say.

Merit realized where she'd seen this scene before: one of those classic Norman Rockwell paintings, the one with the earnest-looking working man standing up at the town meeting to say his piece. But Rockwell might have missed the undertone of hostility in this painting.

It didn't take long for the fur to fly.

"That's all fine and good, Hank," the fellow standing next to Merit said, interrupting the meeting's official proceedings, "but we just want to make sure there's no back room deals going on here. We have something to say about the—"

Bam-bam-bam! Hank swung his gavel with even more gusto. "I meant what I said, Earl." The chairman's face began to turn red. "We've opened this meeting as a courtesy to you, and you're welcome to stay if you'd like to listen. If not, we're going to ask you to leave."

But Earl wasn't backing down, and neither were his friends. "I'm not here to make trouble." He puffed up his chest. "I'm just here to make sure the people of Kokanee Cove have a say in all this."

That brought applause that drowned out even the gavel.

"Problem is," Earl continued, "people from California are coming in and kicking property values so crazy high, nobody's going to be able to afford to live here anymore."

As the crowd murmured their approval, Merit felt like a Daniel in a lions' den, and she could feel all eyes on her and Will.

Earl wasn't done yet. "I hear California developers even came in and bought the old Kokanee Cove Resort, just below where they want to put all those condos, and that it's going to be part of the big mess they're making. Condos up on the hill and a casino down on the water is what I heard. Now we've already got two bars, a coffee shop, and the Buttonhook Inn, and we don't need a lot of outsiders coming in like vultures, buying things up. Anybody else agree?"

More applause and a flurry of comments bounced off the walls. This was getting personal in a hurry. Merit felt her cheeks redden as she tried to back toward the exit. Someone knew from the brother of a friend of a reliable source that all the marinas were being cleared out and rates doubled, probably tripled. Where were they going to keep their fishing boats now that all the out-of-town yachts were coming? And somebody else heard Donald Trump had something to do with the buyout, and that...

"That's a lot of deer droppings."

When Sydney got to her feet, even Hank's gavel paused in midair. She turned slowly to face the crowd and pointed straight at Merit and Will. "My little sister and her husband don't know Donald Trump, and they're not starting any casinos. You're doing this all on your own, aren't you, Will?"

Merit felt every eye rest on her and Will and sensed her husband's discomfort as sharply as her own. If anyone hated speaking in public more than she did, it was her Will.

He cleared his throat, but nothing came out quickly enough to keep the moderator from finally slipping back into the driver's seat of this free-for-all.

"Thanks for pointing out your brother-in-law, Sydney." He still held his gavel up like a threat. Maybe he would use it on someone's head, this time.

He turned toward Will. "Mister, I don't know where all these rumors are coming from, but I hear you are fixing up the place on your own. That right?"

Will nodded, swallowed hard, and finally found his voice. "That's right. Just the resort. I don't know anything about the condos."

"Good," the moderator said. "You've got plenty of work to do, I imagine, just keeping those old docks from sinking. My uncle built those docks back when Sandy Johnson owned the place. When was that, the sixties?"

"Sixty-seven," someone volunteered from the back of the room.

"Yeah, could be." Hank rubbed his chin. "That was the year we had that big freeze, I think."

"No, it wasn't," someone else corrected him. "Sixty-seven was the year they had that huge forest fire up by Sandpoint. The one that burned out fifty-some thousand acres."

"Before my time." That got a chuckle from the crowd, but Hank was done recollecting. He waved his gavel with new menace as he turned back to the newcomers. "Anyway, it's the Sullivans, right? Good luck to you. You're going to need it."

"Thanks," Will replied. "Will and Merit. We're glad to be here."

"Just the two of you?" Hank demanded, continuing the interview. Merit was glad she wasn't answering the questions.

"No, actually…" Will seemed to be warming up. "We have two young girls and an older son who's joining us the day after tomorrow. He's driving a truck with the rest of our stuff—tools, that kind of thing. He's a pretty good mechanic. Just out of the service."

Hank squinted at them. "So where you all from?"

"Uh…" Will hesitated, "south of Boise."

Merit almost giggled. They were from south of Boise, all right. Almost a thousand miles south, but no one needed to know that yet. Not the way these people felt about California.

"And you're all invited to the grand reopening in two weeks," Will added. Merit gave him a warning look. What was he saying?

"Good." Hank waved his gavel for effect. "On behalf of the chamber of commerce, I want to welcome you to Kokanee Cove, home of the best kokanee and rainbow trout fishing in North America...or it was, until the Corps of Engineers started messing with the dam downriver, and the lake levels, and...well, anyway, welcome."

Merit noticed only a couple murmurs of agreement this time.

"Fine," interjected Earl the Rebel Leader, "but what about the casino?"

Here came the murmurs, and several people glanced at Merit, the enemy.

"Actually..." For a crazy moment Merit considered correcting the man, setting him straight and extending her neck out onto the chopping block on behalf of all the Sullivans. These people would find out they were California refugees sooner or later. Instead, Sydney held up her hand to make her own announcement.

"Merit's grandfather—my grandpa too—came to the lake in 1925. He fished the lake and helped build the Navy boot camp back in 1943." She looked around to make sure everyone got her point. "Our family goes back several generations around here."

Sydney's challenge was unmistakable. No one replied. Finally, Sydney sat down, her arms crossed, and Hank picked up the meeting agenda again. Earl's gaze never left Will and Merit. Maybe he was still wondering about the "south of Boise" remark.

Merit wasn't sure what folks would do when they found out the truth. Or how she and Will would get the resort ready in time, now that he'd announced it to the world.

twelve

If you woke up breathing, congratulations! You have another chance.

ANDREA BOYDSTON

M erit paused to catch her breath, wishing the paint didn't make her stomach tumble, the way everything seemed to do these days. She swallowed and ran the roller through the tray once more. Two coats of fresh, white paint would cover a multitude of stains and scratches on the wall above the stove. She took down the little Gone Fishing fish she'd given Will. Well, given herself really. The rustic fish sign looked cute in the kitchen. It matched the resort décor.

Will's pounding stopped for a moment, and she imagined having to rescue her husband from under the house. *Please,* she thought, *at least not before Michael shows up with the truck this afternoon.* How long could they convince their son to stay?

The pounding started again, followed by a clunk and a loud groan. She could hear Will's yell plainly through the floorboards.

"Stupid pipe!"

"Are you all right down there?" she called. "Do you need me to bring you the plumbing book again?"

More grumbling, and the pounding started anew. Merit smiled. *Apparently not.*

She took another breath, trying not to gag on the paint fumes, and Abby flew through the open front door out of breath.

"Somebody's coming, Mom!"

"Oh good." She needed an excuse to put down the paint roller. "Your brother is finally here?"

"Uh-uh." Abby shook her head. "Somebody else. Lots of somebody elses."

Visitors? Already? At the town meeting, Merit had gotten the clear impression that people were anxious about the resort's rejuvenation, but she'd never expected they'd all just show up. Unannounced. *And* several days early.

As Merit pushed open the screen door, a pickup pulled in the little gravel parking lot, followed by a few cars and an older couple on an ATV. A tall man with enormous eyeglasses and not much hair on his head disembarked from the pickup and led the parade. A pleasant-looking woman and a college-age girl joined him, each carrying a towel-draped load in their arms. Something about the girl looked familiar.

"Welcome to Kokanee Cove!" boomed the man. His thundering bass voice perfectly matched his ample frame, the kind of voice that used car dealerships would hire for their radio ads.

"I'm Pastor Bud Unruh, Kokanee Cove Bible Chapel." The man's smile wrapped around his face as if his lips had been unzipped a couple inches wider than normal. "My wife, Bonnie, our daughter, Stephanie. And…"

He waved his hand at the advancing invaders, all of them carrying picnic baskets, coolers, or grocery sacks in their arms. The pastor's wife gripped Merit's hand between her own and finished his sentence for him.

"And we brought a few of our church families with us."

Merit didn't realize until too late that she'd shared a paint smudge with her new neighbor.

"I'm terribly sorry." Merit looked for a rag or a handkerchief. "I'm a mess. I've been painting."

"So you're an artist?" Pastor Bud asked.

His wife scolded him. "Bud! These people don't appreciate your odd sense of humor yet."

Yet. Merit smiled at the exchange and wiped off her hand before shaking any others. "Not a problem," she said. "Actually, my husband is trying to fix something under the cabin. Will?"

Will appeared a moment later, inching out of the crawlspace. Cobwebs wrapped his head like a turban, and his dusty faced appeared several shades darker even in the noon sun.

"Oh!" He patted the dust off his work clothes and blinked his eyes. "I thought I heard someone drive up."

That signaled the start of another round of introductions, not just from the Unruh family, but from everyone in the welcoming party. Several of the ladies parked overflowing plates of poor boy and tuna fish sandwiches with pickles on the picnic tables, along with bowls of chips, slices of bright red watermelon, and pitchers of lemonade spiked with tangy huckleberry juice.

"I'm really glad we caught you all here," Pastor Unruh said. "Because if you weren't—"

Bonnie chimed in. "We were going to have to eat all this ourselves."

"Actually, we're still waiting on our son, Michael." Merit explained about the rest of the equipment and tools on their way and how Michael had agreed to help them out for a while. "He's about the same age as your..."

She looked at the Unruh girl, who had taken a quick liking to Abby and Olivia.

Bonnie laughed. "She's mature for her age," explained Bonnie, "except when it comes to taking care of younger kids. I don't think anyone ever explained to her that twenty-one-year-olds don't usually get down on all fours and pretend they're turkeys or..."

Her voice trailed off as they watched Stephanie pull herself up into the branches of the old maple in the corner of the lawn, then reach high for an abandoned bird's nest.

"I'm sorry," Bonnie whispered. "Like I said, she's otherwise really very mature for her age."

Merit grinned as her own girls followed Stephanie's example, and soon all three girls were swinging from branches.

Another truck came chugging down the gravel path. Someone else from the church welcoming committee? Will craned his neck and squinted.

"I think it's Michael," he said.

That would have been good news, except that the top of the tall rental truck was raking the bottom branches of the trees lining the drive—including the one Stephanie and the girls were in.

"Girls!" Will shouted and waved for them to get down. "Out of the way of the truck!"

In a moment, the two younger girls had swung down and scampered safely back to the picnic. Stephanie, however, didn't seem to notice the danger as she swung off a large branch—right into the middle of the driveway and directly in the path of the oncoming truck.

☙

How had she not heard it coming?

The truck barreled down the hill, and by the time it rounded the last corner, Stephanie still stood planted in the gravel road, staring into the startled eyes of the driver. He skidded to a stop in a cloud of dust.

Now she knew how deer felt. She moved to the side of the drive, still clutching the bird's nest she had retrieved for the two Sullivan girls. Possibly a robin's nest, judging by the size of it—about five inches across. The driver, a boy about her age or maybe a little older, leaned out of his window, elbow first.

"You always stop trucks like this?" He grinned as though disappointed he hadn't plowed her down. And still she dumbly clutched the nest.

"I was just showing Abby and Olivia a...a robin's nest up in this tree." She hid it behind her back.

"Oh. Well, I'm Michael," he told her as he looked at the picnic crowd. "Michael Sullivan. And except for my parents up there by that cabin, I'm not sure if I'm in the right place."

"You are. They said you were coming."

"That's good."

She thought he would pull the truck ahead now, but his two little sisters raced their way, waving and shouting.

"Michael!" Abby and Olivia shouted in chorus.

"We thought you were never going to make it," Olivia told him.

"What are you talking about?" He yanked at a brake lever and hopped out of the cab. "I had to come visit my two favorite little sisters, right?"

"Visit?" Olivia picked up on his choice of words as she gave him a hug. "Aren't you coming to stay?"

Stephanie noticed he didn't answer her question directly, just laughed and wrestled his sisters out of the way.

"This a friend of yours?" he asked them, indicating Stephanie with a nod. "She never told me her name."

He looked like a soldier or a professional wrestler. *Hadn't his parents mentioned he was just out of the service?*

"Stephanie." She shifted the nest to her left hand before holding out her right and bracing for the bone-crunching squeeze that was sure to come. "Stephanie Unruh."

He took her hand but didn't squeeze too hard. Big grip, but gentle. In fact, very gentlemanly. And very...something else that she wasn't quite sure of.

"Pleased to meet you, Stephanie Unruh. I'm really glad I didn't run you over before I even got your name."

"Uh, right." She backed up and nearly squatted on a tree stump before catching herself. "Me too."

She shook her head. She sounded like an idiot, but no one seemed to notice her twitterpated tumbling, least of all Michael Sullivan. She noticed something in his gaze, though—a flash of disapproval as he looked at the resort, at his parents, at the rest of the church people.

But only for a second, and then he turned his attention back to her.

"You work here, Stephanie?"

"Actually, no." She shook her head. "I used to. Before your parents got here, obviously."

"Hmm. Right. Well, between you and me," Michael leaned in, away from his sisters' ears, "I have no idea what they think they're doing here. My dad's not exactly a handyman, and even if he were, this place needs more work than two people can do in ten years."

"They told me you could fix anything."

"Anything?" He chuckled. "Maybe they don't know me very well. And they think they're going to open in a few weeks? This is nuts."

"It's not nuts," Stephanie said. "They've been working hard."

"Yeah, killing themselves." He chuckled again but didn't smile. "So anyway, I got here just in time for the party, huh?"

She didn't answer, and he didn't notice the frown that crept across her face. If that's all he came for, then fine. He could come for the party while his parents killed themselves working.

"Come on, Michael." Olivia jumped into her brother's arms and let him swing her around. "We'll show you where all the bird nests are. There's some down on the docks."

"Okay, Lady O. Show me."

And with the thought of bird's nests, Stephanie needed to return hers to its place in the lovely old maple. She didn't watch as Michael Sullivan's little sisters hustled him away.

thirteen

—— ❧ ——

*There's nothing written in the Bible...that says if you believe in
me, you ain't going to have no troubles.*
RAY CHARLES

He'd been in the military, right? So he was twenty-six or twenty-seven,
she guessed. Maybe older, which surely made him too experienced.
He certainly looked like it. He'd probably had a string of girlfriends, left the
requisite trail of broken hearts. Maybe he was even divorced and had kids.
She wasn't about to ask.

Stephanie continued pedaling, taking a deep breath of fir-scented morning air. A chipmunk scolded her from its perch in a tree.

And what about the little tattoo of an eagle on his arm? That didn't make
him a birdwatcher. He probably didn't know the difference between a canyon
wren and...

Not that it mattered. And it didn't matter how good-looking a person
was. He wasn't her type.

His parents, on the other hand, had taken on an impossible job, trying
to fix up the resort in a matter of weeks. Despite his lousy attitude, Michael
was right about one thing: they were going to kill themselves trying to get
that old place renovated in time for their first customers.

She hadn't had a chance to talk much to Mr. Sullivan, though he seemed
nice, but something about Mrs. Sullivan made her pause. Something made
her want to pray for the woman, the way she would for a bird with a broken
wing. Stephanie knew something was very broken about Merit Sullivan. Her
certainty of it made her wonder how she could be so sure about something
like this when she had so much trouble deciding what shoes to wear in the

morning. Even so, the odd assurance remained: behind Mrs. Sullivan's warm face and grateful eyes laid a secret that hurt.

Stephanie knew her little gesture wouldn't help one way or the other, but she gripped her package as tightly as she could under one arm anyway. She trundled past the lakeside Navy Acoustic Research Center and its secret test equipment on her well-used, around-town mountain bike. The road clung to the side of the hill, keeping a respectful distance from the tall, barbed-wire fence that spelled the base's southern boundary.

"Take the truck, Stephanie."

Her mother always said the same thing. Stephanie appreciated the concern, but her mother couldn't fathom the idea of good exercise, honest sweat, and the feeling of mounting the top of Cape Horn on her own aching legs, up where the huckleberries grew so profusely she sometimes had to whistle to shoo the bears away from their lunch.

"At least carry some pepper spray, girl!"

She'd resisted that idea too, but gave in when Mom got her a little can and planted it on her dresser. Though Stephanie doubted she would ever have occasion to use it, she had to admit that she had checked her belt clip once or twice, just to be sure she still carried the compact little spray can. It wasn't the bears that made her do it, though. The higher-elevation forest north of Cape Horn was also home to cougars. Once, she thought, she'd heard a growl, though it had sounded pretty far away.

No, her mother would never understand why Stephanie always hiked on her own or why she chose to ride her mountain bike around town instead of taking the truck like everyone else. But Mom didn't have to understand everything.

Stephanie glanced up at the gathering clouds, the dark ones that could sweep in from the west and overtake a sunny day faster than—

The deep report of a thunderclap rolled across the granite face of Bernard Peak, echoing and crackling across the near-vertical face that ringed the lake at its southern end. When one followed the severe slope of the surrounding hills as they dashed into azure water, it wasn't hard to see how depths could easily reach a thousand feet or more.

Stephanie quickened her pace. She might have misjudged this storm. It was coming in faster than she expected, and she was concerned about making it to the Kokanee Cove Resort before the impending thundercloud dumped a big load of wet on her. She could nearly smell it—a rolling wash of cool damp moisture that prepared the way for a summer storm. Gasping for breath, she pushed the pedals, hanging on to the package like she was a Pony Express rider delivering the United States mail.

She hadn't quite reached the resort when the first curtain of cool rain swept across the treetops and pulled her into its undertow. She could hear a freight train coming—the real rain shower—and the thunder and pyrotechnic flashes of lightning buried her in their grand show.

"Not good," she mumbled and wondered if the paper sack would keep her cargo dry until she made it to the resort.

The full force of the storm hit her, and it took only a few moments to feel as if she had stepped into a full-blast shower with all her clothes on. She might have turned back if she'd been closer to home, but she coasted down the hill, brakes squealing, rounded a bend, and finally bumped down the gravel road that led to the Kokanee Cove Resort. She remembered the exact spot where Michael Sullivan had nearly flattened her in his truck earlier that day.

She continued right up onto the porch of the caretaker's cabin, and in one fluid movement, she bailed from the bike, let it park itself under the cabin's eaves, and stumbled to a stop by the front door.

For a minute she caught her breath while the rain pelted the metal porch roof in a staccato rhythm. Rain, like drumsticks on a snare drum, madly kept time to a wild beat, faster and slower, louder and softer. Thunder added its kettle drum; lightning, its cymbals. Stephanie didn't knock on the door, just leaned on the front porch railing, listening and watching.

The church folks had left a few hours ago, or their welcoming picnic would have been washed out. As it was, purpose-driven rain rivers rushed across the yard, past the cabin, and down the hill toward the lake. If it kept up much longer, this mountain downpour would take the Sullivans' meager little patch of grass and transplant it right down into Kokanee Cove.

But it wouldn't keep up. These things never did. So she drip-dried a bit and unwrapped the package, checking to make sure it wasn't as damaged as she feared. With the racket overhead, she almost didn't hear the friendly screen door screech behind her.

"Well, look who's back."

Stephanie turned to see Merit had joined her on the porch. "A little wet out there." Stephanie didn't need to explain further.

"Yeah, I can see. Do you always go out in this kind of weather? Pardon me for saying, but you look like you could use some drying off."

"It kind of caught me off guard." Stephanie smiled and swiped a strand of wet hair from her eyes. "I should have known better."

Merit invited her inside, and Stephanie followed her into the living room. Boxes still lined the walls, even more now, Stephanie imagined, after Michael's arrival, though much had already been unpacked.

"The boys are down at the boathouse with Abby and Olivia," Merit said, "if…" Her shy look hinted that she might have seen more than she let on earlier in the day. But Michael wasn't Stephanie's type.

She held out the package, soggy wrapping and all. "Actually, I just came to bring you this."

Merit unwrapped it with a question on her face.

"It's an old painting somebody did of Kokanee Cove," Stephanie explained. "See the mountain up there in the corner? That's Bernard Peak. It used to hang in the snack bar—the store—when I worked there. When the other owners left, they said I could have it, but it seems like it really belongs here, so…"

"That's very sweet of you." Merit beamed as she held the painting to the light. Even with the cracks and fading, it was easy to make out Bernard Peak and the lake below. Stephanie guessed the painter had been a fairly accomplished amateur. "Are you sure? You should keep it."

"No." Stephanie shook her head, and she meant it. "It was hanging in the same spot on the wall behind the counter for years and years. I'll bet there's still an outline on the wall so you can see where it was. People who come back are going to expect to see it there. Besides, I didn't really have any place for it at home."

"Tell you what." Merit brightened even more as she settled on a flowered couch. "We'll accept it on one condition."

Stephanie shifted her feet. "What condition?"

"You know we've only been here a few days," Merit went on, "but Will and I can already see we've bitten off a little more than we can chew."

At least they weren't fooling themselves. Stephanie sat next to her and nodded as Merit continued. She really did have a nice smile, but there was that *something* behind it again.

"We talked last night about maybe getting more help. To tell you the truth, I haven't been feeling very energetic lately. I'm not sure what it is. Flu bug, I thought, but it's a little different. I'm just weak and achy. Maybe it's the stress of moving."

"I've never moved before, but I can imagine," Stephanie said.

Merit smiled. "You're lucky. But here's the thing: you and your parents coming by today, and all those sweet people from your church, I just felt as if...I don't know. I know it's kind of a cliché, but it seemed so much like a God-thing to us. And then Michael showed up in the middle of it all."

"But you were expecting him to visit, right?"

"Oh, yeah. That's not what I meant. It just seemed like God was bringing it all together in our life. I mean, finally. We've been in kind of an odd funk for the past few years. Always busy, always late for something, but more in a treadmill kind of way, if you know what I mean."

"Sure," Stephanie said but had no idea. She let Mrs. Sullivan talk for a while, about the move and how it worked out for Michael to join them for his vacation, after all. God's hand. Merit even explained how her book club friends back in California had given her several boxes of books to set up a little lending library here in Kokanee Cove, and how she was missing the people but not California too much—she straightened.

"Oh! I said 'California,' didn't I? I've been told I'm not supposed to do that, or everyone in town will think we're evil and just buying up the town to boost real estate prices. You won't tell, will you?"

Stephanie laughed. "If anyone asks, I'll just say you're from south of Boise."

"Oh dear." Merit cradled her forehead in a hand. "You heard about that."

"It's kind of an old joke around here." Stephanie didn't tell her that Will hadn't been the first to use that line.

Merit got to her feet—slowly. Stephanie could see exhaustion written in lines across her face.

"All right," said Merit, "I guess I should have known. But I haven't told you what my condition is yet."

"You said the flu, maybe."

"No, no." Merit laughed. "Not that kind of condition. Maybe we should call it a swap."

"Oh, I get it." Stephanie didn't. Merit motioned for her to follow, and they headed out the door with the painting.

Stephanie had been right; the cloudburst hadn't lasted long. Already it was heading north along the lake. If the dark storm clouds kept moving the way they had been, they would descend on Sandpoint in less than an hour.

"We've got so much work to do before we open." Merit held the door open to the familiar floating store and snack bar. The glass doors of the coolers in the back hung open, display racks stood jumbled and crooked, and dusty piles of junk littered the floor. Someone had stacked several boxes on the counter, each marked "M books." Stephanie twirled one of the old vinyl-covered stools while Merit examined a tangled pile of life jackets, fishing lures, poles, and who knew what. "But you know Will wants to open in a few weeks, in time for the Fourth of July Fishing Derby."

"By the Fourth of July?" That sounded pretty optimistic, but Stephanie wasn't about to say so. She knew where the painting went, though; the little nail was still in the wall. She gingerly reached up and hung the painting in its place.

Merit leaned against the counter and smiled. "So I was just wondering if you had another job."

"Oh, well, I'm kind of between jobs, thinking of going back to school. Not really sure what—"

"Perfect," she interrupted. "I want you to work for us. That is, if you're interested, of course. Help us get the place ready, then work in here again, the way you used to."

"That's the condition? And that's okay with Mr. Sullivan?"

"We talked about it already. Not specifically, but I know he'll think it's a great idea."

"You're sure?"

Stephanie thought for a moment. What else was she doing besides taking long walks, filling up her birdwatching notebook, helping Mom around the house, and generally feeling sorry for herself?

"Don't act so surprised," Merit said. "It's like the painting, Stephanie. People who come back will expect to see you here."

Stephanie nodded, and the same rock-solid certainty she'd felt about Merit's weakness now overtook her about her place here. She picked up a broom and dustpan and attacked the mess.

"I guess I'd better get started then."

fourteen

————— ❧ —————

I went to a general store. They wouldn't let me buy anything specifically.

STEVEN WRIGHT

Merit smiled as she picked a day-old loaf of bread off the shelf at the little Kokanee Cove Mercantile. Back in California, she hadn't imagined places like this still existed. Outside of Kokanee Cove, maybe they didn't—unless you counted reruns of *The Waltons* or one of those nostalgic small-town Disney movies.

She looked at the shelves, brimming with one of everything she could think of, including chicken noodle soup, bug repellent, ShureTrout fishing lures, and candy bars. She picked up a dozen local brown eggs, a can of refried beans, and another bottle of headache pills. She checked items off her mental list and gathered the rest of her groceries. Summer was already passing too quickly.

Jingle bells draped on the front doorknob announced another customer. Merit peeked over a shelf of cereal and canned fruit to see her sister walk in. It had to happen sometime.

"Oh, hey there, Sydney." Mr. Mooney peered over his glasses from behind the cash register. He still kept an old 1940s antique register for fun, but he didn't use it. "Haven't seen you in here for a while."

Merit opened her mouth, but she couldn't speak. Instead she watched for a moment, remembering what Sydney had told Will about never shopping at the Mercantile. Why was she here? Thankfully, Mr. Mooney didn't reveal Merit's presence.

"Just needed to drop off this package for the UPS man today." Sydney set a small parcel wrapped in brown paper on the counter. "Do you mind?"

"Of course not." Mr. Mooney pulled the package across the counter.

"Like I always say, bring your packages by anytime you like. The driver usually checks in just before lunchtime these days. 'Bout eleven-thirty."

Sydney rested her hands on her hips and nodded at the injured kestrel that watched their progress from its perch.

"You're not keeping that bird as a pet, are you, Mr. Mooney? Because if you are—"

"Oh no. That's just the bird Steph brought in some weeks back, shaken out of its nest. Hurt its wing a bit, but we fixed it up, and I think it's healing okay but slow. Would have died if she hadn't brought it by, you know."

"But it belongs in the wild."

"No argument from me. Soon as he's strong enough in a few weeks..."
Sydney nodded. "Good."

"I do have a permit for keeping those birds, Sydney."

"I know that. One more thing. Uh..." She paused, hands still on her hips. "I saw a car outside that looked familiar, like my brother-in-law's car. Have you seen him?"

Merit knew she should step forward, say hello to her sister, and finally put the past behind her. How many years had it been since that horrible argument? Still, she couldn't open her mouth.

"No ma'am." Mr. Mooney shook his head, but the corner of his mouth twitched, like he had a smile hidden. What did he know about the feuding sisters? "Not for a couple of days. You might try down at the resort, though. I hear he spends a lot of time down there."

"Hmm." Sydney headed for the door. She scanned the rest of the store as she walked, possibly to check if there was anything else she could criticize. When her gaze rested on Merit, she froze by the door.

Merit took a deep breath. "Well, what do you know!" She smiled shyly. "Small town!"

Sydney made no move closer, letting the door bump her on the backside as she shifted from foot to foot. "I thought I saw your car."

"Yeah. Just picking up some groceries." Merit held up a can of peanuts.

"Did you know they have one of just about everything here? Even a little pharmacy section. They don't have stores like this in..."

California. She let her "gee-whiz" comment slide, as did the rest of their conversation. She decided to try a few questions.

"So how are your, uh, cats doing?"

The cats were doing as well as could be expected. To Merit's surprise, Sydney asked a question of her own. And how were the girls?

"Oh, great. They seem to enjoy living here at the lake almost as much as we do."

"Good, good." Sydney inched out the door. "Uh...Will said you had a nice little place up on the hill. Sorry I didn't get to visit."

Well, yes, Sydney thought it was just fine. It suited her.

Merit went on. "I never thought we'd live in the same town again." The can of peanuts slipped out of her hand, hit the floor, and rolled under a shelf. "And now we run into each other at the store."

Yes, how about that.

A bird screeched in the back room, and Mr. Mooney excused himself for a moment to check on the noise. That reminded Sydney that she'd better run too, before the post office closed for lunch.

"Right, right. Well, come visit us soon." Merit made her way to the front counter, balancing beans, eggs, and pills, as Sydney waved and hurried out the door.

Sure, she would visit. Maybe.

A burly looking guy with a ponytail and three-day beard turned himself sideways to get past her, then headed for the beer cooler. As Merit piled her purchases by the antique register, Mr. Mooney returned to take her money.

"You two really sisters?" He punched in her totals.

"Wouldn't have guessed it, huh?" Merit said, trying to lighten the situation. "Actually we didn't really grow up together. She's a few years older than me. I guess we, uh, didn't have that much in common when we were girls."

And we still don't.

"I would never have noticed," Mr. Mooney commented.

Merit wasn't sure whether or not to laugh at Mr. Mooney's playful jab but decided it couldn't hurt. She hoped he wouldn't make a big deal about the last item she had placed on the counter hiding it behind everything else.

"You need a bag for that?" He didn't even wait for her reply before slipping the item into a recycled plastic sack from Target along with the rest of her groceries. Silly thing to buy but oh well. Thankfully, he didn't make a show of it as the burly man sauntered up behind her and hoisted his twelve-pack on the counter with a thunk. Merit nonchalantly squeezed the top of the bag shut and extended Mr. Mooney her Visa.

"Uh…" The shopkeeper hesitated. "Actually, Mrs. Sullivan, we're not set up for credit cards yet. Cash and local checks are all I can accept."

"Oh dear." She fumbled through her purse and found three wadded ones and a handful of change. Not nearly enough. "I'm so sorry. I left the checkbook at home, and I only…"

"Don't worry." He handed over the bag. "You just pay me next time."

Merit hesitated for a moment, but he nodded his reassurance. She took the bag with a thank you and exited through the door with a jingle of bells, relieved that Sydney was long gone. She only had to sidestep the back end of a pickup and the eager Labrador retriever leaning out for a sniff of her bag as she hurried to her car.

Not now, she prayed silently. *Please don't let me run into anybody else I'm supposed to talk to.*

She didn't relax until she'd turned the key in the ignition, hit the door lock button, and slumped back in the Rover's leather seats.

"That went well." She sighed and ran a hand through her hair, wondering how she would ever get to know her mysterious, standoffish sister. Of course, to Sydney, Merit may have seemed mysterious and standoffish. She supposed it depended on whose perspective one considered. How had she gathered the courage to try building a bridge now?

But a bigger question bothered her. Had she moved here for this? to repair a once-close relationship, strained over the years? Maybe it was too late after all. She couldn't help imagining God shaking His head at her wimpy witness just now. At this rate, she and Sydney would get around to discussing spiritual things…when?

"It's a start, Lord," she mumbled, pulling the Land Rover into gear. Now she just had to get home before anyone else saw her.

She nearly went through the car roof when someone rapped on the glass.

"Goodness!" She looked out the window, hid her sigh with a smile, and rolled down the window.

"Sorry!" Pastor Bud leaned against her side mirror. "Didn't mean to startle you."

"Not at all," she lied, stuffing the little grocery bag below her legs while trying not to appear overly obvious. "I was just thinking how amazing it is to live in a place where I can't go anywhere without running into people I know."

"Not like California, huh?" He smiled. He just wanted to tell her how much he and his wife appreciated the Sullivans hiring Stephanie, how much Steph liked the job, and how much they'd love to see them all at church on Sunday.

"I'm working on him, Pastor. Will's just…" She hoped he would understand and leave it at that. "I can tell you, though, that he was really impressed when all of you showed up to help us move in. I don't know that we've ever seen that kind of thing before."

"Well, you tell Will that you can always call if you need anything. An extra hand, prayer, whatever."

Merit studied the man's face and saw no trace of the spiritual *Let's Make a Deal* mentality that would have scared her away immediately. Was Pastor Bud really as sincere as he looked and sounded? She thanked him and started to roll the window back up.

"Now, if we can only get through to your sister," he said, "*that* will be the true miracle."

Amen to that.

fifteen

The grace of God means something like: Here is your life. You might never have been, but you are because the party wouldn't have been complete without you.

FREDERICK BUECHNER

This isn't possible."

The impertinent pink wording on the pen-shaped instrument told her plainly: *You're pregnant!*

The kit she'd purchased at Mr. Mooney's store must have passed its expiration date. This was August, after all. That was the only explanation.

She fished the package out of the trash, replaced her reading glasses, and checked the fine print on the back, but she couldn't find anything to indicate she'd done something out of order or misunderstood the directions. But who could read all that small print, anyway, without a magnifying glass or eyes that hadn't passed their fortieth birthday?

Merit closed her eyes. She knew her body well enough to recognize the mounting similarities between the way she had been feeling the past several weeks and the way she'd felt with each of the girls. Though she didn't remember feeling as weak, achy, or generally ill as she did now.

Father, she prayed, more fervently than she'd prayed in a long time. *Is this what You want? at this stage of our lives? Because I'm not at all sure I'm ready for this.*

She stared into the mirror over the sink, trying to think of another way to deny what she knew to be true. But how?

Unfortunately, God gave no immediate answer, not like He had with Mary. Merit thought she understood, for the first time in her life, the questions the mother of Jesus had asked.

"How will this be," Mary asked the angel, *"since I am a virgin?"*

Merit had never imagined the words in her own mouth.

"How will this be," she asked the Lord, "since my husband had a vasectomy over a year ago?"

For a moment, she wondered how this would look to her husband—if Will would have a Joseph moment and think the worst. But only for a moment, and the shame of it made her cheeks flush. Will knew her much better than that. Still, she checked the test strip one more time, in case it wanted to change its mind. It hadn't.

She threw the tester into the trash, a bit harder than she'd intended, and stared once more at the pregnant woman in the mirror. This wasn't supposed to happen to forty-four-year-olds. At that stage in life, didn't they say there was more risk of complications, more chance of…

She pushed the thought from her mind, stood on her tiptoes, and turned her profile to the mirror, wondering how soon she'd start showing. She told herself not to worry about everything that could happen but wouldn't. Nothing bad had happened with Abby or Olivia. They had both been enthusiastic womb gymnasts. Now *there* was something to look forward to. The signature nausea she had taken for a flu bug had already started waking her at four or five every morning. Will, bless his snoring heart, slept through it all.

Of course, when she'd found out she was pregnant with Abby—or Olivia, for that matter—the news hadn't been confirmed by a little plastic stick. Their family doctor had been the one to deliver the good news. Despite that, Merit didn't need a little test kit to tell her what she knew in her mother's heart.

She couldn't deny it anymore. This was real.

She couldn't forget Mary's line after the angel explained what would happen as a result of her historic pregnancy. Funny how it came back to her now, several years after Merit had heard it at a women's retreat—back when she and Will still had three good reasons to attend church. She didn't remember anything else about the retreat, just that line from the Bible the speaker had repeated over and over.

"I am the Lord's servant," Merit told the mirror, unable to keep the tears in check. "May it be to me according to Your word."

If anyone saw her now, they'd know what a hypocrite Merit Sullivan really was. Smiling Merit, always upbeat. Pious Merit, who made Will pray before meals, sometimes, and always at Thanksgiving. Their new employee and her pastor father would be shocked if they knew how shallow and weak-kneed her faith was. But they would never find out. Merit would see to that.

A fluttering of new life reminded her that she and Will had another new beginning on its way. She had to tell him.

"Merit?" Will knocked on the bathroom door, which she rarely shut all the way. "Honey? Are you all right?"

"Just a minute!" She dabbed at her eyes and stuffed what was left of the incriminating kit back into her pink bathroom bag, then stashed it in the lower drawer of the vanity. She straightened her hair and wiped the last tear tracks from her cheeks with a tissue before pulling the door open and smiling.

Will stood in the middle of the hallway, arms crossed. He'd have looked like an investigative reporter if not for the gray paint all over his face.

"You still think it's something you ate?" he asked.

She'd thought so the last time he'd asked, days ago. Now she knew better, but she couldn't tell him yet. The time had to be just right for news of this magnitude now growing in her womb.

"It's nothing that won't work itself out, dear." That much was true.

He didn't look satisfied with that answer.

"Well, if you're not feeling better in a day or two, promise me you'll call a doctor."

"I promise," she said. "And you promised you'd walk up the hill with me this morning before it got too hot."

"Uh…I still have to replank that broken section of dock, and there's a leak in the—"

She stopped him with a gentle finger to his lips.

"You've been working your tail off all week. Just walk with me for a little while, and then I'll let you get back to it."

"Well…"

"Besides, we've hardly talked since we got here. How late did you get to bed last night? Eleven?"

"Actually…" He rubbed the back of his head and looked sheepish. "More like midnight. I was trying to fix that compressor and kind of broke something in the process."

"And you're painting the boathouse." Merit licked her thumb and tried to rub a spot of paint off his forehead. "Restocking the snack bar. Repairing the roof. Fixing the gas pumps. Then you sleep like a dead man until the alarm goes off at five thirty."

Even if he did have two right thumbs, no one could say Will Sullivan wasn't a hard worker.

"You're not complaining?" he asked.

She shook her head as they headed down the hall. "Of course not. We both knew what we were getting into, and I'm proud of you for tackling all those jobs. Of course, I haven't exactly been sitting around eating bonbons or watching soap operas."

The idea sounded strangely appealing all of a sudden. At least for the next seven and a half months, she would have a convenient excuse for weird cravings or incoherent thoughts.

"I could use a couple bonbons right now." Will sighed and unbuckled his tool belt. It gave him a macho look Merit had never seen when he wore business suits and striped ties. Right now, though, she'd settle for a little of his attention, away from the bustle of renovation work. He closed the front door behind them.

"Sorry, I'm all out of those." She gripped his hand to help her up the trail behind the cabin, walking as slowly as she could. He just laughed.

"Look up there." She pointed to a fish hawk circling the thermals above the lake. "Stephanie says they can spot a trout underwater from all the way up there."

"Better eyesight than I have." Will smiled, finally seeming to relax.

At the top of the hill, they paused to survey their new world. Merit pointed out a canoe launching from the dock behind the boathouse.

"Speaking of Stephanie…" Merit smiled. "See that?"

"Hey, I'm not completely blind." Will leaned against a boulder in the shade as they watched Michael paddle, more crookedly than he probably realized. Stephanie, who couldn't know she was being watched from the hillside, had stepped outside the floating store to observe. The two younger girls joined her a moment later. Michael had somehow managed to lose his paddle and pushed the water with his hands, soaking himself in the process. They could hear Stephanie giggling.

"I hope he doesn't fall in," said Merit. "That water is still ice cold."

"If he does, I think she'll go after him."

"As long as Abby and Olivia stay where they are."

They watched the little comedy unfold below them. Stephanie and the girls hopped up and down on the dock, waving and shouting encouragement.

Will turned to Merit. "So you think it was a good move after all?"

She thought for a minute, smiled, and nodded. "You know," she said, "I wasn't sure at first, but this place has already won me over."

"Just the place?"

"Well, the people too. I think we have a chance to start something new here. Get back into a church. Don't you think?"

Will said nothing but after a moment, finally nodded.

"It's a good place to raise our kids." She was certain Will could hear the thumping of her heart. "I mean, Michael obviously doesn't need any more raising from us."

They looked down at the canoe, and Will laughed.

"But the girls, they still need us." She took a deep breath. "And they're going to love being big sisters."

In the distance a crow called, and they could hear the whisper of wind in the firs behind them on the slope. A laugh drifted up from the canoe, and Will looked at Merit out of the corner of his eye.

"I thought we already talked about adopting again." His jaw tightened, and he sounded as if he thought ice was about to break under his feet. "I mean, after adopting Michael... I thought we already decided against it, a long time ago."

"I know we did." Merit slipped her hand into his. She'd never been very good at being coy. "I'm not talking about adopting. I'm talking about having another baby."

He chuckled and pushed himself off the boulder. "You had me going there for a minute. Sorry, I can't help you in that department."

"You already did, Will." She didn't let go of his hand, and she felt him tighten up. "Come on, don't be so dense. I'm trying to tell you I'm pregnant."

The tentative smile on his face froze and then his mouth dropped open.

"I—how—I..."

"I wasn't going to take the test at first, but there was a couple it happened to back in Walnut Creek, remember?" She knew she'd better start explaining before this took a turn for the worse. "And then I read about it online. They say there's a tiny, tiny chance of your plumbing...you know, growing back together. They call it recanalization. It depends on what they did to you in the first place, exactly, and—"

"All right, all right. You don't have to get medical on me."

"Well, we can check with the doctor, but I think that's what happened."

Will's eyes glassed over, and Merit wondered if he was going into shock.

"Will?" She nuzzled his shoulder. "It's not as if anything terrible has happened. I know we decided a long time ago not to have any more, but last time I checked, we were still married."

Will slipped his hand from her grasp and hugged his arms to his chest as he paced around the boulder.

"So," he finally croaked, "how long have you known? I mean, how far along are you? Are you sure? You haven't been to a doctor yet, right? Is it a boy or a girl?"

She smiled and touched the tip of his nose. "I looked at the calendar, and I think I'm about six weeks along. I've taken a home test twice, and it indicated the same thing both times. The test doesn't show if it's a boy or a girl, though," she said smiling.

"Wait a minute," Will said, the squint releasing from his eyes. "You never ate a bad chicken wing, after all, did you?"

"Oh, aren't you the clever one."

She didn't have to tell him about every ache and pain. She assumed getting pregnant in her forties was different than in her twenties or thirties, that's all. Right?

Will headed down the hill, raking his fingers through his hair and mumbling, "Oh wow, oh wow," over and over.

"What are you doing?" she yelled after him. "Where are you going?"

Over his shoulder he informed her this would take some getting used to, and that he might have a word with the surgeon who had supposedly performed his operation.

Halfway down the hill, he skidded to a stop and turned around.

"Wait a minute." He put out his hands, signaling her to stay put. "I'll help you down. In fact, from now on, be sure Stephanie helps you with everything. No reaching, no running, no working up a sweat. Got it?"

She laughed as he returned to escort her back to the cabin. "You go from acting like you're in shock to acting like I'm an invalid."

"You better believe I'm in shock," he managed. "Aren't you?"

"Oh yeah." She arched her back as if she were already in her third trimester. "Just give me a couple of months, dear, and I'll *really* give you something to be in shock about."

sixteen

——— ❧ ———

*Give a man a fish and he has food for a day; teach him how
to fish and you can get rid of him for the entire weekend.*
ZENNA SCHAFFER

I'm glad you took us up on our invitation, Michael." Stephanie's dad, Pastor Bud, adjusted the brim of his faded Montana Outfitters cap, the one with fake seagull poop on top that Mom never let him wear at home. "Especially on the spur of the moment."

Our invitation? Stephanie thought it a casual use of the word *our*. Dad could have at least warned her, given her the chance to find an excuse not to come. She watched an osprey in the distance working the far shore and paying no attention to the men.

"Yeah, Will's going to be sorry he didn't come," replied Michael. "What about Mrs. Unruh, though? Does she ever—"

"My mom doesn't like fishing," Stephanie explained. "She never has. The scales, the smell, the hooks. She thinks it's all yuck."

"And you don't?"

Stephanie shrugged but never took her eyes off the distant bird. "Doesn't bother me. Dad and I have always been fishing buddies."

She held on to the side of the boat and let the wind whip her hair back like a flag. In the bright morning sunlight, the freckles on her face would stand out—but so what if they did? She let her father tell the rest of the story as they bounced over a light chop in their trusty old aluminum boat. Dad had stenciled *Amazing Grace* on the side, which explained how it had held together over the years.

"Steph's right," Pastor Bud told Michael as he leaned against the steering wheel. "I never could convince her mother to come out with me. I think the boat's too small for her."

"Small?" A waved rocked them from side to side, and Michael clung to his seat. "Well, I can see her point."

Stephanie's father grinned and gunned the outboard motor once they passed the line of buoys marking the entrance to Kokanee Cove and the end of the no-wake zone. The motor stuttered for a moment, wheezing and smoking. It had seen just as many summers as the *Amazing Grace,* which was several. The motor caught, pushing them straight through a wave and slamming them down on the next one. The wind whipped a shower of spray over the boat.

"Hoo!" Michael whooped. "That's as chilly as the other day."

Stephanie didn't step through the door he opened for her, but she hid a smile at the memory of Michael demonstrating the finer points of paddling a canoe without a paddle. Too bad her father hadn't been there. He might have harvested a sermon illustration from the incident.

They plowed across the southern end of the lake, where the floor rested over a thousand feet below the boat's thin aluminum skin, heading for the western shore. Her father aimed for the abandoned limestone mine, his favorite place to drop his lines. The deep shadows of the Selkirk peaks sheltered the waters there, holding off the choppier waves.

"Stephanie tells me you're a mechanic at your folks' resort," Pastor Bud said to Michael, charging off on a new topic of conversation. Michael would be able to show his better side now, wouldn't he?

Michael explained that he took engines apart and put them back together again and that he'd been a mechanic in the service for a few years, where he'd worked on Humvees and personnel carriers in Iraq and Afghanistan. But it wasn't anything special, he said. A motor was a motor no matter where he found it. Here in Kokanee Cove, he'd already tackled the pile of broken outboard motors in the boathouse.

He crouched next to the pastor and looked at the blue green blend of mountains and horizon, speaking just loud enough to be heard over the drone of the motor. Stephanie wondered again why her father had asked him to come along.

He seemed different when he talked about things that he liked, things that mattered to him, like fixing things and delivering people safely, without incident. Her father kept asking questions, and she couldn't help listening. Out here Michael didn't sound like someone who thought he was anything special, like so many other guys she'd met.

"We prayed for you." Her dad looked at their guest out of the corner of his eye to check his reaction. He got a puzzled stare. "Of course, we didn't know who it was at the time, just the soldiers in the Middle East who needed our prayers."

"Oh." Michael nodded. "You mean, in general. I appreciate that. Really, I do. And I appreciate you taking me out like this. I don't think I've ever been out fishing in a boat before."

"Really?" Stephanie asked before she could stop herself. "Never? What did you do in California for fun?"

"Oh, you know." He shrugged. "California stuff. I was big into skateboards when I was a kid. Broke my arm in three places. Then motorized skateboards, then motorcycles, then cars. Drove my parents crazy."

"So you were never a surfer?" her dad asked. He throttled down, and they drifted into a calmer patch of water, close to a steep, wooded shore with a narrow, gravel beach.

The question made Michael laugh—a light, pleasant chuckle. "No surfers where I lived. That's the other California, L.A. I grew up in northern California. Suburbs. About fifty miles east of San Francisco."

Stephanie had never thought of it like that, as if there were two Californias. She'd never thought much about California, period, except to realize that a lot more people were coming here from there, and there wasn't much she could do about it.

There was also a lot to Michael that surprised her, like how he handled a fishing pole.

"Uh…" He fiddled a bit with the reel, caught himself in the finger with a hook, then looked to see what Stephanie and her father were doing. "Are we supposed to put worms or something on these things?"

Pastor Bud laughed and helped extricate the barb from Michael's thumb. He didn't flinch, just popped the thumb in his mouth, but it had to hurt.

"You could use worms if you wanted to," said her dad, "but that wouldn't help us catch what we're catching today."

"Which is…"

"Rainbow trout, my friend." Pastor Bud expertly cast off the side of the boat with a flick of his wrist then turned to help their guest. "They're all over Lake Pend Oreille, and we catch 'em first because they eat the kokanee hatchlings, which are protected and, if you noticed, we named our town after the kokanee, so—

"Yeah, what's the deal with that name?" Michael asked in a curious tone. Here came the history lesson. Her dad smiled.

"*Kokanee* is from the Salish Indian word *kikinee,* for the little landlocked salmon they liked so well. Our town's founders liked the fishing here too. And I'll tell you, if you haven't had fresh trout cooked up in my wife's frypan before, boy, are you in for a treat."

Stephanie gritted her teeth and wondered if her dad would invite Michael to dinner as well.

"That's the one reason she puts up with our fishing," she said. She switched off the drag to free up her line and flicked her silver spoon lure several yards out to the side—every bit as expertly as her dad. That got Michael's attention, and she had to keep herself from grinning.

Were girls supposed to enjoy fishing the way she always had with her father? She wasn't sure, but right now she was getting a kick out of watching this tough GI wrestle with a rod and reel.

"You've really never been fishing before?" she asked. She wouldn't have believed him if she hadn't seen his fumbling.

"We caught crawdads in the creek behind my house." He smiled. "Does that count?"

"Hmm. Your dad's not a fisherman, either, I guess."

As soon as the words slipped from her mouth, she wished she could rewind the moment.

Michael winced. "Will, uh…he was always gone while I was growing up. Sales trips, conventions, you know. I ended up doing my own thing."

That was the second time he'd said *Will*—not *Dad* or even *my father*. Stephanie exchanged looks with her own father, who gave her a subtle shake of the head—his signal to back off. She would have anyway, but she had a hard time imagining growing up like that. And what kind of man called his father by his first name?

"Well, it's good that you guys can work together now," Stephanie finally said.

Michael didn't answer.

"I don't know about you two," said Pastor Bud, "but I'm planning to catch Old Joe today."

Michael lifted his eyebrows in a question. "You're going to have to explain who Old Joe is."

Stephanie did, grateful for the change in topic. Old Joe had been swimming these waters since she was seven, never mind that fish didn't live that long. The legend of Old Joe was enough to keep them coming out time after time, looking for the big one that would bend their poles and nibble their lures—only to swim off with everything from hook to sinker.

Michael nodded, and it occurred to Stephanie that he might be a good listener.

"That Old Joe has been good for a sermon illustration or two," her father said, studying his line as they trolled just offshore. By this time, Michael had his own line in the water, lure and sinker properly attached.

"You think?" Stephanie laughed. "You've got to watch out for my dad. He sees a sermon illustration just about everywhere, but especially out here on the lake."

"Out here?" Michael said, looking around.

"Out here. Like the time I fell off the boat when I was four, and I wasn't wearing a life jacket."

"That was a good one," her dad said. "The illustration, I mean. Not what happened."

Stephanie smiled. "And the time I came home with an owl chick when I was ten."

"Another sermon illustration?" asked Michael.

She nodded and pointed to a spot just under her left eye. "Especially when I got my face too close, and it nipped me right in the face."

"Ouch."

"Wasn't his fault. He was just hungry. See this little scar?"

He leaned closer, which made her flush and turn away. What was she thinking?

"Oh, and the time—" her dad started, oblivious. He didn't finish, though, as his pole dipped. "Hold on, hold on!"

They sprang into action, Stephanie grabbing the net as her dad slowly reeled in his prize. She throttled down the outboard motor even more, and it sputtered and died.

In all the excitement, no one noticed Michael's pole until it was too late.

"Holy cow!" Michael yelled as it jerked out of the place he had wedged it. He reached for it and missed, and they watched helplessly as it went over the side of the boat and—plunk—into the lake.

Before anyone else could react, Michael tossed his wallet into the bottom of the boat and launched himself over the side in a perfect dive.

"You're kidding me!" Pastor Bud shouted.

Stephanie couldn't believe it, either. But if Michael didn't know anything about fishing, he knew how to move through water on his own power. With a couple powerful strokes, he overtook the pole just below the surface. Stephanie wondered if the net would be big enough to land both her dad's fish and the crazy Californian.

What do I do now? she wondered.

Michael tread water, holding his pole. Pastor Bud started laughing as he pulled in his fish, and Michael whooped and pulled on his lines, as well as he could from that angle.

"Here, here." The pastor gestured to his catch. He brought it close to the side, and Stephanie scooped it up, as they'd done so many times before. They tossed their gear aside—along with the smallish rainbow trout Pastor Bud had caught—and turned their attention to landing Michael. The trick would be getting him back in the boat without swamping everyone in the process. He'd been in the frigid water for several minutes and had to be tiring. The waterlogged fisherman came in fairly well, though—Michael tossed his pole into the boat and then flopped over the gunwale with a grunt and a heave.

"The fish!" he gasped, out of breath and teeth chattering from the cold. But his line had gone slack, and from his knees, he reeled in the last of it.

"Oh, *man!*" Michael dangled the lure, sans fish. Old Joe had slipped out of his grasp.

"Yup, that's what he does," Pastor Bud reassured him. "Old Joe just grabs the lure and spits it out. What he's been doing for years. He's a crafty one."

Stephanie wasn't worried about Old Joe. She grabbed a towel from the front of the boat and tossed it to Michael. "You better dry off before you freeze to death."

"Thanks." He took the towel with a smile, then looked at the pastor. "So how's that for technique? Does that give you another sermon illustration?"

Pastor Bud shook his head. "I couldn't believe it when you went over the side like that."

"Well, I didn't want to get in trouble for losing your pole. Especially not on my first fishing trip."

Stephanie started giggling, then chuckling. It spread to the others, and soon they were all laughing. Her dad held up his prize, still wiggling. That set off a new wave of laughter, until they were all helpless and out of breath.

"If I ever lose my pole, Mike," Pastor Bud finally gasped, "I'll know who to call."

"Sure. Anytime."

Michael dried his hair with the towel, glancing quickly at Stephanie. He looked less like a cocky ex-soldier now and more like a waterlogged little boy, who was only here on vacation.

She looked away, finding lures in the tackle box that needed straightening.

seventeen

———— ❧ ————

I believe in Christianity as I believe in the sun—not only
because I see it, but because by it I see everything else.
C. S. LEWIS

Will leafed through the year-old *Field & Stream* magazine for the third time, checked the pregnancy growth chart on the wall once more, and paced. Merit smiled at him from her seat on the examination table, looking like a child in the silly green gown they'd made her wear.

"Come on!" He slapped the magazine down. "Is it really supposed to take this long to tell us what we already know? She said they'd be right back with the exam results."

"Patience."

Easy for her to say, he thought.

He checked his watch again and thought about poking his head out into the hallway and hollering for someone. "I thought this was going to take an hour, tops. You know, 'Yes, Mrs. Sullivan, you're pregnant. Have a nice baby, and we'll see you in eight months.'"

"We're not the only ones in the clinic, Will. Don't be so impatient. I told you I could have come to this first checkup myself."

"No way. I want to be here for everything, especially if they do one of those ultrasound snapshots."

"You know they're not going to do that yet. There's hardly anything to see."

"But he's in there."

"He?"

"Father's intuition." He pushed through a small pile of *Sesame Street* books, knowing he'd see a lot more of that brand of literature soon. "How long have we been here now? Three hours?"

"Not that long, dear. Just—"

His ears perked up like a dog's when he heard footsteps.

"Somebody's coming." Will stood next to his wife and tried to look casual. This wasn't supposed to be such a big deal. People had babies all the time. Just because they hadn't planned it this way…

The door swung open, and their doctor hustled in. *Now* she was in a hurry?

The pinched look on Dr. Mindy McCauley's face caught Will off guard. From smiles and congratulations to this? A young nurse's aide followed the doctor, pushing a wheelchair. Wait a minute—

"I don't mean to startle you, Mrs. Sullivan," Dr. McCauley said, her tight expression betraying the nature of her news, "but I've looked at your tests, and we need to do some quick follow-up."

Will took his wife's hand and asked for both of them. "The baby? Is he all right?"

The doctor regained her composure and stepped aside to let the girl with the wheelchair roll closer.

"The fetus appears to be normal for this stage of its development. That's not my concern at this point."

"What do you mean?" Will asked again. Merit's face had turned to ash. "If the baby's normal, then—"

"Like I said, Mr. Sullivan, we just need to do some follow-up testing. At this point, I can't really speculate beyond that."

"Wait a minute," Will said, digging in his heels. "You're not speculating, but you're scaring the snot out of us. Something's wrong. What are you looking for?"

Dr. McCauley held her clipboard to her chest and pressed her lips together. "All right. We found a few things we didn't expect. Our initial blood tests indicate leukocytosis, which is—"

"And for those of us who don't speak Greek?" Will demanded.

"Er…" The doctor hesitated, checking her clipboard. "We're looking at an extremely high white blood cell count. But I need to take a closer look before we jump to any conclusions."

"Wait a minute, wait a minute." Will needed more than that. "What conclusions could you be jumping to?"

"Like I said, Mr. Sullivan, I really think it's best we do further tests without delay, before we speculate. We'll need to do a bone marrow aspiration and a biopsy for starters."

Merit squeezed his hand before they trundled her off in the wheelchair. A wheelchair—like she couldn't walk on her own.

"It's okay, dear," she told him. "I'm sure I'll be right back."

Will tried to follow them but was stopped at the doorway.

"Please wait here, Mr. Sullivan," Dr. McCauley said firmly. "We'll take good care of her. Back before you know it."

Will didn't believe a word of it but did as he was told. He paced the tiny exam room for the next hour…and a half…two…

"God, what is going on?" He leaned his forehead against the door and prayed to the God he'd largely avoided—*ignored* seemed too strong a word—for the past several years. He desperately hoped this wasn't God's way of getting his attention. If it was, it was working.

But please, God, no.

He did the only thing he knew a good lapsed Lutheran should do—stare at the wall and recite the creed he'd memorized as a thirteen-year-old.

"I believe in God the Father Almighty, Maker of heaven and earth…"

That part he remembered well, but the words sounded as hollow as they always had. Especially now, since his whispered words only bounced off the white antiseptic walls right back at him. There was no way God would be excited by this wimpy display of faith.

"…in Jesus Christ, His only Son, our Lord…"

Pastor Dahlberg would have been proud to know his old student still remembered the creed, especially after all the trouble Will had caused during confirmation classes.

"...who was conceived by the Holy Ghost, born of the Virgin Mary, suffered under Pontius Pilate, was crucified, died, and was buried."

It occurred to Will that whoever wrote this creed hadn't wasted...any words. What if they described his own life that way?

Conceived, born, suffered, died, buried.

"He descended into hell. On the third day He rose again, according to the Scriptures. He ascended into heaven, from thence He shall come to judge the quick and the dead."

He'd always wondered about that "the quick and the dead" line. It rolled off his tongue but held little meaning.

"I believe in the holy catholic Church, the communion of saints, the forgiveness of sins, the resurrection of the body, and the life everlasting. Amen."

Nothing in there about Lutherans. He supposed the Catholics were around first, so they could word their creed any way they wanted. Besides, it would have gotten pretty lengthy including every denomination in the phone book. Not that he had anything against Baptists.

Will took a deep breath and wondered why he'd bothered with the creed. On the other hand, something about his prayer attempt didn't seem all bad. Maybe it hadn't accomplished much, but—

The door clicked open, and Will jumped. Didn't anybody knock around here? Another young nurse, unsmiling and silent, motioned for him to follow her down the hall and into a conference room. Will's sense of foreboding grew.

Merit sat in her wheelchair next to the conference table. She looked pale.

"Mr. Sullivan." The doctor motioned to a chair. "Your wife wanted you to be here when I explained some of the preliminary results we're getting from the lab. Please sit down."

Will nodded and sat, reaching over to hold his wife's hand. It felt clammy. He couldn't stop thinking that this was how people were supposed to take bad news—seated.

"First of all, let me tell you both that there's good news—despite the fact that many of my worst fears appear to have been realized."

"So enlighten us," Will replied. Maybe Merit had pried more answers out of her, but Will felt as if they'd been stumbling through a dark tunnel with this lady. "I don't have a clue what you're talking about."

The doctor sighed and crossed her arms. "All right. Initial tests show highly elevated white blood cell counts, as I mentioned earlier. The bone marrow biopsy, including the core biopsy, leads me to suspect that we could be looking at AML."

"Which is…" Will curled his lip. Why couldn't these people ever speak English?

"Acute myeloid leukemia."

Will's throat went dry. Leukemia. It all made sense in a twisted, horrible way—the worried looks from Dr. McCauley, the hurried trip to the lab. Will's head began to spin, and he was glad he was sitting.

"Is that what's made me feel so weak these last couple months?" Merit's voice shook, and it surprised Will that she was able to say anything. Despite her wide-eyed expression, she looked a little better than he felt.

Dr. McCauley nodded. "Fatigue, fever, shortness of breath, loss of appetite, weight loss—they could all be symptoms, but…"

But the doctor wasn't sure and still couldn't tell with absolute certainty. Possibly it was a combination of Merit's illness and the pregnancy, she told them. And before they jumped to any conclusions, they would need to do more tests.

"You said there was good news." Will needed some of that. Something to shine some light on this nightmare.

"Absolutely." The doctor put on her game face, leaned in, and gripped both their hands in hers. "Now you both listen to me. I've seen this kind of thing before, and I'm not going to mislead you. This could be quite serious. But what I'm saying is that we have a fighting chance. With aggressive, immediate treatment, and with the right support system and attitude, the odds are—well, it wouldn't be right to guess at the odds just yet, but they're not insurmountable."

"That's the good news?" Will asked, just to be sure.

The doctor nodded. "Time is not our friend right now, however. We're making arrangements, as we speak, to admit Mrs. Sullivan directly to the oncology unit. First we'll do the D and C, and then we'll go right into some aggressive treatment. With any luck—"

"Wait, wait a minute." Merit held up her hand, as if asking the teacher a question. "Why would I have a D and C?"

Will tried to remember what that meant. He'd heard the term before but never paid much attention to the female medical abbreviations.

Dr. McCauley's voice turned deliberate and syrup-sweet, as if she were talking to someone far younger. "Listen to me carefully, dear. This is an accepted medical procedure, and these are the steps we need to take. We don't have a lot of time, and there really is no other way."

A storm broke on Merit's countenance, one that Will recognized. She set her chin and crossed her arms protectively over her chest. "No one is going to take my baby."

The doctor shook her head in obvious puzzlement for a moment, then tried another tack. "Mrs. Sullivan, no one's saying you couldn't get pregnant again. Although frankly, at your age, I wouldn't advise it. In fact, even without the cancer, we'd be talking about higher risks of fetal abnormalities. You're forty-four years old."

"I do remember my age." Merit's eyes narrowed. "Let me ask you this: if I went through chemo and radiation without the abortion first, what are my baby's chances?"

"At this stage of development?" The doctor shook her head. "And with aggressive radiation treatment? Not good. It would not be a responsible move on your part—or mine as your physician."

"That's what I thought you'd say."

"So we'll get you over to—"

"No." Merit shook her head. "I can't allow you to kill the child in my womb any more than I could stand by and watch you strangle one of my other children."

Will shuddered at the comparison.

"Don't you see, Doctor?" Merit pleaded. "I'm their *mother*. Do you have children?"

Dr. McCauley gazed down at the table for a moment. Will noticed she'd pulled back her left hand—the one without a ring.

"We're not talking about me here," she said. "We're talking about—"

"You don't know what it's like, do you?" Merit asked, hitting hard. "You don't understand that I can't risk his life with radiation or chemo. I won't."

Will sat stunned as the reality of her words soaked in and chilled him to the bone. He couldn't speak, but he could hold on to her hand for support, and this he did, as though clinging to life itself.

The doctor changed tactics again.

"Mrs. Sullivan—Merit—please don't do this. Don't throw away your life over an embryo. I have nieces; I think I know what you're going through. You need to remember that you have a responsibility to the children you already have. And if I can say so, a *God-given* responsibility. Think of them."

At this, the tears welled up in Merit's eyes, and for the first time she seemed to soften. She reached across the table to grip Will's hand in both of hers. She looked at her husband with a pleading in her eyes he'd never seen before.

"I need you to back me up, Will. Say some—"

"Your husband can't back you up," the doctor snapped. "You know how he's going to feel about this. You know what he's going to say. Merit, you know what's right in your heart. Now you have to do the right thing. At least begin a modest chemo treatment."

Will wanted to say something, but the words caught in his throat.

The doctor pushed a clipboard across the table. "This is the consent form I need you to sign, Mrs. Sullivan. And if you can't sign it, I'll see that your husband does for you."

Could she do that? Will wasn't sure, but by this time, he wasn't sure of anything. The awful truth was that, despite Merit's protests, he wasn't sure he wouldn't sign it.

Dr. McCauley pulled a pen from the front pocket of her lab coat, clicked it, and handed it to Merit.

Will finally found his voice. "Honey…" he said, "we should talk about this."

Merit's lip quivered and tears began streaming down her face. She took the pen and looked at the doctor.

"Will's right," she croaked. "We need time. We need to talk—"

"I understand," the doctor broke in, looking at both of them sternly. "Take a few minutes. Talk to your husband. I'll wait."

What were these—pressure tactics? Obviously the two women had entirely different ideas of how long it would take to make this decision. They needed days for this, not minutes.

The doctor stood watching as Merit's hand wavered over the form. Will held his breath when she lowered her hand as if to sign the form.

"No." Merit dropped the pen on the table, yanked the form out of the clipboard, and deliberately tore it down the middle. "You're right."

The doctor's eyes widened.

"I *do* know the right thing to do in my heart," Merit explained. "I'm sure Will does too. God would never ask me to hurt our baby, no matter what. Besides, I could have the abortion today and still die in a few weeks or months, right?"

The overhead fluorescent light hummed the answer.

"I'll start whatever treatment you want," Merit finished, "but not until after the baby's born."

"I don't think you understand, Mrs. Sullivan. That's going to be too late. I'm afraid the leukemia may already have spread to your lymph nodes. We may *already* be too late."

"Then it will be. But I won't do it. I *can't*."

Merit dropped the clipboard on the table and headed for the door. "I need to get my clothes and go back home," she whispered.

Will stared at the door as it clicked shut behind Merit. He felt the growing heat of the doctor's gaze.

"Please, Mr. Sullivan. You're not going to let her do this." Dr. McCauley's jaw thrusted and her eyes blazed. "Do you know how unreasonable this is? I—I'm sorry to be blunt, but I should call social services if you don't consent."

"What? Social services can't—" He swallowed hard.

"All right, I'll tell you what." Her voice softened a notch, leaving her threat dangling. "I'll prepare another form for you to take home. Talk it over. She'll change her mind if you talk to her, especially when she sees the girls. Please, just don't delay more than you have to. Certainly not more than twenty-four hours."

Will shook his head sadly as he headed for the door. "I'm sorry," he told the doctor, "but my wife's decision is…"

What could he say? He reached for the door handle.

Conceived, born, suffered, died, buried.

"… her decision is her own."

eighteen

I've noticed that everybody that is for abortion has already been born.

RONALD REAGAN

Will hadn't expected a lot of conversation on the drive home, but the silence in the car nearly crushed him. He drove on, his knuckles white on the steering wheel, his mind racing as fast as the car engine but going nowhere except in circles.

Merit, meanwhile, pressed her nose to the side window as the scenery flashed by.

What was there to talk about? Besides the new baby, and the cancer treatments, and whether Merit would live another year, and what to tell the girls, and how, and when. Besides what would become of the resort, and how to tell people in Kokanee Cove.

Other than that, there was nothing to say, so he squinted at the road ahead, trying to keep silent tears from blinding his vision and their Land Rover from wandering into the oncoming lane.

Their dreams together, this new place, this new life…gone, gone, gone.

As they took the lake cutoff road, Will could taste blood, and he realized he was biting his lip. The visit to Dr. McCauley's had numbed all feelings, all pain.

Gravel sprayed as he hit the shoulder going around a curve.

"Will!" Merit warned him. "Slow down."

"Or else what?" He straightened out the car, and they flashed past a road sign telling them Kokanee Cove lay nine miles ahead. What mattered anymore? After what they'd been told, what really mattered?

"Please." She rested a hand on his knee.

He sighed and let the car coast down to the speed limit.

"You think I made the wrong decision?" she asked. "I'm sorry we didn't have a chance to talk it through."

"We didn't, did we."

"I just wanted you to say something, and then there she was, with the pen and that form and everything. I guess it was just my gut reaction."

"I know. I'm sorry I didn't...the words were just stuck, you know?"

She looked at him. "You think I should have signed the form, had the abortion, and started the treatment?"

He didn't answer right away, didn't even know if it was a serious question.

The highway widened in the flatlands above their lake, where an old barn stood sentinel at the edge of a hay field framed in green hills. The Idaho State Historical Society had erected a historical marker here about one of the gold rush-era towns that had lured settlers to the region.

He'd once thought it was a beautiful spot. Now he knew he'd better pull over there or risk running into oncoming traffic. For the briefest moment he considered it. Then just as suddenly, he stomped on the brakes and raked the roadside gravel in a sliding skid.

"Will!"

He stared at the dead, empty barn, a blurred picture of what his life had suddenly become.

"Answer me, Will. There was no choice in my mind. But do you think I made the wrong decision?"

He rubbed his temples and took a deep, jagged breath, holding on to the sobs as long as he could before giving in. Then he could only close his eyes and bury his head in her lap, shaking and sobbing like he hadn't since he was a little boy.

She held him close, adding tears of her own. He didn't know how long the waves would continue, and he didn't know if the little life inside her could hear, but he knew that with his ear against her stomach, he could almost feel the pulse his wife now shared.

He finally sat up, wiping his face. He still hadn't answered her question.

"I...I would give anything to trade places with you right now, Merit. If God had any sense of justice, He would let me die for you."

The words sounded as cheesy coming from him as they did on daytime television, but he meant every pain-filled word.

Merit raised a hand to her cheek and shook her head. "Don't talk like that about God, Will. Please."

"You asked me." He shrugged. The pain swept over him again like a tide that had nowhere to go but back and forth over the same wound, and it stung more than brine ever could. "I can't make myself say that you're doing the right thing. I'm sorry. I just can't."

"But the baby." Once more the pleading in her eyes melted his spirit. "Dr. McCauley kept calling it a fetus, but I know better. It's our *baby*, Will. Maybe it's still tiny, but it's our baby, no matter what they try to call him. Or her."

"I know it's our baby." He cradled her glistening cheek in his hand. "I know you're doing what you think is right. What can I say? You've always been the better parent, the better Christian than me. Don't you think?"

He knew it was a question she could never really answer. Which one of them had a clearer connection to heaven? Who was more spiritual? Right now, though, he thought he knew the answer.

"I never thought that, Will."

"I know you didn't. That's not what I mean."

"What *do* you mean?"

He raised his hands. "I don't know. But how can I be your husband and not do everything I can to protect you? How can I just sit here and say, 'Yeah, sure, you have an aggressive case of cancer that's going to kill you in a matter of months. But we don't have to do anything about it, we're not going to do anything about it, and I'm okay with it'? Well, I am not okay with it. I am not okay with this decision, Merit."

They stared at the meadow as five minutes passed, then ten. With their arms around each other, they watched a fawn and its mother tentatively step into the open and sniff the breeze. The doe looked suspiciously at the vehicle, then flicked her large white tail into the air and disappeared once more into the woods, youngster in tow.

Couldn't it be that simple? Just hide in the woods? If only.

Once in a while, Will kissed away Merit's tears, though he knew in the end it could make no difference—like trying to kiss away the raindrops before an oncoming thunderstorm. The flood had already come upon them, and there was nothing he could do to stop it. Once his wife made a decision, she would dig in her heels and never turn back. It was one of the things he loved about her. And one of the things he now hated as well.

"You're not going to try to make me change my mind?" Merit asked, her voice wavering.

"Every day," he snapped, but he knew he couldn't. He straightened and took the wheel once more. "I mean, no."

She waited for him to explain.

"I might pray you'll change your mind," he said, "but I'm not sure God is in the listening mood."

"Will, don't—"

"I told the doctor it was your decision, and it is. You know how I feel about it, but…" He shook his head, searching for a way to explain.

"Promise me one thing?" Merit asked. She dabbed at her eyes with a tissue from her purse.

He shook his head. "I'm not sure I can promise anything anymore. I'm sorry. I'm just…out of promises."

"Okay, but all I'm asking right now is that you don't tell the girls yet. We have to figure out a way to break it to them. And maybe we don't have all the facts yet, either."

He groaned. "They're going to have to find out sooner or later. And later is—"

"I know, I know. Just not now. Not today. They were so excited about having a little brother. They're not ready for this yet."

"And you think *we* are?"

He wished he hadn't said it and tried to restart the car, then jumped when it made a horrible metal-grinding screech. The motor had already been running. He hadn't turned it off.

"It's not about us, Will."

"But do you really want them to think everything's fine and dandy?" He pulled back onto the lake access road, then realized he hadn't checked for traffic. "Do you really want them to think everything's just like it always was? Because the more we wait, the harder it's going to be for everybody. You know that."

It was her turn not to answer. Her look begged him—*please*—and he could only nod his feeble yes as they crested the ridge and neared Kokanee Cove. What else could he say to her? He knew it wouldn't matter much what he said or did not say. The kids would know, soon enough.

And then no amount of pretending would hold off the storm descending to sweep away the fragments of their once-perfect life.

nineteen

❧

*The hardest thing to learn in life is which bridge to cross and
which to burn.*

DAVID RUSSELL

W hat's this?" Merit smiled as she walked down the ramp to the floating store. "Somebody's birthday?"

Will and Merit both knew the answer, but Will admired how she pushed
away the tears when it was time to be cheery for the girls. Never mind the
news they carried with them from the doctor's office, like from a funeral.

Abby and Olivia had hung a homemade balloon bouquet on the store's
swinging front door. They'd also hand lettered a couple of cute construction
paper signs and hung them by the door.

Congratulatuns, MoM!

They could work on their spelling, but the gesture was nice. Even so, it
hurt to smile, and Will wasn't sure he could keep his chin up as both girls
rocketed out the screen door. Good thing Michael was out running errands.

"What'd the doctor say?" Abby reached them first and wrapped her arms
around her mom.

"Is it a boy or a girl?" Olivia asked as she hopped up and down on the
dock.

Stephanie leaned in the doorway with a faint smile, looking more like a
parent than a babysitter. She still held a broom and dustpan. It was impressive what she had done in the past few days to bring the store back to life.

"I'm sorry," she told them. "They're so excited about their mommy
having a baby, they've been telling everybody who'll listen: the guy who was
down here fixing the gas pumps, my parents, everybody. I hope it's not
inappropriate."

"Of course, they're excited." Merit smiled and hugged her girls. Will wanted to scream, cry, break something. Just not here in front of the kids.

"Excuse me, please." He hurried through the store, slipped into the storeroom, and shut the door behind him with a sigh. Stephanie had already organized the newly stocked shelves, probably alphabetically. He'd never met anyone so organized. How old was she anyway? Nineteen? Twenty?

In the dark, he couldn't tell what had been done or which way was up. He fumbled for the light switch but only found something that made a lot of racket when it hit the floor and spilled all over his feet. Fishing lures or licorice whips, he wasn't sure.

"And you know what?" he asked the darkness as he slammed his fist against the wall. "Ask me if I care!"

He fell to his knees, groping in the darkness for whatever had spilled and fighting the emotion once more. He imagined himself alone for the first time, trying to raise the kids without his wife, then scolded himself for thinking any of this was about him and not about Merit.

He found himself kneeling in a squiggling mess of plastic worms, probably SquiggLures or some other lame invention that was supposed to attract bigger fish.

Ask me if I care. He grabbed a handful of lures and flung them against the far wall. He thought he had run out of tears back in the car with Merit, but somehow his frustration found more.

"A boy?" he challenged the darkness. "Or a girl?"

His fingers closed around a stray can, and he sent it flying as well. It must have hit a shelf, as fishing lures rained down in the dark. He wildly swept them away, swept away the sobs, gasped for breath.

What kind of God…

He would have done more damage, but the door squeaked open and the tall figure of Pastor Bud Unruh stood framed in the light from the store. Fortunately, Bud found the light switch a bit more handily than Will had.

"You all right?" What else would someone ask if they discovered a man with tears streaming down his face kneeling in a pile of plastic worms? "Steph said you were back here, but…did you lose something?"

Will cleared his throat and sniffled. Maybe the tears didn't show.

"Couldn't find the light switch."

Bud looked at him sideways. "You sure you're all right?"

Will dropped the worms and got to his feet, brushing himself off as he did. He would have pushed his way out, but the large man still blocked the way, and he didn't look like he planned to move.

"My boat's at the gas dock," Bud told him.

Will turned his face to wipe away the last tears as discreetly as he could. Probably too late.

"I'll get you some gas," he said. "Pumps are working now, I hear."

"Thanks, I have plenty. That's not what I mean. I'm going out for an hour or so to clear my head before I jump back into next week's sermon. I thought maybe you'd want to come along."

"Uh, no thanks. I've got a to-do list as long as your arm."

Bud didn't move. "Just an hour then? I could use the company. Sometimes it helps me get my thoughts in order when I have someone to bounce them off of. I'd really appreciate it."

Will thought for a moment before giving in to the man's persistence. What did it matter now anyway? Another hour? Another week? Today the entire rotation of his world had been turned on its head.

He sighed. "All right. Sure."

He followed the big man through the store, trying not to look at Stephanie and the others, who were unpacking boxes and setting up a small candy shelf. They must have heard him wrecking the storeroom. Maybe they wouldn't notice the mess until later.

"We'll be back in an hour or two," Bud announced with a wink at his daughter. "Sermon preparation, you know."

"Don't forget your fishing pole," she replied, but her concerned eyes were on Will, like he was a puppy in need of extra care.

Bud held the door open, and they walked to *Amazing Grace*. He watched Will looking at the house.

"I saw her heading up there," he said. "She looked fine."

Appearances can be deceiving, Will thought.

A minute later, they were powering away from the dock and out toward the middle of the bay. Bud waved and shouted at all the sailors he recognized, which was just about everyone.

"Looking for some wind, Jake?" he called to the first sailboat, motionless on the glassy water.

Jake waved back. "You pray some down for me, Pastor."

Bud laughed and turned his attention back to driving.

Once they were past the no-wake zone, he glanced at Will. "Sometimes the point out here is not going anywhere in particular." He stood and vacated his seat. "Here, you take the wheel for a while."

"Uh…" Will hesitated, but Bud waved him across. And since the little boat tipped when the big man moved to the other side, Will did as he was told and got behind the wheel. Why had he agreed to come?

They settled into their respective seats, and Will edged up the throttle. Where to? He guessed Bud had already given him as much direction as he was going to get.

They headed south toward Buttonhook Bay, which seemed to suit Bud just fine. He asked how the cleanup at the resort was going, though he must have had a pretty good idea already.

Will told him it was going great and that Stephanie was quite the worker. The docks were floating again, the gas pump was working, and the store was almost ready to reopen.

Pastor Bud listened and nodded at all the good news. "Cognitive dissonance." He pronounced the words like a college professor giving a psychology lecture.

"I'm sorry," Will said. "Did you say what I thought you said?"

"Yup. Cognitive dissonance. The stress you get when you hold on to two ideas that clash. You know, when people actually start believing their own lies?"

"Yeah, I guess I knew what that meant."

"Like the UFO doomsday cult. Remember those poor folks? Even after their leader was ousted—arrested, I think—and none of his end-time predictions came true, they still went out and recruited more suckers. In fact, more than ever."

"I remember that. They were on the news."

"Yeah," continued the pastor, "they had to know the truth, but somehow they conned themselves. Despite everything, even when their world had collapsed around them, they kept up appearances. They believed the lie that all was well, even when life had blown up in their faces. You understand how that works?"

Will shook his head. "I sure don't."

Or maybe he did.

"Hmm. Anyway, I thought I'd tackle it in my next sermon on Genesis. All's not right in the garden, but God is still in control. If we look outside ourselves, there really are answers. But if we don't, all we have left is cognitive dissonance, and we're just fooling ourselves big time. Why don't you come?"

"Oh, you mean *this* Sunday?" Will stalled. So that was why the pastor invited him out here. "I still have a lot of—"

"I know. You have a lot of work. We all do."

Funny how Pastor Bud could lob that kind of jab into the conversation with a gentle smile. If he were a boxer...

"Sorry," Bud said, backing off. "I didn't mean to drag you out here and corner you into coming to church. That's not what I had in mind."

"You had something in mind?" Will asked.

They rounded a point at the south end of the lake, where it narrowed to form an anchorage. Half a dozen sailboats were tied up at the docks and a couple others were anchored in deeper water. Will cut the motor, and they drifted in the crystal clear bay.

"Well, sort of." Bud stretched and dragged his hand in the cool water. "I know you and Merit have a lot on your plate. In fact, congratulations are in order, aren't they?"

"Oh, that." Will forced a low-grade smile, knowing it wouldn't convince anyone, much less Pastor Bud. "Thanks."

"You don't look too thrilled about it, which I can understand. Tell me if I'm wrong, but it's a bit of a shock, right?"

"A shock?" Will chuckled the way someone did at a cruel joke. "That's an understatement."

"Okay, but you have to admit it's still a gift from God."

The kind of gift Will would much rather decline.

"Merit might agree with you," he said.

"But you don't."

"Listen. I know what it looks like. I know the girls are excited. It's just…they don't know the whole story."

A cabin cruiser coasted by, throwing up a small wall of water behind it. As they bobbed in the wake, Bud waited for Will to finish. Before he knew what he was saying, Will had explained nearly everything that happened that morning, from the doctor's diagnosis to the conversation on the way home. Bud listened, wide-eyed but quiet, nodding every once in a while to show he understood. Finally, Will ran out of story, proud he hadn't broken down this time.

"I'm so sorry, Will," Bud said. "I could tell something was wrong—and I had a feeling it was more than just your wife being pregnant."

Will nodded, suddenly feeling foolish for unloading the whole story the way he had. "I feel like…I don't know—like my heart has been ripped apart. Like I used to know what was right, but now everything's washed away."

"So you don't agree with Merit's choice."

"This is my wife's life we're talking about. I thought we should at least try some kind of treatment. Do you blame me for thinking that way?"

"I don't blame you for anything, Will. I know it's easy for me to spout the spiritual answers. But for you and Merit, and the kids…"

"Hey, I'm not the evil pagan you think I am."

"I know you're not, Will, and I didn't say that."

Will explained how he was raised in a good Missouri Synod Lutheran church, how his folks took him to services, most of the time. How he was confirmed when he was thirteen. The shadow of a fish darted below them, and Will's words trailed off as he followed it with his eyes. On the shore, a kid swung from a rope out over the water and dropped with a whoop.

"Do you remember Rita Fedrizzi?" Bud asked him.

Will slowly pulled his attention back to the pastor. "No. Should I?"

"She was in the newspapers a few years back. Italian woman, Catholic family. They ran into the same dilemma as you two, or similar."

"No kidding?" Will wasn't sure he wanted to know, but he couldn't *not* know, either.

"If I remember right," Pastor Bud continued, "she was diagnosed with melanoma about the same time she found out she was pregnant with their third child. She was in her forties, I think. They wanted her to have an abortion, too."

"And she wouldn't?"

"She wouldn't. She refused all cancer treatment until the baby was born, a little boy. I just remember there was quite a media storm about it at the time. All the pro-abortion people thought she was crazy or that the Pope had some kind of power over her."

"I never paid much attention to that kind of thing before." Will didn't want to know how the story ended. He guessed it wasn't happily ever after.

"The other thing I remember about the Fedrizzi story is how strong the husband stood by her, no matter how much heat she took for the way she protected her baby. Will, Merit's going to need that kind of support from you. No matter what you're feeling right now—and I can understand that—you two are going to have to stand together on this."

"Listen, I appreciate your concern." Will felt his fists clench and fought to keep his voice steady and civil. "But what happened to some Italian family has nothing to do with us. Nothing at all!"

Will turned to the old Evinrude outboard hanging on the back of the boat, checked the throttle, and gave the starter cord a yank, nearly pulling it out of the motor. The engine sputtered but didn't catch until the third try.

"I know you're upset, Will"—Bud raised his voice over the roar of the motor and rested his hand on Will's shoulder—"but I want you to know we'll be praying for you. We're going to pray for healing, and we're all going to be here for you. For both of you. Do you hear me?"

Will nodded but gritted his teeth and looked straight ahead. He jammed the throttle forward, and the little boat leaped ahead, careening around the point and back into the wider part of the lake. They passed the no-wake sign at full throttle, and Will turned to look at Bud.

"So what happened to Rita Fedrizzi?" he asked.

Bud didn't answer right away, just held on as they bounced over a wave and headed north, back toward the resort. Finally, at Will's glare, he took a deep breath.

"Every case is different, Will. Like you said, it's not fair to compare her to Merit. I shouldn't have brought it—"

"Quit playing games! What happened to her?"

Will already knew, but he had to hear what was now almost impossible to hear over the drone of the motor and the slap of waves.

Bud stared at the floorboards as he answered. "She died a few weeks after their son was born."

twenty

—— ❧ ——

If you were going to die soon and had only one phone call you
could make, who would you call and what would you say?
And why are you waiting?

STEPHEN LEVINE

Only twenty-four hours had passed, and her secret was already out.
Partially.

But what could she do about it? Merit climbed the trail above the resort,
the one that looked down at the water as it skirted the lakeshore. She couldn't
go far this morning, just far enough to stretch her legs. Maybe out to Blackwell Point and back.

Pastor Bud knew, and he would share the predicament with God, who,
of course, already knew. How long, though, before she and Will had to tell
the girls and Michael? How long before her sister and the rest of the town
found out?

And then, how long before they all looked at her with the kind of pity
reserved for Romanian orphans, hurricane victims, and starving African children with bloated bellies?

Poor Will. He'd already begun to torture himself over this. It hurt her to
watch him, almost more than it hurt to think about her own situation.

Oh, but the girls! They were the only thing that made her take the doctor's pen. The only thought that nearly pushed her to close her eyes and
blindly sign her name to the permission form. Will had no idea how close
she'd edged to the brink of that cliff—and the thought of what she'd nearly
done made her shake.

But the moment in the doctor's office had come and gone like an icy wind, and she'd done her best to slam and lock the small window of *maybe,* even as the horrible temptation still beat on the shingles of her soul. Did it matter how close she'd come to destroying the life that grew inside her? That tiny spark of Will that God had fanned to life, probably right here in their new home? She'd counted the days, and it always seemed to add up.

She shuddered at what had almost been and apologized over and over to God for being so arrogant as to even think about sweeping away such a precious gift, like yesterday's trash. She knew better. And now, with every ounce of her strength, she hugged her new life as she walked and gazed out at the lake.

"No one's going to hurt you now, little one." She knew exactly who she spoke to, exactly where he lived. Though he might not recognize the words, she prayed he would somehow sense the mother's vow behind them. "I promise I'll do everything I can to protect you."

And when I can't, then what? she wondered for a moment, afraid to think how short her road might now be.

"And if I can't," she concluded, "then your daddy will."

Your daddy, Will. That made all the sense in the world, just now. It helped to make this vow out loud, as if she stood in a court of law, her right hand in the air and her left on a Bible. As if she stood before the Judge. She knew with rock-solid certainty that she was accountable to Him even more than she would have been in the county courthouse.

The wind off the lake made her shiver. Though it was August, it might as well have been December. With the shiver, a rain of doubt beat on her heart—sudden and unbidden, with a fury that made you duck for cover and hope lightning would not strike.

"Why did You give this to me, God?" She decided to address Him aloud, since no one else could hear her. Campers from the state park occasionally wandered this far, if they knew where Blackwell Point was or wanted to read the historic marker overlooking the lake. But at this time of the morning, she usually had the point to herself.

Except today.

Before she could scold herself for paying more attention to the beautiful view than noticing if anyone was sitting on the "view bench," as she liked to call it, she had already walked too close to back up. She had to either keep walking or stop and chat with Stephanie.

Merit decided on the latter. No use being antisocial.

"You come up here a lot, don't you?" Merit asked.

"Oh!" Stephanie jerked her head around to see who had spoken, then softened and smiled. "I didn't hear you coming."

Merit leaned against the back of the bench, next to Stephanie's parked mountain bike. She stooped to pick up a flattened soda can someone had left in the dust.

"Sorry," Merit told her. "I didn't mean to intrude."

"Not at all." Stephanie hurriedly closed a small, leather-bound pocket Bible and scooted over to make room. Merit remained standing, though, clutching the can.

"Good place to watch birds?" she asked. And pray, from the look of it. Merit supposed she could use some of that.

"Sometimes," Stephanie answered. "I saw a boreal chickadee here once. Right over there on that log." She pointed. "I think it was lost. Boreal chickadees don't come to this part of Idaho. Not on purpose anyway."

"I have no idea what kind of bird you're talking about," Merit said, returning the smile, "but I'm glad you do. And I'm glad you came to work for us too. In fact, I know we wouldn't be nearly as far along with the renovation if you hadn't pitched in. Will and I both appreciate it very much."

"I'm not the only one." Stephanie deflected the praise in the same way she shooed away a yellow jacket buzzing around the bench. "Everybody wants to see you guys do well. It's not like the development—you know, outsiders. People here like what you're doing."

"Maybe. Unless you talk to my sister. She'd rather we tear the place down and replant it with wildflowers, I think."

"My dad tried to witness to her once." Stephanie smiled. "She wasn't very interested in Jesus, but she had a lot to say about karma."

"That's my big sister."

"Yeah. But I think people appreciate you guys because you're here to stay, if you know what I mean."

"Here to stay…" Merit repeated the words, wishing they could be true for her.

Stephanie would know the whole story soon, though it appeared she didn't yet. That was only appropriate. Merit assumed Stephanie's father had discretion and didn't go home and tell his family every personal detail of every confession he heard. One wouldn't call their story a confession, but people like Will probably confided in him all the time.

Even so, Merit felt the weight of her charade, felt the pain in her shoulders from carrying a load for too long. She wasn't far enough along in her pregnancy to feel the strain in her back. This pain parked itself in her neck and would not release its grip. She rubbed her neck and arched it to the side.

"Feeling all right, Mrs. Sullivan?"

Stephanie's parents had taught her well. Plenty of kids couldn't see or hear beyond the range of their own ear buds, their own little worlds, and they certainly would never speak with an adult this way. Funny how Merit connected so easily with someone only her son's age.

That didn't mean she was going to answer the question.

"You know the only thing that could get you fired from your job, Stephanie?"

It was worth saying something outrageous, just to watch Stephanie's animated facial expressions.

Merit patted her on the shoulder. "I'm just teasing, Stephanie. Relax."

"I know, Mrs. Sulli—"

"That's *it*!" Merit interrupted with a jab of her finger. "You need to stop calling me Mrs. Sullivan or I'll fire you on the spot. Call me Merit, and that's all. Understand?"

"Sure." Stephanie nodded as she gathered her things and rose to her feet. "I understand, Mrs. Sullivan."

Now who was teasing whom?

With a little smile, Stephanie wheeled her bike around and started pushing it down the path toward the resort.

"I didn't mean you had to run off, Stephanie."

"I know. But I really should get to work. We're cleaning out the coolers today, and Mr. Sullivan wants me to do some painting on the outside before more customers start coming next week."

"You paint too? Is there anything you don't do?"

"Well, I don't think it's the sort of thing your husband wants a pregnant woman doing."

Merit forced herself to laugh a little, enough to convince Stephanie that all was right with the world. She wasn't sure, however, that Stephanie was fooled.

"I'll walk back with you then," Merit told her, "if you don't mind walking your bike. A pregnant woman can do that, can't she?"

Stephanie flashed a concerned look at her—as if she saw right through Merit's mask. What would happen—in a day, or two, or five—when Stephanie did find out? Because one thing was sure: she would.

Merit sighed as she looked out at the sparkling waves. Even if this wasn't the way she'd planned it, well, nothing else was either.

"Listen, Stephanie," Merit felt the load on her shoulders tighten, "there's something I need to tell you."

twenty-one

——— ❦ ———

*I have heard there are troubles of more than one kind. Some
come from ahead and some come from behind. But I've bought
a big bat. I'm all ready you see. Now my troubles are going to
have troubles with me!*

DR. SEUSS

Merit paused to take in the view before heading down the path to the
house. Down on the lake, a couple of fishermen pointed their craft
toward deeper water, but the breeze hadn't picked up enough yet to attract
any sailboaters.

Merit rested a hand on Stephanie's shoulder. Maybe she shouldn't have
been quite so honest with the girl about her condition.

"I wish…" Stephanie wiped the last tear from her eye with the back of
her hand. "I wish there was something I could do."

"You just keep doing what you're doing." Merit tried her best to smile.
"You're a big help to us that way."

At the resort, the girls weren't climbing trees or chasing each other like
they were when she left. Michael wasn't clattering about in the boathouse, or
Merit couldn't tell if he was. And where was Will?

"I'll get started with the coolers then." Stephanie parked her bike and
hurried down to the floathouse, leaving Merit to wonder. Wood smoke
drifted across the water from a shoreline bonfire, adding a pungent accent
to…what was that?

Good thing that awful smell isn't coming from my house, she thought, sniffing the smoke. Even from a distance, Merit could tell someone had left the
burner on far too long.

"Will?" She stepped on the front porch and poked her head in the door, still wondering. Abby met her, wearing one of Merit's old aprons and motioning her to come inside.

"It's almost ready, Mom!"

"Oh." Merit took another whiff. The burnt breakfast smell had intensified, leaving no doubt as to its origin. Merit stepped into the house, leaving the door propped open for ventilation. "Is someone cooking?"

"Me!" Olivia squealed from the kitchen.

Merit reached the kitchen doorway and squinted through the smoke. "Oh, honey…" She tried to part the clouds without success. "Looks like you need some help in here."

"No—stay there!" Both girls joined voices and circled their wagons so Mom couldn't interfere. Abby escorted her mother to the couch.

"You sit here with Daddy," Abby commanded with the most authority her ten-year-old voice could muster. "We're making scrambled eggs and pancakes and sausages, and you can't come to the table until we're ready."

"Hmm." Merit wondered why the smoke alarms weren't chirping. "Where is your father?"

"Over here."

Will shuffled down the hall from the direction of the bathroom, still in his slippers and tousled morning hair.

"They wouldn't let you help, either?" she asked.

He shook his head. "Are you kidding? They've been working on this since you left for your walk. It's turning into a brunch, I guess."

How could Merit complain? The girls had hand-decorated paper napkins with pictures of hearts and flowers. They'd set the table—spoons on the left, forks on the right, no knives. While Olivia stirred the orange juice, Abby brought out the eggs.

"Oh, my." Merit tried not to look too surprised. "How many did you make?"

"Just one package." Abby smiled as she ladled out three or four eggs on each plate. One package probably meant a dozen. Merit suppressed a sigh. They meant well.

"You can sit down now," Abby told them, and they found their assigned seats according to cute name tags.

"They wouldn't tell me what was going on," Will said, eyeing his plate. He didn't seem to mind the enormous pile of eggs and blackened sausages.

"It's a cheery-up breakfast," Abby told them.

"Cheery up…" Merit prompted.

"To cheer you two up." Abby looked as if she had just solved all their family's problems right there at the kitchen table. "Livvy and I thought maybe it was because you had so much work and we weren't helping enough. So from now on, we're going to make breakfast."

Merit looked into the kitchen, where the smoke was finally starting to clear. It appeared the girls had used every bowl in the cupboard and every utensil in the drawer. Most were piled in the sink, others on the small counter next to the stove. Despite the mess, she couldn't help smiling.

"That's a very sweet offer," she said, "and I know you want to help. We have plenty of jobs for you, but tell you what. How about you help Mommy cook during the week, and I can show you some tricks for cooking on Saturdays?"

The girls looked at each other before nodding.

"Will that make you stop crying all the time?" Olivia asked.

"Livvy!" Abby scolded. "You're not supposed to say anything about that."

"But I just wanted to know."

The lump in Merit's throat returned, along with more unwelcome tears. She couldn't hide them any more than the girls could hide the smoke from that morning's breakfast.

"See what you did?" Abby turned on her little sister, but Will held up his hand.

"She didn't do anything wrong," he told them, with a quick glance at Merit. "In fact, your mom appreciates it more than you know. We both do."

"Then why is she crying again?" Olivia asked.

At her daughter's innocent misunderstanding, Merit couldn't hold back gentle sobs. Just like she couldn't hide the truth from her children anymore, no matter how long she wanted to pretend everything was okay.

Will was right. For their sake now, she would have to tell them.

She nodded at her husband and saw in his eyes that he understood.

"Girls…," he took a deep breath, "there's something we need to tell you."

Abby and Olivia looked uncertainly from parent to parent, and Merit knew she needed to pull it together. If she fell apart here, so would the girls. She dabbed a napkin to her eye, streaking a colored heart. No telling what had just rubbed off on her cheek.

"I still don't know what we did wrong." Olivia bit her lip, and Merit motioned for her youngest to sit in her lap.

"Daddy already told you, sweetheart. You didn't do anything wrong. None of this is your fault."

"None of what?" Abby asked, going straight to the heart of the matter. "Don't you like the breakfast?"

"The breakfast is wonderful," Merit began, searching for the right words to say what should never be said to a tender, trusting heart.

"Listen, girls." Will took over. "You know your mother had to go to the doctor the other day?"

"To check the baby, you mean?" Abby asked, and Will nodded.

"Couldn't they take pictures of the baby," asked Olivia, "the way you said they would?"

Again Will nodded. Even at their age, his daughters never missed a beat.

"They'd wanted to take pictures," he explained, "but they found something…wrong."

Merit's mind spun with second thoughts. Couldn't they wait a little longer to dump this horrible news on their daughters? Wait until later. Wait until after. Wait.

But Will continued, and there was no stopping him now.

"They found a kind of cancer inside your mother." Will struggled with each word, and his tears would tell the girls more than anything he said. Merit pulled Olivia closer, afraid to look in her daughter's eyes. "You know what cancer is."

"My friend Crystal's dad had cancer." Abby sounded like a grownup when she added to the conversation like that. "Remember?"

Merit and Will both nodded.

"And now he's better," added Abby, "since they gave him a lot of pills." She looked straight at her mother. "You can get the same kind of pills, can't you, Mom? They can make you better. God can make you better."

"Of course, God can make me better, dear." Merit nodded and rocked Olivia slightly. "I'm just not sure if that's what He wants to do."

"Of course it is!" Abby crossed her arms, pushed back her chair, and stood up. "We'll pray, and that's what'll happen. And you can take the pills, just like Crystal's dad."

Merit shook her head and reached out to stroke her daughter's long, beautiful hair.

"I can't, Abby." Why did she have to tell her daughters this part?

Abby looked at her with a frown. "But you have to! If you're sick, you have to! That's what you always tell me."

"Maybe the pills wouldn't work on Mom," suggested Olivia. Wisdom from an eight-year-old.

Merit shook her head. "It's not that," she told them. Will started to say something, but she wouldn't allow it. This was hers to finish. "I can't take any strong medicines because they would hurt the baby. Do you understand?"

Most likely not, but they nodded.

"After the baby's born, though, I promise to take all the medicine I can."

"And *then* you'll get better," Olivia told them with the faith of a child. She looked from face to face, as if testing the truth of her theory on the emotions of her parents. Merit wasn't sure how to send the right message. She could only look at her husband, the tears blurring her view.

"Right?" Olivia persisted, her voice quavering with doubt.

What else could they say? They sat in silence while Merit rocked Olivia in her lap, and Abby sat off by herself, looking as if she could come up with a better way to solve their dilemma, if only she thought hard enough. No one ate their eggs.

Eventually Olivia sat up, having reached some kind of decision.

"We should tell Aunt Sydney."

Merit wasn't sure where that had come from, but she knew her determined daughter had reasons of her own.

twenty-two

———— ❦ ————

Some of God's greatest gifts are unanswered prayers.
GARTH BROOKS

W ell, Merit was crying and everything, but…"
Michael wasn't sure how to explain it. He hardly knew this girl. Stephanie kept up with the traffic on I-90, changing lanes way too often and nodding at all the right times, like she cared about him and his parents. Did she?

"I'm so sorry about your mom," she told him. "I can't imagine…"

No, she probably couldn't.

"Thanks." He watched the Welcome to Washington State sign fly by as they continued west toward the Spokane airport. "Although actually, she's not my birth mom."

Stephanie glanced at him out of the corner of her eye. Almost as if she thought he might be joking.

"Is that why you sometimes call her Merit?" she asked. "I wasn't sure if that was just a California thing, or what."

"It's not a California thing." He chuckled, even though it didn't seem funny. Nothing did anymore. "I don't really remember my birth mom. I think she was into drugs when I was really little, and we lived in this tiny apartment. I kind of remember sleeping on a big purple couch with ripped cushions, and there were always a bunch of crazy people coming and going all the time. Lots of screaming and yelling, and nobody my age to play with, so I did my own thing, played by myself. But that's all I really know. Merit and Will adopted me when I was five."

"Wow."

Maybe she hadn't heard a sob story like this before. He'd tell her the other side of it, as well.

"Yeah," he continued, "as I understand it, they didn't think they could have their own kids, so I was their second choice. You know, like the prize losers get? What's that called?"

"A consolation prize? Michael—"

"That's it. Consolation prize. Anyway, I've always known I was different than the girls. Sometimes I think they regret it."

"Oh, come on. I'm sure they don't regret anything. You talk about it like you didn't want life to happen that way."

"I didn't say that. It's just…sometimes it's weird thinking you're some-body's second choice. Didn't you ever get picked last when kids were choos-ing sides for basketball?"

She didn't answer.

"That's right," Michael said. "You were homeschooled, weren't you? I should have known. You never—"

Michael stopped and held his breath. If that sounded snarky, he hadn't meant it to. Taking it back would only make things worse, though, and he could already feel the tension tying his neck into knots. Just like in the Mid-dle East.

He turned his face to the window, but Stephanie apparently didn't think the discussion was over.

"Okay, so you would have rather stayed in a drug house? Sounds like your parents took you out of that."

Michael turned and stared at her. Was she defending Will and Merit now? As if they needed defending.

He turned back to the window. "I shouldn't have said anything."

"No, I'm glad you did. It helps me understand where you're coming from a little better. I'm really sorry, Michael."

"I don't think you understand."

She didn't answer the last jab, just drove silently while he stewed in his own words. He wondered what Will and Merit were going to do now, wondered what *he* was going to do now.

"You've never lost anybody, have you," he said.

It was not a question; he didn't need it to be. He would have bet his next month's salary that Stephanie Unruh, the perfect girl from the perfect family in the perfect town, had never lost anyone she'd loved. Certainly not a mom.

And certainly not two.

"Because if you had…," he started, but then let the words die in his throat. He didn't want to finish that train of thought.

He turned toward Stephanie, ready to apologize, and was surprised by the dark storm in her eyes.

"Whoa, I—uh—" he stuttered. "I didn't mean to upset you. I mean, she's not *your* mom."

"Apparently you don't think she's yours, either."

"I didn't say that."

"Yes you did. You said the woman who gave you up for adoption was your real mother. I guess we have different definitions of what a real mother is."

"And what's yours?"

He wasn't sure why he kept provoking her, but they would be at the airport soon, and it wouldn't matter anymore.

"I think a real mom is the one who raises you," Stephanie said. "I think a real mom is the one who's always been there for you. The one who would give up everything for her kids."

Not that again. Michael rested his forehead against the window and closed his eyes. He tried to picture the woman who had given birth to him, but all he could recall now was the screaming, and he wasn't sure if it was a bad dream or a real memory.

But his real mom? The only picture in his mind was Merit, cheering for him as he hit his first youth league home run. Merit putting a bandage on his knee when he cut it open doing a motocross flip on his bike. Merit crying when he left for the Middle East, crying even more when he got back.

"I know what you're saying," he admitted. "Guess I'm just upset about Merit's...you know."

She looked at him with those big eyes, completely ignoring the semi in the lane ahead. Michael put his hand on the wheel, just like Merit always did when Will drove crazy.

"Look," he told her, "I'm sorry, but can you keep your eyes on the road? You're making me nervous."

She returned her gaze to the freeway, shaking her head. "I thought you were different, Michael. All the guys around Kokanee Cove were always so into themselves." She bit her lip. "And I guess maybe you are too."

"Excuse me?" He arched his eyebrows. "When did this turn into a beat-up-on-Michael event? I'm not even sure if—"

"I'm not even sure why I..."

Michael wondered what she'd been about to say. She could have finished that sentence a dozen ways. Instead she sniffed and pulled in front of a mini-van without signaling, just as they reached downtown Spokane. Michael resisted the urge to grab the steering wheel from her. This girl was a worse driver than Will.

"My mother was born there." She pointed to a tall building looming on the left. "Deaconess Hospital."

Michael blinked at the building, then at Stephanie. "Why did you just tell me that?"

"Habit." She shrugged. "Every time we drove by here when I was a kid, my mom pointed it out to me. I guess it was important for her to know where she came from. And that big church over there?" She pointed at a tall spire to the right. "That's where my folks were married. They were raised here in Spokane, met at Whitworth College, and then Dad got called to the pastorate out at the lake."

He let the tour guide comments go, then took a breath.

"Look, Stephanie, I'm really sorry. It's good of you to drive me to the airport like this, and all I can do is spout off like an idiot."

"I had to pick up those books for my dad, anyway," she said.

"I know, but it was still nice of you. And I'm sorry. I have a big mouth sometimes."

"So do I." She paused as they neared the airport, then veered toward the terminal. "I hope your boss isn't too upset with you for taking this many days off."

"I wouldn't be surprised if he's already hired somebody to replace me, just for being gone so long. The war hero thing probably won't get me out of this."

Stephanie veered across several lanes of traffic to bring them into the curbside loading zone. Michael dug his fingernails into the dash, bracing for impact.

"You said United?" she asked, pulling to a halt. When he opened his eyes, he noticed they had almost run into a young couple standing in the drop-off area ahead of them, locked in a passionate kiss.

Michael choked on his saliva.

"Are you all right?" She patted him on the back, which was nice but really not necessary. He held up his hand and tried to breathe.

"Uh." More coughing and gasping. "Yeah, I'm fine. And really, thanks again for the ride."

He grabbed his bag from the backseat and hurried away, slamming the car door behind him. He caught her reflection in the plate-glass windows of the terminal and watched as she followed his progress…just a little too long.

"Please, Will? I just can't tonight." Merit had already closed her eyes. "Will you tell them goodnight for me? They don't have anything clean to wear tomorrow. There's a load of dirty clothes next to the washer. And the dishes…"

Will rested his head against the bedroom doorjamb and checked his watch. Eight fifteen.

"I'll take care of it, babe. You just rest. Do you put the whites in cold water or hot?"

But Merit didn't answer, didn't move, only rested her head with a backward tilt on the pile of pillows she'd collected.

Will stepped forward and leaned over her. She didn't look right. Her cheeks too pale, her lips too blue...

"Merit?" He tried not to panic but couldn't help leaning closer. "Are you asleep, or—?"

He tried to tell if the covers moved over her chest but couldn't. Tried to hear if she was breathing, leaned so close he should have been able to feel her breath on his ear, but still couldn't tell. Surely—

She gasped and he jumped, nearly falling over backward. But she had breathed. Thank God. And now he recognized her light, regular breathing. He waited for his heart to settle down before he stepped back up to the bed and pulled a light blanket over her shoulders. He kissed her cheek.

"Sleep is good," he whispered. "Just sleep, Merit. That's all you need. And when you wake up, you'll have your old energy again, and you won't be throwing up all the time. Right?"

She sniffed and rubbed her nose.

"Sleep," he told her again. "You'll prove those doctors wrong. You can do it, Merit. I know you can do it."

She stirred again, and he straightened and wiped his eye—too late.

"I'm sorry." He hoped the tear that dribbled off his cheek onto hers like a raindrop under a darkening thundercloud would not startle her awake. She whimpered softly but did not open her eyes, as if a bad dream had already taken hold. Now she moaned, a little more loudly, her lower lip quivering, and her eyelids flickered. This time he reached down to wake her, then thought better of it.

"No," he decided. "You go ahead and dream too."

He watched her for a few minutes, quiet now. He thought of praying but didn't know what to say that God didn't already know or that hadn't already been begged for. Why couldn't God just hear him the first time, instead of making him grovel?

Of course, if that's what God wanted, he wasn't above that. He would climb the mountain on his knees, if that's what it took. He tried to imagine what kind of deal they could strike.

What do You want, God?

No answer. He could have put his fist through the wall. Instead, when he heard soft giggles from down the hall, he turned away to pad down to the girls' room.

"Where's Mommy?" Olivia asked. She held her pony under the covers. "She always—"

"Mommy went to bed early again tonight. She's feeling tired."

Olivia groaned. "She's always feeling tired. She slept all afternoon and all day yesterday too."

"That's how she's going to be for a while."

"Because of the baby? Or because of…the other thing?"

Will hesitated. "I don't know, Liv. Maybe both."

"Then I'm going to pray." Without warning, Olivia launched into her nighttime prayers. Her pony with the red and green hair still hid under the covers because she was a big girl now, and according to Abby, big girls didn't sleep with dolls or horses anymore. Abby eyed her sister from her own bed, then obligingly bowed her head and folded her hands.

"Good night, Lord," Olivia began, "and thank You for the lake and the mountains and the rivers and the sky—"

"You don't have to thank God for all that," Abby interrupted. "He knows—"

"It's my turn to pray!" Olivia said, not backing down. "You prayed last night, and tonight you just have to shut up!"

"Olivia." Will stepped in to referee. "We don't say shut up. Where did you learn that? Abby, let her finish."

Abby frowned but closed her eyes again, letting Olivia start over. And she did, restating her thanks for the lake and all the rest. Abby pretended to snore.

"Abby…" Will warned quietly. Olivia didn't seem to notice.

"And I pray that Michael would come back home right away," Olivia prayed. "Also that Mommy wouldn't be so tired and sick all the time, that You would make her feel better, and that You would help the baby inside her grow big and strong."

Will nodded his agreement. That would be nice.

"And please help Aunt Sydney to be a Christian…"

This was getting deep.

"Help Abby not to be so snotty all the time…"

He peeked at the older sibling, but she'd already laid her head back on the pillow, her mouth open in sleep. She looked too much like her mother when she did that.

"… and please help Daddy not to be so sad," Olivia concluded, "because I just *know* You're going to make Mom better. In Jesus' name, amen."

For a brief moment, before the amen evaporated, Will entertained the idea of staying in Abby and Olivia's Pollyanna world just a little bit longer. What would it take to own the kind of faith that seemed to come so naturally to Merit and their daughters?

"Tell us a story before you go, Dad?" Olivia's voice sounded heavier, farther away. She was fading fast. "One where they live happily ever after?"

Will wasn't sure he knew how that kind of story went anymore.

"Maybe tomorrow, Liv." He forced a smile in the darkened room and mussed Olivia's hair, then gave them both a kiss. "Maybe tomorrow."

twenty-three

———— ❧ ————

God has not been trying an experiment on my faith or love in order to find out their quality. He knew it already. It was I who didn't.

C. S. LEWIS

Will stood at their dining room window a week later, ignoring its taped-over crack in favor of the view of the lake beyond. He twirled a postcard from Michael between his fingers.

Not an e-mail, not a phone call, just a postcard of a dated aerial view of downtown Walnut Creek, California, taken before several twenty-story office buildings had sprung up and changed the city's landscape forever.

"Where did you get that?" For a woman early in her pregnancy, Merit could sure sneak up on a man. He jumped, and she giggled—which was nice, since no one had been much into giggling lately.

"You're always doing that to me!" He turned around and displayed the card.

"I don't know where Michael finds those old things." She took it from him and began to read. "So he still has his job, after all," she mumbled, scanning the message. "You think Stephanie will want to know?"

"Stephanie?" Will acted surprised, though he shouldn't have bothered. They both knew.

"Oh, come on. Don't tell me you didn't see something going on when he was here. They spent almost every afternoon together."

"Maybe, but they didn't seem to have much in common. I think she annoyed him."

"Don't be silly," Merit said. "Stephanie's such a sweet girl. They would make—"

"Stop right there," he interrupted. "Let's not get into the matchmaking business. I don't think that's our job."

"I'm not matchmaking. I just want to make sure our son realizes when a young lady is interested in him. What if he comes for another visit?"

"Then he does, dear. But it's none of our business one way or the other. And besides, I'm pretty glad I couldn't talk him into staying on with us."

Merit lowered the postcard and looked at him. "You meant that the other way around, didn't you?"

He'd been waiting for the right time to tell her his idea, and this looked like it to him.

"No. I meant what I said. Because here's what I think we need to do, Merit…"

She leaned against the back of the couch, chin in her hands, as if bracing for another hit.

"Listen, I'll just come out and say it." He had to. This was for her own good. "I've been thinking hard about this, so I called up the real estate agent in Coeur d'Alene, the one Uncle Fred dealt with when we bought the place. He understands that things can change, and he thinks if we put this place on the market right now for a low enough price, we could probably turn it around in a matter of weeks, maybe days, and cut our losses. Then we can get you back to Walnut Creek, where they can take care of you—and the baby—much better. I even called Bruce at the office, and he told me he'd take me back with open arms whenever I wanted, part-time if I needed, at first."

He expected a reaction, just not the one he got.

Merit stared at him with blazing eyes, then wadded up the postcard from Michael and threw it in his face.

"Walnut Creek?" she nearly screamed at him. That couldn't be good for a pregnant woman, could it? "Are you crazy?"

Will raised his hands for protection, but he was too late. The postcard hit him in the eye.

"Hey! What are you doing? I'm just trying to think about what's best, Merit."

"You could have fooled me."

"Come on." He felt the heat rising in his face, and his words came out like bullets. "You know that some of the best hospitals in the country are in the Bay Area. You'd have a much better chance down there than we do here."

"Oh, so now we're playing the chances, are we?" Her face had turned as red as his. "There's nothing wrong with the hospital in Coeur d'Alene. You act like it's some kind of hillbilly clinic."

"I didn't say that."

"Of course you did! You dragged me up here, kicking and screaming, then I fall in love with the place, and now you want to give it all up?"

"Looks like that decision's already been made for me," he snapped.

"What's that supposed to mean?"

"Do you want me to spell it out for you, Merit?" He punctuated his words with a wave of his hands. "You have leukemia, you're pregnant, and it's going to get worse every day."

"Pregnancy gets *worse*? That's not the word I would have used."

"You're twisting things. You know exactly what I meant. The point is, you need a lot more help and support than we can give you here, so—"

She tried to interrupt but he talked over her.

"—so I think we made a huge mistake bringing the family here—bringing you here—and now the only thing we can do is take a step back and deal with this situation with the best resources we can find."

How could she not see the logic in that?

Merit shook her head. "You still don't get it, do you?" she asked, setting her jaw.

"What's there to get?"

"God moved us here for a reason, even if we don't see it yet."

He started to groan but bit his tongue. "Let's not bring God into this again. That's way too convenient."

"It is *not* too convenient. In fact, it's not convenient at all, the way I see it."

"How do you see it? Are you even thinking about how *I* might feel?" Will asked.

"How *you* feel? Since when is this about how *you* feel?"

Will rolled his eyes and sighed. This was like trying to reason with a can of paint.

"Okay, Merit. Can we agree we have to think this through?"

"Sure, but—"

"Use our brains. The doctor said—"

"I know what the doctor said." She sounded ready to spit. "But I am not going to let you run at the first sign of trouble. I'm not going to let you do that, Will Sullivan. I still believe God moved us here, no matter what you say."

"Yeah, great argument." He crossed his arms and hid his hands so she couldn't see him making fists. His head throbbed. "Pretty nice when you can just spiritualize it and hide behind God. Easy out."

She looked at him, and her eyes filled with tears. But he'd expected that to happen, and she couldn't make him take it back, not a word of it.

"Will, please tell me you didn't mean that."

He didn't answer, and she didn't look away.

"You love this place," she said, her voice softening, "don't you?"

Will turned to look out the window, away from the woman he loved more than his own life. Would he trade places with her? In a heartbeat. Did he love this place? Without a doubt. But that wasn't the question here. Why couldn't she see that?

He uncrossed his arms, let his hands dangle, and dropped his shoulders.

"Whether I love this place or not," he began, his voice almost matching hers, "it doesn't matter anymore. Don't you see, Merit? It's not about *what* I love. It's about *who*."

Neither of them spoke until he felt her arms slip around his waist and draw him close. She wouldn't be able to do that much longer before someone came between them.

Her voice came in a hoarse whisper. "Sometimes you're totally impossible, Will Sullivan. But you're my knight in shining armor, and you always will be. Always."

"I sure don't feel like one."

"Shh." She turned him around and planted a finger on his lips to silence further protest. "Listen to me. *Please* listen to me. It was no mistake to come here and we can't go backward. We can't go back to the Bay Area. I want to live in this place with you for the rest of my life, however long that is, Will. Eight months or eighty years. Please? We can't sell this place. It would never be the right thing to do. I just know it."

Will had seen more tears this past month than in the past twenty-four years of marriage combined—except, maybe, for their first month of marriage, which didn't count. Despite this, his heart melted as he traced the warm track of Merit's tear with his finger.

"I'd already made up my mind," he said. "I was going to be the strong head of the house and make an executive decision for you and for our family."

She nodded and looked up at him, a sob catching in her throat. "And what is best for our family?"

Will held her in his arms, fighting the answer, wrestling the truth—whatever it was.

He sighed. "Sometimes you make me so angry, Merit."

She nodded. "I know. Likewise."

"Other times, I feel like I'd walk through fire to make you happy."

The corners of her lips turned up in a small Merit smile. "Say that again, mister."

"Don't push your luck. Most of the time you just puzzle me, like there's something driving you I've never quite been able to understand or tap into."

"Like now?"

"Like now."

He paused and she didn't pull away from him.

"You never answered my question, Will. What's the best thing for our family?"

He kissed the last of Merit's tears from her cheeks and forced himself not to think about how much longer he'd be able to hold her this way. Finally he sighed, knowing he couldn't win this battle, and not knowing if he really wanted to.

"We'll stay," he whispered. "How can I say no to you?"

"You can't."

He breathed in her sweet scent and buried his face in her hair.

Someone knocked on their front door. "Mrs. Sullivan?"

Stephanie.

Will backed away from his wife, wishing he could hold her just a little longer. Maybe take an entire weekend to hold her. The knock at the door came again.

"Just a minute, Stephanie," Merit called. "I'll be right there."

But not before she grabbed Will and gave him a kiss that nearly knocked him over.

"I love you forever, Will Sullivan," she told him, their noses almost touching. "And no matter what happens, you'd better not forget it."

"Who said anything about forgetting?" He squeezed her hands, knowing the subject of moving away would never come up again—not like this.

As Merit headed for the door, she paused to retrieve the crumpled postcard she'd thrown at Will.

"Stephanie!" she called as she reached the door. "Are you still there?"

"Still here, Mrs. Sullivan."

Merit looked at Will and winked. "Good. Because you're fired."

Will blinked. "What did you just tell her?" he asked.

Merit laughed and pulled open the door.

"I'm really sorry, uh…Merit." The expression on Stephanie's face matched Will's own. "It's just hard for me to get used to calling you that."

Merit chuckled. Whatever hurt on the inside, his wife put on a convincing show.

"As long as you're working on it, *Miss* Unruh."

"Please," Stephanie said, getting into the game. "Just call me Stephanie."

Merit laughed, and it seemed to melt away some of the gloom. "I'm glad you came by," she replied.

Of course, just a little later would have been nice, Will thought, but he didn't mention that.

Merit smiled and lifted the postcard. "I just got something in the mail, and I thought you might want to see it."

twenty-four

———— ❧ ————

Sisters never quite forgive each other for what happened when they were five.

Pam Brown

N o, I hadn't heard." Sydney sat in her orange beanbag chair on the floor, yoga-style, stirring her chamomile tea. "Should I have?"

"Not necessarily," replied Merit. "I just thought, you know, word gets around in a small town like Kokanee Cove. Will and I are still getting used to it ourselves."

"And you mention this because…"

"Because I didn't want you to hear it from someone else."

Merit shivered despite the late morning sun heating up her sister's trailer. What was it about this place that gave her the creeps? It could have been the smell of incense, the crystals, or the seasick feeling she got twirling around in the hanging wicker chair that looked like a New Age parakeet cage.

Making her the parakeet.

"I see." Sydney took another sip of her tea. "Of course, I don't know much about rumors. I suppose it depends on who you tell."

"For instance?"

"For instance, Foster Mooney at the Mercantile. He knows everybody's business, more than a man has a right to. If you want a rumor started, I suggest you talk to him. As for me…"

"I think he is a nice man. He and Stephanie seem to get along, with the birds and all."

Sydney sniffed and Merit leaned forward to hear better.

"I haven't bought anything at the Mercantile in years," Sydney said. "I just drop off my dreamcatchers there for the UPS man to pick up."

"That's right. I forgot you sell those. Do you place an ad in a magazine?"

Sydney nodded. *"Mother Earth News.* I've run a classified ad in the back for ten years. I get orders."

"But the Mercantile—why don't you shop there?"

"I've asked Foster to carry more organic foods, but he always laughs and tells me they're too expensive. He has no idea what kind of pesticides and hormones his produce has."

"Organic foods are good," Merit said, trying to agree with her sister on something.

"How expensive can poor health be, I ask you? All these things the government slips into the food chain to quiet the masses—next they'll be fluoridating the water. Anyone with eyes can see that."

Not again. Merit hadn't stopped by for a diatribe on global warming and the latest conspiracy theory.

"Oh dear, Sydney." She tried to extricate herself from the wicker chair as well as the direction the conversation had taken. "You seem to know a lot more about these things than I do."

"You got that right, Sister." Sydney took a deep breath. "I just don't know when we're going to stop depleting the planet's resources and overloading our population."

Merit gave up trying to escape the chair and faced her older sister squarely. "Is that what you think Will and I are doing by having another child? overpopulating the planet?"

Sydney's face flushed. "No, I didn't mean—"

Merit wasn't through. "Well, that's pretty ironic, coming from a woman who lives in a town of five hundred people, out in the middle of nowhere. Overpopulating, huh?"

"That's exactly the kind of attitude we need to change," Sydney fired back. "Just because it's not a problem in northern Idaho doesn't mean we don't need to meet our global responsibilities."

Merit snorted. "So you don't eat red meat, you recycle, and you meditate on world peace, just the way Mom and Dad taught you, and that makes everything right."

"You don't need to bring Mom and Dad into this, Merit. Just because you never saw things their way—"

"You got that right. The original hippies. Beatniks, or whatever they called themselves."

"You've got to deal with that negative energy, dear. Otherwise—"

"Like they did? I guess they were dealing with their own negative energy when they dragged us to that awful commune in Mendocino. I don't know how I survived."

Sydney blanched.

"What?" Merit asked.

"You remember that place?" Sydney whispered.

"Barely. I was only six, so you must have been sixteen. Not a very good memory for you, either?"

"Ha." Sydney looked away. "You have no idea."

Merit studied her older sister for a moment, trying to decipher the comment. "Care to enlighten me?"

"No." Sydney shook her head. "It was a long time ago. Let's just say I learned early that men can be pigs."

That didn't sound good. "I'm sorry, Sydney," Merit said. "I didn't—"

"Forget I said anything. You wouldn't understand, and I don't want to talk about it." She gave Merit a long look and her shoulders drooped in surrender. "I suppose I should congratulate you. Maybe it's your karma to help overpopulate the world."

"Overpopulate? This is your nephew we're talking about." Merit swallowed her anger. Arguing with Sydney about this wouldn't accomplish anything.

"Oh, so you know already."

"Not officially." Merit stifled a yawn. "Will's just convinced it's going to be a boy, so I've gotten used to calling him a he."

"Hmm." Her sister leaned over and checked Merit's eyes. "You're anemic. I have some organic soybeans and spinach extracts you need to take."

"Anemic?" Merit asked, slightly off balance at her sister's sudden change in topic. "My doctor didn't say anything about that." Of course, she'd said plenty of other things.

"I'm not joking, Merit. Let me get you some dong quai pills, and I'll make you some gentian tea."

Merit felt a familiar queasiness and held up her hands. "No. I mean, I appreciate your concern and everything, but if you don't mind, I'll just handle it like I did with the other kids."

"You mean by continuing to eat processed poisons, junk food, and animal products?"

"I'll cut out coffee and eat plenty of fruits and veggies. How's that? And meat has iron in it, right? I always eat pretty well."

"Meat?" Sydney made a face. "Don't make me ill. And if that's true, then why do you look so bad?"

They were skating a little too close to the line, and Merit resumed her efforts to get out of the wicker basket. How did she explain this?

"Listen to me, Sydney." She ran a hand through her hair and willed the tears not to appear. "There's something else I need to tell you."

Before her sister could interrupt, Merit gave the condensed version about the cancer and what the doctors had told her. As she talked, her sister's face clouded over more and more.

"So your religion…" Sydney barely forced out the word. "Your *religion* forces you to take this insane position?"

Merit gulped. What else had she expected from Sydney?

"No, I wouldn't put it that way. But it's true my faith and what the Bible teaches does color my thinking."

"*Color*? Sounds more like it spray paints the sense out of you." The tint of Sydney's cheeks matched the doctor's when Merit had refused the abortion. "In fact, this is more like some crazy, right-wing brainwashing we have to deprogram out of you. Is this what the Pope told you to do? Listen to what you're saying, Merit!"

"You know I'm not Catholic. But I don't disagree with the Catholic position on life, if that's what you're getting at. In fact, they're right on the mark, as far as I'm concerned."

"So you're going to sacrifice your life for a fetus, leave your children without a mother, and the Pope is just going to sit back in his robes and applaud, is that it?"

"I don't know why you keep bringing the Pope into this, Sydney. I told you—"

"I know, I know, you're not Catholic." Sydney jumped to her feet and paced around Merit's chair, wagging her finger at the air.

"It just kills me," she went on, "to see someone like you throw her life away—and for what? Keep in mind the gender of the people pulling the strings here."

"I don't see it like that." Merit was surprised how calm her words sounded. How, for the first time, she felt a measure of peace. "And gender has nothing to do with it, unless you consider my gender and what someone of my gender would do to protect her own children."

"Well, who runs your church then? Men. And they sure as *your* hell have never had to carry any unwanted pregnancies. Ever thought of it *that* way?"

"First of all he—our baby—is not unwanted. He's a gift from God. And second of all, you don't have to curse."

"I thought you were the religious one." Sydney's smile twisted into something unpleasant. "Don't you believe in a hell where your God sends people who don't believe exactly the way your men have told them to believe?"

Merit sighed. Wrong battle, wrong time. She let it go.

"It's all about power, and it's all about men." Sydney launched into one of her rants. "Men write your Bible. Men tell you what it says. Men tell you what to think and what to do. And men tell you to die when they're done with you or when they want you to make a point for them."

Merit remembered the "men are pigs" comment from earlier and thought about bringing it up again but decided against it.

"The only point I'm making is—"

"The only point *worth* making," Sydney interrupted, "is that we don't need them. Me? I don't buy into the men's-only club, and I don't understand why you do."

"This is not—"

"Would you let me finish? This is suicide, Sister. Don't you see that? And your man-God is—"

"That's enough." Merit managed to push herself out of the wicker cage and face her sister head-on. Whatever peace she'd felt had heated to the boiling point.

"Finally we agree." Sydney stood her ground, balanced like a boxer. "Are you really going to let yourself be oppressed like this?"

"First of all, I am not being oppressed. You don't understand anything about my decision, even after I explained it to you."

"It's what I *do* understand that scares me, Merit."

"Maybe. But I didn't expect this from you."

"If you didn't want my opinion, you shouldn't have come here."

Something else Merit could agree with—she shouldn't have come.

"Okay, but I don't appreciate the way you talk about the Lord. He's the One who died…"

Sydney rolled her eyes. "Here we go again with the 'Jesus died on the cross and you're going to hell if you don't believe' thing. You don't think I've heard that on late-night TV? Some of those clowns are funnier than Letterman reruns." She pointed at the tiny black-and-white set in the corner of the room, a rabbit ears antenna balanced on the top. "Those hypocrites are just another part of the system that keeps you oppressed. Or didn't you notice them always asking for your money? Come on, Merit, you're not that dumb. Or maybe you are."

"I have a book back at the store I'd like you to read, Sydney. It's really good, by—"

"By a man with 'Reverend' in front of his name, right? That's even worse. No thanks."

Merit broke her promise to herself about those tears. She couldn't keep them from rolling down her cheeks. Sydney was just so…hard.

"You were right about my coming here, Sydney," she said. "Will said I shouldn't, that I should wait a few more days. I should have listened to him."

"A few more days? What would have been different then? Aside from the fact that you'd be that much closer to dying, I mean."

Merit took a step back in shock. Sydney didn't have to say it that way.

"And that's another thing!" Still her sister railed at her. "Does your Will really think this suicide is a good idea? Then he's as bad as the Pope and all the other religious male medievals who want to keep women in bondage. In fact, these religious fascists—"

"Don't you *ever* talk about Will that way!" Merit would have slapped her if she'd had a clear shot. She headed for the door.

A hand grabbed hers, holding her for just a moment.

"Sister." Sydney's voice had softened, even after all this. Merit didn't turn, didn't look. "I hate what you're doing. I don't want to lose you now. Not after you've just come back."

But Merit was done with this, done with the conspiracy garbage and the goddess nonsense. She'd fulfilled her family duty by coming here, and now she wanted to go home.

She pulled her hand away, stepped out into the sunshine, and slammed the trailer door behind her.

It didn't feel any better.

twenty-five

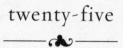

It has always been my private conviction that anyone who pits his intelligence against a fish and loses has it coming.
JOHN STEINBECK

When Merit looked at her floating castle, she could easily imagine how right everything could be.

Stephanie scurried from the store to the gas dock, pumping gas and selling bait and snacks to an unending parade of out-of-towners here for another late summer fishing derby. The pleasant buzz of an outboard motor filled the air as it propelled a boat of eager fishermen out to deeper water. A sailboat fluttered its sails just off the dock, preparing for a morning outing. Merit took a deep breath, catching the lake's fresh scent in a breeze that caressed a flag overhead. A pair of mallards whistled by.

Just a normal morning, until one noticed the dark clouds hovering over Bernard Peak. Fishermen and tourists alike tried to forget the storm they knew approached from beyond the mountains, but denial, Merit knew, would not hold it back for long.

She could imagine a hundred other horrible situations in which she would rather find herself, and none of them included a case of acute myeloid leukemia. Why had God dumped this in her lap? She couldn't keep herself from thinking, *I could end this all today if I just took the doctor's advice.* Or maybe just a small start on her treatment? Who would think any less of her? Who would even need to know?

No no no! Merit grimaced as she leaned against a piling on the dock. She knew exactly where those questions could take her, so instead of answering them, she gently patted her stomach.

"Don't worry, little guy. Your mommy's still taking good care of you."

God knew she could do no less.

All right, then, she told herself, this would be their arrangement—not a deal, just an understanding. She would take care of the life growing inside her, the life God had entrusted to her. No questions, no complaints, no buts. And then, perhaps He could take care of her as well as she took care of the baby. So if she honored her end of the arrangement—

"How are you doing today, honey?" Will broke into her thoughts as he stumbled down the walkway, manhandling a pair of oars and a small outboard for a rental customer. She still wasn't sure how she'd convinced him to go back to work after everything they'd been through.

"Fine," she moaned, and the lake's spell evaporated like morning mist. "Just fine."

"No headache today?"

"I took a couple of Tylenol. The doctor said it wouldn't hurt the baby."

Although she wasn't sure how much she could trust a doctor's advice anymore. That thought only made her feel like Sydney, afraid of every conspiracy theory, mistrusting any authority. Pretty soon she'd be drinking that awful tea.

"Well, let me know," Will added, " 'cause if you want Stephanie to give you a hand behind the counter today, she said—"

"I can handle it, okay?" She cut him off, regretting it when she saw the stricken look on his face.

"Whoa." He dropped his load and held up his hands. "I'm on your side, remember?"

She knew he'd only been trying to help, but he didn't seem to realize how his help was coming off. She turned and escaped across the dock to her post inside the floating snack bar and bait shop.

Merit hadn't been inside two minutes, pretending to be busy sorting gas receipts, when jingle bells on the door announced yet another customer.

"You've got to see this one, Merit!"

She didn't recognize the younger man, but he obviously recognized her.

"I think we've got a winner out here!" he said, waving for her to follow.

Merit reluctantly stepped outside. Out on the dock, the stranger made Fred Martinez hold up his string of three rainbow trout for the camera. They were good-sized, but Merit didn't know anything about prize-winning fish.

"Dick Pullman's got a bigger fish," Fred told them. "Of course, he's always got a bigger fish."

"Then I'll have to track him down too." The photographer smiled and adjusted his lens before pressing one of the buttons. Nothing seemed to happen. "Uh, hold on a minute."

"Nice camera," offered Fred. "What'd it cost you?"

"Actually, it belongs to a friend." He wrinkled his nose and squinted at the camera, but it only beeped and flashed in his face. "Shoot. I had it figured out this morning."

"Here." Fred reached over. "I think you want to press this one on the top."

The camera flashed again.

"Hey, thanks." The stranger smiled, showing off a set of whitened teeth. "Us fishermen have to stick together."

He didn't look like a local fisherman with his Boston Red Sox cap and spotless running shoes. He was probably from the derby organizing committee, since he seemed awfully excited about Fred's catch. Fred didn't seem to mind the attention, either.

"You want a shot with me and my new pole?" Fred held up his pole in one hand and the fish in the other. "Maybe this is good enough for second prize?"

"I think it could be." The photographer lined himself up for yet another shot, and this time the camera worked the way he wanted.

Merit turned to go back to her post, but the stranger called to her.

"Let's get the resort owner in the picture with this winner."

"Oh no." Merit backed away. "You don't want a picture of a pregnant lady to ruin things."

"I hadn't noticed." He shrugged, not giving up. "But you do own the place, don't you?"

"Well..."

"Go ahead, Merit." Stephanie walked up and gently pushed her to stand next to Fred. Merit looked around for Will, hoping for a rescue, but he was cleaning rest rooms or doing some other glamorous chore. She'd already chased him off.

"Here we go." The photographer backed up a couple of steps before anyone could warn him about the edge of the dock.

"Hey, uh—" Stephanie held out her hand but not quickly enough.

He tottered on the edge...and barely pulled back.

"Whoa." The guy never stopped smiling. "Almost took a dip there."

"No kidding." Fred chuckled. "That would have been good."

The stranger recovered quickly and held his digital camera up again. A red light flickered in their faces. Merit tried not to turn her barely-showing profile toward the camera and did her best to smile.

"Cheese."

Satisfied after three more shots, the photographer released them—only to follow Merit back into the store.

"Can I help you with anything else?" she asked him, noticing he had an eye on her books. "Borrow a book—or a life jacket maybe?"

"Right. Actually..." He selected a bag of chips and set them on the counter in front of the cash register.

"Eighty-nine cents, please," she said.

"Do you have change for a fifty?" he asked, holding up a bill.

"That kind of cleans out my till. Do you have anything smaller?"

He didn't, so she counted out forty-nine dollars, a dime, and a penny into his hand.

"So you and your husband are from California, is that right?" He'd been chatting with Stephanie, he said, who had been kind enough to tell him all about them.

Merit nodded, but the furrow on her brow must have given her away.

"I don't mean to sound nosy!" He held up his hands. "Just getting to know my new neighbors."

"I see." Merit relaxed. That was different.

"So…" He headed for the door, munching his chips. "Do you have plans to host another derby next year?"

"We're not the derby organizers, Mister, er…"

"Chris." He flashed a smile, one foot out the door. "Chris Davidson. And I just meant, you'll be around, right?"

Merit's throat went dry. He couldn't know how his question made her feel.

"Sure," she mumbled. "We're planning to be here."

He nodded his thanks and slipped out into the once-perfect day. She almost followed him to tell him where to find Dick Pullman's boat, but someone else would help him if he still wanted another photo.

Stephanie entered the store a few minutes later.

"Strange guy, huh?" Merit commented.

"Asked a million questions." Stephanie tucked a bill into the register and rang up a gas sale.

"Hmm."

❧

By the middle of the next week, Merit had heard the rumors, just like everyone else: Pastor Bud had reeled in several good-sized trout, none of them record-breaking, but still exciting enough in local fishing circles.

"So how big was it?" Will asked over the cup of coffee Merit poured for him from the snack bar coffee maker.

She held out her hands as if measuring the imaginary prize. "Uh…thirteen inches?" she guessed. "He told me last night. Fourteen?"

"In other words, you're not quite sure."

Merit smiled and sipped her gentian tea, then grimaced and nearly spit it out.

Will gave her a worried look. "You sure you want to drink that stuff?" he asked. "I can smell it from here."

"It's great." She nodded and tried not to gag. Her sister would have been proud. "Just wonderful."

"I don't believe you."

"You don't have to." She took another sip, longer this time.

Her husband shook his head and shrugged.

The door bells jingled, and Stephanie and her father stepped inside.

"Well, here's the man who can tell us about that fish." Will grinned. "Bud, how long was that monster rainbow you caught yesterday morning?"

"Thirty-five inches." Pastor Bud beamed. "Came to twenty pounds, three ounces. Guess there still are a few big ones out there."

"Did that fellow from the derby committee get your snapshot?" asked Merit.

Bud's face went blank. "Don't know anything about that. But I've got to show you something."

He pulled a grocery store tabloid from under his arm, the kind that regularly related Elvis sightings and UFO abductions. Merit wondered if her sister subscribed. She also wondered why Pastor Bud was carrying one around.

"You actually read those things?" asked Will.

Bud shook his head, licked his finger for traction, and flipped through the pages. "Nope. One of our people saw this when they were grocery shopping in Coeur d'Alene. Thought you should see it."

His grim tone made Merit pause, but her heart truly stopped as she stared down at the half-page photo of herself standing next to Fred and his runner-up trout. Across the top, a bright red headline screamed to the world: "Resort Owner Trades Her Life for Unborn Child."

She closed her eyes and tried to keep her head from swimming as Will took the paper and quietly read the article.

"It says you're defying doctor's orders, refusing treatment for life-threatening cancer, and that you have less than nine months to live."

"Who told him *that*?" asked Merit. She turned to Stephanie, who shook her head.

"Oh no, Mrs. Sullivan." Stephanie's face paled. "I didn't share anything like that."

"But you said he asked a lot of questions, right?"

"He did," Stephanie answered. "But mostly it was just stuff about the resort, how long you've been here, what people are saying about you and Mr. Sullivan, that sort of thing. I would never…"

"I'm sorry. I didn't mean to accuse you. It's not your fault." Merit turned back to her husband. "What else does he say, or do we not want to know?"

Will looked ready to shoot someone—probably their visitor with the camera. He stabbed the paper with one finger.

"He says you're predicting a total recovery, in spite of what the doctors say. That you're a fundamentalist who runs a right-wing religious library and doesn't believe in doctors, and that you're undergoing herbal therapy, mail order, from some clinic in Mexico."

"Oh brother." Merit sighed. "That's pretty creative. I wondered why he asked me if I was planning to be around for next year's derby."

"Well, that's a stretch." Will read on, then grunted. "And all this stuff about the girls and Michael. Did you tell him any of that, Stephanie?"

"I am so sorry, Mr. Sullivan." Stephanie's voice quivered and she looked down at her feet. "I thought he was from the derby committee and was just being friendly. He never said who he really was. And I never said anything about your…Merit's cancer."

"Well, he found out from someone." Will slammed the paper down on the counter. "Maybe somebody at the hospital. Whatever happened to patient privacy? Something's really screwy here."

Merit looked at her husband with tears in her eyes, as if she could—or should—apologize for this man.

"I didn't mean for us to keep it a secret forever," she told him. "But this wasn't how I wanted to announce it to the world."

"What can we do about it, though?" wondered Stephanie.

Merit thought for a moment before she turned to the second page of the tabloid, picked up her phone, and dialed the News Tips contact number below the New York address.

After several levels of "to subscribe, press…" or "to leave a message, press…," she finally got through to a live voice.

"Luna Publishing, how may I direct your call?"

"Chris…" She checked the byline. "Chris Davis. This is Merit Sullivan."

"One moment."

She waited for the inevitable voice mail then jumped when a live voice answered—a voice she recognized.

"Chris Davis here. I was hoping you'd call. This is—"

"This is Merit Sullivan. Sullivan is my real name, by the way, and you have a lot of nerve, Mr. Davis."

She ignored the stares from everyone in the snack bar. Will's eyes had grown the largest.

"Listen, I'm really sorry about the mix-up with the name and all," Chris Davis told her. "You know how writers sometimes use pen names."

"I don't think we're talking about pen names here, Mr. Davis."

"Please, call me Chris."

"No, Mr. Davis. You violated our trust. You misrepresented yourself. You invaded our privacy, and—"

"And the good news is that I'm talking to you and not your lawyer. You don't have a lawyer, do you, Mrs. Sullivan?"

"I didn't call to sue you, if that's what you're afraid of. Though now that you mention it, it's not such a bad idea."

"All we're doing at *National Exposure* is giving the public inspiring true stories, Mrs. Sullivan. Yours is one of them, and you've got to embrace that."

"That's pretty tough to do when half the story was made up, and the other half was private information."

"Your employee didn't seem to have any problem answering my questions."

"Let's not bring her into this."

Merit could feel her blood pressure rising. Only Will's hand on her arm kept her from melting down. He motioned for her to hand over the phone, but she shook her head and held on.

"Well, like I said," Chris Davis continued, "I'm sorry you're upset, but when I heard about your story, I knew it was hot."

"Hot is the last word I'd use to describe this. In fact, there are so many mistakes and outright lies in your article, I don't know where to begin. That's only secondary, though, to the way you deceived us."

"But you like the photo, don't you? I thought it turned out really well, with the fisherman there and everything. Really cute."

"Cute?" She felt the pressure returning. "Why didn't you tell me who you were? If you were going to pry into our lives, why didn't you at least have the courtesy to identify yourself and then ask your questions?"

"What would you have told me if I'd done that?"

Merit didn't hesitate. "I'd have told you to jump in the lake. Although you seemed quite capable of doing that on your own."

"Uh…I'm not always that clumsy. But see? You wouldn't have given me the time of day. I rest my case."

"That still doesn't give you the right to invade our privacy, Mr. Davis. And how did you find out about us in the first place?"

He didn't answer right away, then laughed. "You know how it is with the press, Mrs. Sullivan. We all have our sources."

"Even slimy tabloids like yours."

"Even…tabloids like mine, yes. So what do you say to a follow-up interview to set the record straight?"

So that was his tactic—publish a bunch of lies as bait, then sucker the victim into another interview.

"I wouldn't talk to you again if my life depended on it, Mr. Davis," Merit said.

"But you're talking to me now. And you called me, which I really appreciate. You don't mind that I've been recording this conversation, do you?"

"I do mind. Good-bye, Mr. Davis."

"Oh, come on. You're not going to be rude and hang up on me, are you? Tell me your opinion of Rita Fedrizzi. You know about her, don't you?"

Rita Fedrizzi. For a moment it stung her almost to tears to realize what was going on. She even almost answered him. But she would not be a poster child for the cause, especially not in this man's horrid tabloid. It was much more satisfying to slam the receiver down, making sure Chris Davis knew she had done so.

And then she hung her head over the phone and wept as Will wrapped his arms around her. Stephanie and Pastor Bud headed for the door.

"No." Merit reached out her hand and called to them through her tears. "Please don't go. Not yet."

They stayed, and the four of them waited for the storm together, knowing it had just begun.

twenty-six

———— ❧ ————

Faith is like radar that sees through the fog.
CORRIE TEN BOOM, in *Tramp for the Lord*

T he storm hit even sooner than Merit had imagined and with more
    ferocity than she could have dreamed. It slammed into Kokanee Cove
the next morning as Merit and Will stepped into the Mercantile to pick up a
few groceries.

Foster Mooney didn't turn as they entered. His focus remained glued to
the portable radio parked on the shelf behind his register next to the clock
with fisherman hands that ran backward. Merit ducked as a sparrow of some
kind dive-bombed them and then settled on the storekeeper's shoulder.

"They're talking about Kokanee Cove on the *Ross Aden in the Morning*
show," Mr. Mooney said without looking at them. "Can you believe it?
National talk radio!"

"Already?" Merit whispered to Will with a look that told him she would
turn around on the spot if he would too.

Mr. Mooney swiveled to see who they were, and his mouth dropped
open. "Oh! I didn't realize. I…"

"That's okay." Merit held up her hand. It was time to face the storm.
"Turn it up. I want to hear too."

She didn't, but the notoriously liberal talk show host had already put
another caller on the air.

"Hey, thanks for taking my call." At first the caller sounded perky and
upbeat, and Merit breathed a little easier. That quickly changed. "I just
wanted to comment on that whacked lady in Montana."

"That would be Idaho," the host corrected. "Out in the wilderness where
shotgun polygamy is still a way of life."

"Whatever. Me, I can only handle one woman at a time."

The host laughed as his guest continued.

"Anyway, I just think this has to be one of the sickest examples of how the anti-abortion crowd has gotten out of control."

"So you're saying, caller, that you don't support this woman's choice not to seek treatment for her cancer?" Even through the radio, they could hear the snicker behind the host's voice.

"Hey, she can kill herself for all I care. That's one less right-wing, religious wacko to worry about. The only thing that worries me is what this says about the mind control these Bible thumpers have over their people. That's the one thing we need to do something about. I heard she was a member of a cult or something."

"Oh brother." Will clenched his fists.

Merit felt another headache coming on, and she rubbed her temples. She wouldn't be able to listen to this garbage much longer, and the host's response didn't help.

"I believe you're talking about the Catholic church, caller. And I have to agree with you, because in this case we're dealing with a hierarchy that is cheering this woman on. I mean, if you can believe it in this morning's statement, which I'm going to read here in just a moment..." The sound of chanting monks came up in the background as the host continued his rant. "...the Catholic church is actually *praising* this woman's decision to spit in her doctor's face. You might understand that happening in a backward, third-world country like Slobovia or Outer Momboland but not here in the USA."

"Yeah," agreed the caller, obviously fired up by this time. "That's gotta stop."

"Thanks, caller. Let's hear what the rest of you think. Everyone has the right to death with dignity. But should we sit by as church officials—who, by the way, did a lot of sitting on the sidelines as hundreds of children were abused at the hands of priests—pull strings to influence an obviously mentally disturbed woman—perhaps spiritually *coerce* her—into a church-sanctioned suicide? What about this woman's kids? One report says she has five."

"Three!" Will blurted. "Three, you moron. If you can't get even *that* detail right, you'd better—"

"Will." Merit gripped her husband's arm, holding him back as she might have done if he was about to hit someone.

"What's going to happen to this woman's kids?" the talk show host asked. "I think somebody better tell her church that she has a *sacred* duty to them too, doesn't she? Tell us what you think. We're taking your calls live on *Ross Aden in the Morning,* your sane alternative for the rest of us…"

"That slime…" Merit could almost see the steam pouring from Will's ears. "He doesn't know the first thing about sacred duty. If he wants to know a little truth, I'll call him and—"

"No, Will."

"But you heard that garbage," Will said, waving a hand at the radio. "They're just building one lie on the next, whipping people up with their warped agendas. Where does it stop? Somebody needs to set him straight."

"Just let it go. This is our fifteen minutes of fame, but I'm not going to let them pull you into the mud."

Mr. Mooney stared at them as if they'd never met.

"Never heard Kokanee Cove mentioned on the *Ross Aden in the Morning* show before." He erased a quick smile with a hand to his face. "I mean, they had no right to say those kinds of things about you." He paused. "Did they?"

Merit had completely forgotten what they'd come to the Mercantile for in the first place. She grabbed her husband's hand and pulled him outside, only to be hit once again by the storm. A young woman in a brightly painted Channel 3 Eyewitness News van pulled up to the store and rolled down her window.

"I'm looking for the Kokanee Cove Marina," said the woman, slipping on a pair of designer sunglasses. "Someone named Sullivan. Any idea where I can find them?"

Merit pointed at the gravel road that led past the Buttonhook Inn restaurant and out of town—the opposite direction from the resort. Plenty of potholes and a couple of nice switchbacks. Good four-wheeling territory.

"Up that road about three or four miles, all the way to the end," she told the newswoman, who smiled her thanks and headed off in a cloud of dust.

Will gave her a wry smile as they climbed into the Land Rover, but they both knew they had only bought a few minutes of peace.

❧

The peace lasted an hour and forty-five minutes before the now dust-encrusted news van came roaring down the hill toward their resort. When the van's windshield wipers cleared dust to each side, Merit could see the determined face of the newswoman glaring out at them.

A moment of understanding passed between them as the van rocked to a stop, and Merit realized the trade-off might not have been worth it.

"You go inside," Will told her, leaning against the shovel he'd been using to transplant a lilac bush next to the parking lot. Sweat glistened on his forehead. "I'll talk to her."

"Thanks, honey," Merit shook her head, "but I've got to apologize to her first."

Merit remembered the day after she got her driver's license when she'd borrowed her dad's brand-new Ford Pinto and scratched the side against a shopping cart in the Save-On Foods parking lot. The week she'd remained silent about the accident had been one of the longest in her young life. She also remembered the distinctly nettled expression her father wore the day she'd finally offered a confession. It looked just like the one worn by the woman now emerging from the van.

Abby and Olivia ran out from behind the house to greet their visitors.

"Are you really from Channel Three?" asked Olivia, wide-eyed. Her older sister held her back a respectable distance.

"We've seen you on the news," reported Abby, her arm around Olivia. "You're the one who's always standing in front of car wrecks and stuff. But you're prettier in person."

That softened the attacking journalist. As a cameraman climbed out of the other side of the van, she paused for a moment to fix her hair and smile down at her two young admirers.

"I'm Shanna Tomkins." The news reporter held out her hand to the girls. "What are your names?"

Abby knew enough to look for permission from her mother. Merit nodded her okay as she stepped up to the van herself. The girls told the woman their names and shook Ms. Tomkins's hand in turn. Finally, it was Merit's turn.

She held out her hand. "Merit Sullivan, and this is my husband, Will. That was a mean trick. I feel foolish. I apologize."

The newswoman flashed a brilliant TV smile. The girls were right. Even without stage makeup, she was beautiful.

"Not a problem, actually. We got some really nice scenic shots from up on that overlook, didn't we, Barry?"

"Mmm-hmm." Barry the cameraman didn't look up as he replaced the battery pack on his shoulder-mounted camera and adjusted a compact boom microphone. Did they just assume it was okay to march in, ask questions, and take pictures?

"Girls, you can watch from the front porch," Will said pointing. His serious gaze dampened the newswoman's smile.

"Actually," she countered, "it would be very nice, with your permission, if we included the girls in a couple of shots. Give it a family flavor."

Will shook his head and told the girls to hurry along. "We've already heard a lot of half truths and things that don't match up with reality." He squared off with the reporter, his voice level and strong. "All Merit and I want to do is set the record straight. We'll keep the girls out of it."

"Whatever you're most comfortable with." Ms. Tomkins glanced at her cameraman, who hoisted the camera to his shoulder and adjusted the eyepiece. The red light on the front of the camera told Merit he was already rolling, that he had already caught a shot of the girls running toward the porch. "But you don't mind if I ask you a few questions."

Her voice, though soft and reassuring, didn't turn up in a question at the end of her last word. Merit shivered as the rose-colored camera eye stared their way and Shanna Tomkins held a Channel 3 microphone toward them.

"Mr. and Mrs. Sullivan, I first want to confirm what we've already heard: When did you learn you were pregnant? Was this before or after you found out about the cancer?"

Merit bit her lip, then opened her mouth to answer at the same time as Will. He gestured for her to go ahead.

"The same time." Merit nodded slowly. "We learned about both things at the same time."

"The doctor told you what you needed to do to live, is that correct? What did he advise you?"

This response came harder, though they all knew the answer already.

"*She* told me to…" Merit looked at her feet and felt Will's arm around her. "She told me to kill my baby if I wanted to live."

"In so many words?"

The questions didn't get any easier from there, couched in body language that said "I care" but tossed her way with enough barbs to sting. No, they had not heard about Rita Fedrizzi in Italy before they made their decision. No, they were not a member of a cult. But yes, her faith had everything to do with deciding to keep the baby. Had this woman been listening to the Ross Aden show on the way to Kokanee Cove?

Ms. Tomkins paused for a moment and glanced at the porch before revealing the full extent of her fangs.

"I hate to ask this at such an obviously emotional time, but you must have discussed it: Did you make this decision with your children in mind? And do they understand? Do they agree with your decision?"

Merit felt the grip on her shoulder tighten just a little, as the question hit Will just as hard. The reporter waited without a word, confident that the editors would cut out all the dead air they wanted. Will's touch reassured her, but Merit's self-control dissolved like sugar in hot coffee.

And still the camera stared, unblinking.

"They understand," she finally whispered, and the boom mike lowered toward her face.

"Could you say that again?" asked the reporter. "I'm not sure we caught that."

"I said, they understand what's going on." But her voice couldn't carry the load and cracked under the weight. Did Abby and Olivia understand the grief their mother carried? How could they?

With camera still rolling, Merit collapsed into Will's arms, hit by the same grief these two innocent ones would have to carry long after their mother was gone.

"Oh, Will." She buried her face in his chest and sobbed, holding even more tightly as her knees gave way. "Will, it's no good. It's not fair to them. It's not…"

"Shh." Will cradled her head in his strong arms and stroked her hair, turning her away from the camera.

"Can you turn that thing off now?" Will asked.

From the corner of her eye, Merit could see that Abby had retreated to the corner of the porch, arms crossed. In a moment, Merit felt another set of arms around her waist.

"It's going to be okay, Mommy." Olivia's sweet voice wavered too.

They held fast to the life they'd been dealt, crying out the pain, but holding tight even so.

Merit heard the reporter ask the cameraman if he was getting all this, and of course, he was. He circled eighteen inches away, probably looking for the perfect angle with her beautiful lake in the background.

And...who knew? Maybe Livvy was right.

twenty-seven

*As the poet said, 'only God can make a tree'—probably because
it's so hard to figure out how to get the bark on.*

WOODY ALLEN

Will popped his head into the snack bar. "Got a minute, Stephanie? I need a hand hauling a trailer from Ed Nieback's place behind the Mercantile."

"Uh, sure. Be right there." She could do that. Since Mrs. Sullivan had gotten sick, she'd been doing just about everything around this place anyway. Not just watching the snack bar, but calling in orders and pumping gas, helping fix docks, and even painting a few boats. Funny thing was, she kind of liked it. Or she would have, if things had been different.

She locked the cash register till, hung the hand-printed Back in 15 Minutes sign on the door, and shut it behind her. Up in the parking lot, Mr. Sullivan waited in his Land Rover.

"Thanks." He put the car in gear and they started down the gravel road. "You know how it is getting one of those things hooked up. One person can do it, but it's much easier if someone else is behind the wheel."

"Not a problem, Mr. Sullivan."

He'd never asked her to call him by his first name, which made working for him more comfortable. Calling Mrs. Sullivan "Merit" was one thing; calling Mr. Sullivan anything else would have been entirely different.

Halfway to town they passed another network TV van with its satellite dish on the roof. A reporter stood by the edge of the road talking to a cameraman.

Mr. Sullivan moaned and slumped in his seat. "This past week has been a little different, hasn't it?" he asked, slowing for a curve.

They passed Tom and Marcia Urban's cabin on the outskirts of town. Tom attended their church, but Marcia watched TV preachers and UFO shows behind the drawn curtains of their cabin and might be mistaken for an alien herself.

"Different?" Stephanie watched the TV crew. "You can say that again. I don't think I've ever talked to so many television reporters in my life. I mean, I never have, before this."

"Yeah, neither have I. But Merit and I really appreciate having you around with all this going on. Otherwise, I mean... And the girls, you're their idol."

"They're sweet." She smiled. "But you know, a lot of people around here are praying for you."

As if to prove her point, they passed the Mercantile. Mr. Mooney stretched from the top of his stepladder, adding another letter to his sign.

Pray FOr the SULlivans.

Mr. Mooney apparently didn't have enough lowercase letters, but that hadn't stopped him. Another TV crew filmed the man's every move.

"Don't you guys have a war to cover?" Mr. Sullivan grumbled as they passed. "Terrorists? Car crash? Something dangerous?"

His mention of the war made Stephanie think of Michael. She couldn't help wondering what he was doing or if he was happy with his life in California. She might have worked up the courage to ask his father if Mr. Mooney hadn't shouted.

"Whoa!"

Almost in slow motion, he waved his arms and lost his balance as one of the ladder legs gave way. Either he hadn't extended or locked it properly, or he'd been standing on the step that said Do Not Step Here, and the ladder just folded underneath him. Sign letters fluttered everywhere as Mr. Mooney fell.

Mr. Sullivan brought the Land Rover to a screeching halt.

"Mr. Mooney!" Stephanie sprinted around the car, praying with each step that her friend wasn't hurt too badly. Mr. Sullivan nearly beat her there, but not quite. Noah McHenry from the Buttonhook Inn restaurant across the street jogged over. Even Mrs. Sullivan's sister, Sydney Olson, burst out of the store to see what all the noise was about.

And the TV cameraman just kept rolling.

"You okay, Foster?" Noah McHenry kneeled by the stricken shopkeeper, who had landed on his back in a bright yellow forsythia bush.

"I think the forsythia might have cushioned his fall," Will said. Stephanie helped him extricate the ladder from the mess of arms and legs and lay it to the side. Mr. Mooney said nothing, however—just moved his mouth like a fish and blinked his eyes.

"I think he got the breath knocked out of him," guessed Noah. The Harley-Davidson biker tattoos on his arms flexed as he gently moved Mr. Mooney's arms and legs. "Didn't you, bro?"

"You want us to call George?" asked Will, looking up at his fellow rescuers. "That's the volunteer medic fireman, right?"

"George is in Alaska fishing for a couple weeks," reported Noah. "But the good news is he always comes back with a freezer full of halibut and salmon. Best stuff you ever tasted, except for lake trout. In fact—"

"Uh." Stephanie didn't want to interrupt, but when guys started talking about fishing... "Don't you think we'd better get him inside or something?"

Mr. Mooney recovered enough to sit up on his own, and he waved off their help.

"I'm just clumsy," he wheezed. He breathed slowly at first, then nodded and rose to his feet, dusting off a few yellow blooms as he did. "Clumsy and not very good with that old ladder."

"You sure you didn't break anything?" Will asked.

Mr. Mooney smiled back at him. "I'll let you know. But I do appreciate everybody running over to give me a hand."

Which reminded Stephanie: what had happened to...

"That's enough!"

They turned to see Sydney Olson advancing on the cameraman, a rolled-up newspaper held high like a club.

"You're like vultures," she screeched, "circling our town, waiting for someone to die. Just like the multinational corporations you work for."

"I'm with Fox, lady." The camera guy backed up and lowered his camera for safety. The red light told Stephanie he was still capturing this attack on film, probably for broadcast on tonight's news. "We report, you decide."

"No kidding?" Sydney didn't lower her weapon. "Well, I'm deciding it's time for you to take your negative aura and leave. You brought it in with all your equipment, and it's polluting the town. Do you understand me?"

"Whatever, lady. I have just as much right to be here as anybody else."

Will tried to break up the unlikely fight. But instead of retreating peacefully, Sydney pulled her arm away from his grip and turned to confront her brother-in-law.

"And *you!*" she shouted, continuing to set the world and its multiple conspiracies in their places. "*You're* the one who's killing my sister!"

Will flinched and turned pale. He opened his mouth to reply but must have changed his mind. He took a deep breath and turned to walk away.

Sydney wouldn't let him. "Don't you run away from me. I have something to say!"

And she'd have millions of viewers. The cameraman filmed the argument from a safe distance.

"I want to know how you think you can get away with this," Sydney demanded, "forcing Merit to sacrifice her life on your altar of male domination."

"Now wait a minute. It's not like that at all," Stephanie interjected. She knew it was none of her business, but she couldn't just stand there and watch, the way the cameraman had done when Mr. Mooney fell off his ladder.

Will shook his head at her and held up his hand. "It's okay, Stephanie," he whispered.

Sydney continued, ignoring Stephanie completely. "She wasn't like this," she told Will. "Not before she met you. She used to have a head on her shoulders. Used to think for herself. She was just a girl, but we marched together in Berkeley, you know."

Mr. Sullivan frowned. "Yeah, I've heard all those sixties stories."

Stephanie blinked. Mrs. Sullivan wasn't *that* old, was she?

"Then you should realize what you've done to her."

"Look, Sydney," Will spoke softly, trying to make peace, "I know you never liked me, and I know your parents never approved of me either. But—"

"Whatever gave you that idea?"

Stephanie wasn't sure how much sarcasm lay hidden in the strange woman's remarks.

"Oh come on," Will replied. "I wasn't radical enough for them. I didn't want to torch society, and I didn't care about joining marches." He glanced at Stephanie. "Pretty strange, huh? They almost wouldn't let me date their daughter because I was too straight."

"Well, they *did* let you date their daughter," Sydney snapped, "and that was their—"

"Mistake?" he interrupted. "Is that what you were going to say? Their mistake, and her mistake. Is that why the two of you had your big blowup? I think everyone's forgotten the reason, except you."

Sydney clamped her lips together and didn't answer.

Mr. Sullivan held out his olive branch again. "Look, Sydney, I didn't come here to fight with you. In fact, why don't you come back to the house with us? You haven't seen what the resort looks like, have you? We could all talk."

"No." Sydney shook her head, her voice growing louder and louder. "Not after what you've done to her. Not now."

"We'll give you a ride, Sydney." Stephanie stepped forward. "It's okay."

Sydney looked at Stephanie as if she were offering a dose of the Asian flu virus. She looked at Mr. Mooney's sign and then back to Stephanie. She sneered. "And you Christians have the nerve to enable this fascism with your *prayer* meeting."

Stephanie's mouth dropped open. She'd known Sydney had some odd ideas, and that she never came to church, but neither did a lot of backwoods folks who just wanted to be left alone. But she hadn't expected this.

"As if your prayers to a *father* would do anything but reinforces this... this...homicide!"

Sydney had run out of words but not out of bile, and she reeled back and swatted Will across the head with her rolled-up newspaper. He flinched but didn't retreat.

"I hate you, Will Sullivan! Do you hear me? I hate you, and I hate what you've done to Merit!"

He didn't answer, so she hit him again and again—on the shoulder, on the face, on the ear—but he stood his ground, not even holding up his hands for protection. When the newspaper finally unrolled from the beating, he took Sydney's beating fists in his hands. Her screams faded to whimpers, and he held her in his arms. But the heartsick look on his face brought tears to Stephanie's eyes, and Mr. Mooney and Noah McHenry turned away. Even the TV cameraman turned off his camera and retreated to his van.

I hate you, hate you, hate you...

Sydney Olson collapsed on her brother-in-law, whimpering softly and clenching her fists on his chest, and he held her as she sobbed.

Stephanie didn't want to hear what he told Sydney, but she couldn't help it as she turned to walk back to the Rover.

"I know, Syd," he said, his voice soft and sad. "Sometimes I hate me too."

❧

No one spoke as they drove back to the resort—the trailer they'd come to town for replaced by an unlikely passenger in a tie-dyed dress. Sydney gripped the side of the door as if ready to bail out at any moment. It wouldn't have surprised Stephanie if she did.

"I'm glad you changed your mind about coming out, Sydney." Will navigated around a pothole, mostly missing it. Stephanie bounced on the backseat. "I know Merit's going to appreciate it."

"I must be crazy," mumbled the older woman. "But she is my little sister, no matter what you've done to her."

Will didn't reply.

"I can make us some sandwiches when we get there," Stephanie said to fill the silence. "How's that sound?"

"Yeah, I'm starving." Will nodded and sounded cheerier than he had a right to. "How about you, Sydney?"

Sydney wasn't so sure, especially when she heard what was on the menu.

"Well, we don't need to have bologna and cheese." Stephanie tried to figure out what else she could put together from the snack bar cooler. Not the ready-made burritos or the packaged deli sandwiches she often microwaved for their guests. "I think we have some turkey."

Turkey was filled with artificial preservatives, Sydney said. So was beef. Eating meat destroyed the body's natural rhythmic need for natural antioxidants.

"I've got it!" Stephanie smiled. "I'll just make tuna fish with pickles. Everybody likes tuna, right?"

Not Sydney. Did they know what kind of damage the tuna industry did to the marine environment?

No, Stephanie couldn't say that she did, but as they turned down the lane to the resort, she got a sixty-second ecolecture. Her stomach growled for a quarter-pound burger with cheese.

"So I can make us a lettuce sandwich." Stephanie wasn't serious.

"Perfect," replied the eccentric older woman. "With sprouts?"

"I'll see if we have any." Stephanie knew they didn't.

"I can teach you how to grow them for yourselves."

"Would you look at that." Will slowed the car and pointed ahead. Had he seen a deer? maybe a buck with an impressive rack of antlers? The dust swirled around them for a moment before clearing.

A silver Hyundai with a broken windshield and a dangling side-view mirror was parked next to the cabin, layers of bugs plastered on the front and crammed full of boxes and clothes and suitcases. The driver must have gone inside to say hello to Merit and the girls.

"You know who that is?" Stephanie asked. "Looks like a homeless person with all that stuff packed in the car."

"He's not a homeless person." Will put the car back into gear. "Not anymore."

He parked the Land Rover behind the visiting car, leaped out the door, and ran up to the porch.

Sydney turned to Stephanie with a puzzled expression on her face. "Do you have any idea what's going on here?"

"I think so." Stephanie jumped out of the car, trying not to look too eager. She'd seen the California license plates.

Will found his guest on the front porch of the cabin. He locked his arms around Michael in a fierce bear hug and lifted him off the deck.

"Dad!" Michael warned. "You're strangling me."

But Michael was grinning just as much as his father, who slapped him on the shoulder blades in a fair imitation of the Heimlich maneuver before holding him out for a better look. Stephanie decided it was safe to approach the porch now.

"You're really back?" asked Will, glancing at the car. "I mean, I assume you're not just packed for another vacation."

"Not a vacation this time."

"But…so quick?"

"Yeah. Felt good, to tell the truth. I quit my dumb job, sold a lot of my stuff. I didn't have much to begin with, so that wasn't much of an…" His blue eyes met Stephanie's as she stepped onto the porch, and his voice trailed off. "Wasn't much of an issue."

"You're sure about this?" Will asked.

"Oh come on." Michael's eyes never left Stephanie's, leaving her unsure who was he talking to. "I had to come back, Dad. You need the help. And there were a few things here I didn't really want to leave after all."

Stephanie felt her cheeks burning and looked away.

"Is your mom inside?" Will asked as he released his grip on Michael. "Have you—"

"She's on the couch." Michael's expression grew serious. "I've already said hi. She was kind of asleep, though. And—"

"I know, Michael."

"Everything you told me on the phone, Dad, is it still the same? Is she still…"

Will nodded. "That's why I'm so glad to see you." He mussed his son's hair—Michael tried to duck—and finally noticed Stephanie. "Oh! I forgot to tell you. Stephanie's taken up a lot of the slack while you've been gone. A lot of the day-to-day stuff, which she has no idea how much we appreciate. I know I haven't made it easy, the way I've been…" His voice dropped off.

"We've all just been doing what we can," Stephanie put in. "It's not—"

"She's even been pumping gas and taking care of dockside chores with me," added Will. "Couldn't run this place without her."

Stephanie blushed and flexed her arm. A silly gesture, but Michael laughed.

"Tell you what, Stephanie," he told her. "I'll take over the gas pump if you don't make me cook."

"Deal." Stephanie looked back at the car, remembering their passenger. "Oh! We brought someone with us from town."

On cue, Sydney emerged from the Land Rover and stepped onto the porch, willing to shake Michael's hand.

"The last time I saw you, young man, you were half as tall as you are now. You ran out of my house screaming."

"No." Michael grinned. "I wasn't really screaming, was I? I don't remember that part."

"You screamed as if someone were trying to kill you. Maybe you don't recall, but I do. And you tried to bury the tofu I served you. You said it looked like it was alive once and needed a funeral."

"Well, give me a break, Aunt Sydney." He wrapped an arm around her. "I was just a little kid. Now tofu's one of my favorite foods."

She looked at him sideways, frowned, and shook her head. "I may live by myself with only animals for company, but I'm not naive. You like tofu as much as I like a Big Mac, which I can honestly tell you is poison from the industrial pit of despair."

Michael laughed, and the sound reminded Stephanie she hadn't heard a real, honest laugh around here for a long time. And though she would not have admitted it to anyone—especially not anyone on the porch with her— it warmed her like a cup of steaming hot chocolate on a cool day.

"Speaking of Big Macs," Stephanie said, heading down the stairs toward the docks, "I'd better make those sandwiches."

No one objected, so she kept going.

"I think I know why you came back, Michael Sullivan." Sydney's pronouncement caught Stephanie off guard. What would this odd woman say next? Stephanie slowed just enough to listen.

"You do, Aunt Sydney?"

"I do. And I don't think you came back just to work on outboard motors or pump gas at your father's gas dock. I think there's a young woman involved in this somewhere."

Stephanie caught her breath but continued down toward the docks. She didn't wait to hear Michael's response.

twenty-eight

Yes'm, old friends is always best,
'less you can catch a new one that's fit to make an old one out of.
SARAH ORNE JEWETT

O
h, Cheryl, I'm so glad you and Rick decided to come." Merit squeezed
her friend's hand. "You don't know what it means to me."

"Well, you made me promise, right?" Cheryl squeezed back.

Minutes after the Millers had arrived with their pop-up travel trailer,
Cheryl's three children had run down to the beach with Abby and Olivia to
throw rocks into the lake and giggle. Next they explored the tree fort Michael
was building them. The two moms watched the scene from the front porch
of the cabin, soaking in the evening calm.

"Amazing how little it takes to entertain them." Cheryl smiled and
sipped her mug of herbal tea as she paced the porch. She took a deep breath
and closed her eyes. "And I can see why you and Will fell in love with this
place. But you lied."

"What?" Merit wrinkled her nose and pushed herself in the porch swing.
"Did you say *lied*?"

Cheryl fought to hold a poker face. "Well, you told me it was pretty, but
that's not true."

"Really? You think we made a mistake? I was afraid—"

Cheryl interrupted with her laugh. "No, I mean, you never told me it
was *this* stunning."

"Oh. Right. I thought I had." Merit returned the smile.

Cheryl pointed across the bay the way Will had done the first evening
they'd stayed here, a lifetime ago.

"Look at those mountains, Merit. How they reflect on the water. I've never seen anything like this. It's like one of those Thomas Kinkade paintings come to life."

"I've thought the same thing." Merit took a sip of her own tea, savoring it for a moment. Caffeine-free, the way the doctor ordered. "Like we've always belonged here."

As they chatted, Will took Rick off on a grand tour of the premises. A few customers wandered here and there, puttering on their boats or cleaning up their catch after a day's fishing. Thank God for Stephanie, who didn't seem to mind putting in endless hours down at the snack bar, answering the phone, or occasionally pumping gas. Between her and Michael, Merit wondered if she and Will were even necessary. Although Will…

"I think it's been the hardest for Will," Merit said. "He's always working so hard, trying to keep things together, scurrying around, asking if there's anything he can do for me. He's sweet, but I worry about him. The look he gets on his face."

"What kind of look?"

"Like the weight of the world is on his shoulders. He's been talking with Pastor Bud, Stephanie's dad, once in a while. But I don't know. I still don't know."

"But…," Cheryl hesitated, "you can understand how he feels."

"Oh, definitely." Merit stared off at the lake. "It's just that…oh, I'm sorry. Here I go again with my problems."

"Not at all. And please don't feel like you're all alone. Like it's just your problem. That's why we're here, girlfriend. And if Will can't see straight sometimes, you know it's only because he loves you to death. I mean—" She slapped a hand across her mouth and groaned.

Merit had to smile at her friend. "Please. Don't worry about it."

"Well, then." Cheryl's hand came down, and she took a deep breath. "What about Abby and Olivia? How are they doing?"

"Oh, the girls. I think they're worried, especially Abby. But they've got themselves convinced that Mommy's going to be okay, somehow. That the doctor is going to figure out how to make me all better. That God's going to send a miracle."

An uncertain smile played at Cheryl's lips as she lingered by the porch railing.

Merit went on. "And you know what? Maybe they're right. Maybe adults are too cynical to recognize a real-life miracle, even if it bites us on our noses. Do you…do you believe in miracles like that?"

Cheryl chewed her lip. "I know that God can if He wants. We've been praying, you know."

"I know, and you know how much I appreciate it. The people here at the church have been amazing. They bring dinner—casseroles—all the time. They're so sweet. They watch the girls… I don't know what I would do."

She hadn't meant to choke up. But that brought Cheryl down to the bench beside her, a comforting arm around Merit's shoulder. They rocked together in silence for a moment, savoring the lake smells and the kid sounds around them. A raven cawed in the distance, and an outboard motor buzzed somewhere off the point. Cheryl was the first to speak again.

"So you remember what it's like to be pregnant?"

"Do I!" Merit gasped for effect. "Only it's so different this time. I'm totally wiped out. I mean totally. Zero energy, like I can't even get out of bed. Some days I don't."

"What does your doctor say?"

"We had to find another doctor." She almost chuckled. "The first one was so upset about what we were doing, so bent out of shape, that she just couldn't deal with it. She said if we weren't going to follow her advice, she wanted us to work with someone else."

"Very noble."

"Yeah, in fact, I wouldn't be surprised if she was the one who told the media."

"Oh, the media!" Cheryl finished her tea and cradled the mug in her hands. "Do you have any idea how many national programs have been play-ing the Merit Sullivan story?"

"Do I know? Ha! They've even been mentioning my 'right-wing' lend-ing library."

"Oh! That reminds me! I brought a few more boxes of books from the Bookworm girls. They're in the car. They wanted you to have some more right-wing propaganda."

Merit released her breath in an easy chuckle. And despite her numbing headache and the claws of fatigue that threatened to pull her right back to bed, it felt good.

"I saw that program where they showed the store and those 'right-wing' books," Cheryl said. "If they only knew what a compassionate liberal you really are."

"Yeah, we saw a lot of those cable news shows."

"At least Sean Hannity was nice."

"He's Catholic," Merit said.

"I heard that too."

"Well, the good news is that the media circus died down after that first frenzy. I don't think I would have been able to take it much longer, the way they came after us."

"Oh, Merit." Cheryl turned on the porch swing and grabbed her friend's shoulders. "I don't know if I've ever told you how sorry I am that—"

"Please don't." Merit closed her eyes and raised a hand. "I mean, I just wanted it to be—"

"I know what you're going to say."

"Do you?" Merit didn't open her eyes, but she suspected her friend was right.

"You wish Will didn't have to worry so much, and that it was just like it always was when our kids played together and we had barbecues on the back patio and Easter egg hunts in the Abells' backyard. When we took them trick-

or-treating around the neighborhood and when we would go camping at Fallen Leaf Lake."

"Exactly." Merit didn't mind a little syrupy reminiscing. A little schmaltz. Let the violins play. "Remember that campground we used to go to, with the store that had the—"

"The swinging screen door that squeaked like the one on *The Waltons,*" Cheryl finished the thought with a chuckle. "And that cute little chapel right in the middle of the campground where they rang the bell on Sunday morning, and we'd all troop in with our wet kids and our unshaven husbands?"

Merit smiled at the memory. "We used to love that place."

"We all did," Cheryl agreed, but her voice was serious now.

"What is it?"

"You know what happened to that campground, don't you?" Cheryl frowned.

"Happened?"

"I just read about it in the *San Francisco Chronicle.*" Cheryl looked out at the lake. "They're tearing it down. All of it. Somebody bought the land for luxury condos, with swimming pools and tennis courts and all that."

"Oh no." Merit assumed Cheryl's blank stare. Will and Rick were finally returning from the grand tour, trooping up the gangplank from the docks, sharing a joke. Merit sighed. It was probably time to get something together to eat. "I guess I shouldn't be too surprised. That kind of thing always seems to happen, doesn't it?"

"Not always. Look at you and Will out here building the Great American Dream."

"You think that's what it is?" She laughed, and it felt good. It was easy to forget reality and talk the way they always had, like girlfriends in high school with big dreams of husbands and kids, of making a difference in a few lives, of maybe traveling the world. Cheryl had always talked about going to France or Italy or Rome. Maybe she would someday.

"The Great American Dream," Merit repeated, clearing her head with a little shake. "Is that what we're doing? Right now I'd settle for getting out of this swing without looking like an idiot."

"Oh, sorry! Here." Cheryl put her feet down to stop the swinging.

"No, no. Actually, if we keep the swinging going, and if I time it just right…oh, this is silly. I don't know why I'm so weak-kneed. I've turned into an eighty-year-old woman overnight. Why I even—"

"Moooooom!" Olivia came screaming down the path, chased by a crew of other kids.

"It wasn't my fault!" Abby insisted, arriving at the same time as her sister to defend herself.

They could see blood between Olivia's fingers as she clutched her knee and grimaced. "She pushed me and I fell!"

The rest of the story came out in a torrent of tears, but the details and the blame didn't really matter. Merit gritted her teeth and pried Olivia's fingers away enough to see that this time she wasn't acting.

"Ooh, that's a nice one."

"No no no!" Olivia squeezed her eyes shut and winced with her entire body. "It's just a scratch. It's just a scratch!"

Merit clicked her tongue and wished somehow she could use the same technique. Just deny it, wish it away, like Dorothy in *The Wizard of Oz.*

There's no place like home, she thought.

"I wish it *was,* sweetie," Merit said, taking stock of the situation and trying not to let the butterflies in her stomach get the best of her. The blood had run down Olivia's shin and soaked her sock.

"Just a bandage. That's all I need, Mom. Please."

"I'm afraid not." Merit sighed and took one last peek at the wound. "This one might need some stitches, honey. Keep pressing your hand down tight, so it doesn't bleed all over the floor. We'll get it cleaned up inside."

She turned to Cheryl, giving her the look only moms can share, a look born from kissing boo-boos, sitting up with feverish toddlers all night, and fashioning splints for sprained wrists. "Like always, right?"

Cheryl paused and nodded, returning the look, the tears brimming in her eyes. "Kids certainly do make sure of that."

"*This* week, at least. I just wish you guys could stay longer."

twenty-nine

———— ❧ ————

You don't get to choose how you're going to die. Or when.
You can only decide how you're going to live. Now.
JOAN BAEZ

Does this mean summer's almost over?" Merit dangled her hand over the
side of the boat and traced rings in the still blue water. Will leaned his
head back and caught the early September sun full in his face. They bobbed
gently in the middle of the lake, and he listened for any sign that they were
not the last surviving people on the planet.

"Summer is not over," he murmured, barely loud enough for her to hear.
"In fact, they've canceled autumn, and this summer is going to last for the
next fifty years. Maybe a hundred."

"Is that why you brought me out here?" she asked. "To end fall?"

"Exactly, my dear Mrs. Sullivan. When all else fails, a little dose of denial."
He felt a cold splash of water on his bare chest. "Hey!" he shouted.

His wife might have been sick and pregnant, but she could still have a
respectable water fight. And so could he, for that matter. It didn't end until
they'd soaked each other like little kids and she lay back on the bench in the
back of the boat, panting and giggling, obviously exhausted.

"You act like you want to be thrown in," he teased, and she weakly held
up her hands.

"Please, no, Will. You don't want to be accused of drowning your sick
pregnant wife."

"Shows what you know." He kneeled next to her and wondered if the
past several months had all been a bad dream. He ran his fingers along her
glistening tanned shoulders, then brushed back her hair and buried his face

in her neck. For all the times he had watched her sleeping, wondering if she might not wake up. For all the times he had caught himself thinking, *This could be the last time...*

"Are you sure there wasn't a rapture, dear, and we got left behind?" Merit asked.

Will sighed at the thought, knowing his turn to be left behind might be coming sooner than he liked. He squinted out at the water and scanned the lake.

"I don't see anyone. I guess we'll have to camp out here and wait for the apocalypse."

With that unspiritual comment, he flipped himself over the side of the boat with a whoop. This time of year, the lake was cooler, but not enough to take his breath away. He swam around to the bow, retrieved the rope that normally tied up the front of the boat, and gripped it in his teeth.

"Honey! There's a walrus in the lake!"

Will turned over on his back and did his best imitation, and Merit's laugh felt like a salve to his soul.

He removed the rope from his mouth. "Well, this walrus is going to tow you into shore, ma'am." He did the backstroke until he had the boat moving along at a good speed, headed directly for the gravel beach just south of the abandoned lime mines and the bare remains of old piers where lake steamers had once docked generations ago. For this generation, the site served as a perfect camping spot, quiet and shaded, with a picnic table and a fire pit.

Will pitched their nylon pup tent, then started a fire and cooked a rather tasty one-pot camp stew of specially spiced sirloin, potatoes, and onions. They ate in silence as an orange and pink sunset lowered against the far western shore, the backdrop of mountains partly covered now by descending clouds.

"This is perfect," Merit whispered, snuggling against him.

"What—the food or the chef?" He slipped an arm around his wife, drawing her as close as he could. The fragrance of sun and the breeze lingered in her hair.

"Yeah."

He felt her shiver. The shadows had darkened, and the lake's chill turned to mist, blending with the smoke of their campfire. Will unzipped one of the sleeping bags and draped it over her shoulders.

She smiled up at him. "What happens if one of the kids needs us…or there's an emergency? or if I want to listen to the Giants' game?"

"I told Michael he could call us on the handheld if he needs us for anything. You know the Heimlich if I choke on a russet. And baseball can stay at home this time."

"No, seriously. Is the radio in the boat?"

"Yeah, it's…" Then he remembered. "Actually, I think I left it on the counter back at the resort. But I'll check."

He went to the boat where he'd tied it to an outcrop of logs a few feet offshore. He waded out and performed a quick search. No radio.

"Oh well," he called back. "We wanted to be castaways, didn't we?"

"Looks like we are, whether we wanted to be or not."

The only signs of life Will could see were a couple lights in cabins on the other side of the lake and the dim outline of a small boat headed north along the western shore, miles distant. A soft chorus of goose music wafted across the water as their local flock of Canadas discussed the possibilities of heading south.

Will cleaned up their dinner dishes and then built their bed in a smooth spot of gravel next to the tent, just under a canopy of firs. With two double sleeping mattresses, his princess would be quite comfy.

"I feel like such an invalid," Merit said. She still huddled under her sleeping bag, though the evening breeze had turned oddly warm. Maybe they would be able to sleep under the stars after all.

"Well, you are an invalid," Will said, "but what are we supposed to do about it?"

They exchanged a look, trying to decide how funny life had a right to be at this point. And as it turned out, it didn't matter. They laughed anyway.

Later, they laughed at a pair of mallards that splashed down at the shore in front of them, investigating the likelihood of a handout. After that, they laughed at the way they couldn't escape the smoke following them and making them cough. Will added a couple of tamarack logs to coax more flames from the fire, hot and high.

"The rescuers will come now for sure," Will said. He sipped a steaming mug of coffee, maybe the best cup he'd tasted in a long time, even if it was from the stash of decaf he shared with his pregnant wife.

"What if we don't want to be rescued?" She rubbed her nose against his cheek, making him shiver.

"I wish we'd come here twenty years ago."

"Me too. But if wishes were fishes…" She tossed a pebble into the water, and they watched the rings spread before fading. The first stars had already made an appearance, each sparkling brighter than the last. So bright that Will almost expected singing from heaven, and he felt himself straining to hear.

"I'm going to learn the names of those stars." He pointed up at a particularly bright cluster that had just appeared. Were they planets? He couldn't even find the North Star, but not knowing didn't diminish the raw beauty that made him shake his head in wonder. The same kind of wonder that filled him when he looked at Merit's profile. "All their names. And then I'm going to teach them to the girls…and him." He laid a hand on her stomach.

Merit snuggled closer under the sleeping bag, and he felt her arms circle his waist in answer. The ducks had left them alone, and the water lapped at their feet. Another warm breeze drifted across the lake, and a cloud covered some of the stars like the blanket covered Merit's shoulders.

"Lots of things he has to learn." She buried her face in his shoulder, and he felt the warm rain of her tears soak through his T-shirt. "But I'll be happy as long as he learns to just be like his daddy."

"His mom too. I'm not going to do this alone."

The words slipped out before he could catch them, and then he could not reel them back in. But they also brought up the question he knew had to be asked: *How do we address this elephant on our doorstep? Pretend he's not there, or rush out with shouts and threats, daring the beast to come inside...or go?* Was this where his faith was supposed to come in? the faith that, if he was being honest, he wasn't sure he'd ever possessed?

"You know the girls have been praying all summer," Merit said. Her voice sounded steadier than Will felt and lacked the edge of hurt accusation she could have tossed back at him for bringing up the dilemma.

"I know," he answered. "And I want to believe the way they do. I wish I could. I'm just afraid, Merit. I'm afraid..."

He wasn't sure how to finish. Afraid of what? afraid that Merit would die the way their first doctor had predicted? or afraid that somehow she might be healed, that God would do something special in their lives? afraid that God would honor their commitment to doing the right thing but might require something back in the bargain? something major? Will couldn't think of anything wrong with the terms of such an arrangement and would have signed on the dotted line without hesitating if he'd been given an opportunity to do so. It even seemed logical, in a God sort of way.

"I know." She held him as though she'd never let go.

The fire eventually faded to embers, and the wind gusted warm around them, laden now with the scent of stubble from far-off wheat fields and ice packs from snow-peaked mountain ranges. Perhaps even the faint signature of brine from a distant ocean.

"Smell that?" He knew then that a storm was coming.

A freight train of thunder rumbled far off then flashed its piercing lights as jagged white raked from heaven to earth. The lightning drew closer with each chest-rumbling clap of mountain thunder.

"I smell it now," Merit replied. "I wonder if we're okay here."

"Too late." He knew he should get up and tie down a few things, but he didn't want to let her go just yet, didn't want to feel anything but the warmth of her nearness. "I don't think we want to be out in an aluminum boat in the middle of a storm."

That meant they had to retreat to their shelter, so Will threw their dinner things back into a Tupperware container before helping Merit with the sleeping bag. An extra tarp over the tent would help shed heavy rain if it got to that.

It did. They stopped for a second at the hissing sound, faint at first, then louder—the first sheet of rain rolling toward them from the southwest.

"Here it comes." Will tossed the bag inside their tent and crawled in next to Merit. They zipped the door closed, leaving just enough open to watch the mighty power display.

"Goodness!" Merit shrank back at a particularly close flash and immediate boom, as if a bomb had been detonated directly overhead.

"One thousand nothing!" Will grinned as lightning illuminated Merit's beautiful face, flushed with excitement. She held her fingers to her ears at the monstrous thunderclaps.

The wind rattled the treetops and shook their tent, sending sheets of horizontal rain to pelt their campsite. They laughed at the sheer force of the thunderstorm, and they had to believe it had been planted over their heads to inspire and entertain them—God's version of a Fourth of July fireworks show. Between flashes, Will leaned closer and kissed the nape of Merit's neck.

Merit entwined her arms around him, and he looked into her eyes as another series of flashes lit up their tent. She leaned closer and her lips met his.

"Shh." She kissed him again and again, and he could not refuse her.

The pounding rain and howling wind made it nearly impossible to speak in normal voices, so he leaned his face next to hers.

"My wife once said she didn't like camping."

"Your wife once said she didn't want to move away from California. A girl's got a right to change her mind."

"And we never had thunderstorms like this in the Bay Area."

"You can say that again. But Will…" Another flash lit up their tent, and he could see the pleading look in Merit's expression. "You said you were afraid."

"I remember."

She paused for a moment, and the old fear caught up to him. This time it was his turn to wet her shoulder with his tears. They held each other through the storm, as it sent wave after wave of thunder and lightning rolling over their refuge. What else could they do but cling to the life God loaned them tonight? It could be their last time to do so.

Will recognized in Merit's face a different kind of fear, a fear he knew she tried to deny, especially in front of the kids or their new friends in Kokanee Cove. Out here, though, the wind and the rain had carried away her mask, unveiling the vulnerable Merit, cuddled up in a sleeping bag with her husband, pretending the past didn't exist and the future might never arrive.

After all, hadn't he told her this summer would never end? Now he was afraid of being right.

Fear? Yes, but with her soul opened only to him and to God, Will knew it had nothing to do with thunder and lightning.

She looked into his eyes as another jagged flash lit up their protected space.

"I'm afraid too," she whispered.

The thunder clapped.

thirty

———— ❦ ————

Thunder is good, thunder is impressive; but it is the lightning that does the work.

MARK TWAIN

O h come on, you guys." Michael poked his head in the bedroom door. "No more screaming. It's just a little thunder. You're acting like a couple of sissies."

To punctuate his sentence, another flash lit up the girls' bedroom. Two shapes hid under Abby's covers, and he could hear their screams over the clap of thunder, which was saying something. Michael groaned.

"It's not just a little thunder," came a shaky voice as the thunder echoed off the mountains. "And so what if we *are* a couple of sissies?"

"Well, you don't want me to tell Mom and Dad you were having a panic attack, do you?"

No answer. Lightning flashed, and he plugged his ears against the screams.

"All right." He sighed. "Bring your blankets into the living room. We'll make some popcorn and tell ghost stories. How's that?"

A pair of eyes peeked out from beneath the blankets, then another.

"Really?" asked Abby. "Mom says we shouldn't talk about ghosts."

"All right, then just stories."

They nearly knocked him over on their way out.

"But just for a little while!" He didn't think they heard him over the next crack of thunder. The girls were right about one thing: they never had anything like this back in California.

In Iraq? Well, that was a completely different story, one he wished he could forget, only this thunder wouldn't let him. The key was to keep his eyes open and focus on *now,* focus on making microwave popcorn and grabbing sodas out of the refrigerator.

Five minutes later, all three of them snuggled under a blanket, munching popcorn and slurping Cokes.

"This was a good—" Olivia flinched at the next roll of thunder but didn't scream.

"Good idea," Abby finished her sister's sentence. "But you have to tell us some stories, Michael. *True* ones."

"True ones? That's not part of the deal."

Another flash, and Olivia started counting *one thousand one, one thousand two...*

"We'll start screaming again," Abby promised as the thunder rattled the windows. Even Michael ducked.

"All right, all right." When their parents asked how things went, he would not include how his two little sisters wrapped him around their little fingers. "What kind of story?"

"About what you did in the Air Force," Abby said without hesitation. She knew what she wanted.

"No." They weren't going there.

Abby didn't give up that easily. "But you've never told us what you did when you were gone. Like, did you save anybody's life?"

"And, and...," Olivia added, "were there any kids over there?"

"Well, sure, but..." Michael swallowed and tried to find a graceful way out of his predicament.

"So do they ride camels and stuff?" Abby asked. "Do they live in tents?"

Michael surrendered to the constant barrage of questions and the racking attack of thunderclaps. Only now he was the one flinching, and his little sisters acted as though nothing bothered them. What was up with that?

"No." He would give them the *Reader's Digest* condensed and sanitized version. Not all the details, just the bare bones. And then they would never ask again. "The ones we saw lived in houses, like in the cities in the northern part of the country where I worked."

"Houses like we live in?" Where did Abby's curiosity come from?

Another strike of thunder shook Michael to the bone, and he shivered.

"More like stucco houses. Flat roofs. Dusty streets. The kids would come out and yell things at us. Dumb things they heard somewhere on TV, I think, like 'Show me the money, American!'"

The girls laughed until another flash silenced them. This thunderstorm wasn't giving up without a fight.

"So is that all they did?" asked Abby.

"Once they had an old soccer ball, totally flat but they didn't care. And one of the guys in the convoy, his name was Williams, he tried to give their ball back after it... Well, he shouldn't have done that, I guess."

"Why not?" Olivia stuffed another handful of popcorn into her mouth. No one-at-a-time dainty bites for her. "What's wrong with playing soccer?"

"Nothing's wrong. It's just that..." He knew from the start he would paint himself into a corner, but he hadn't guessed it would hurt this much. He wrestled to find a safe way to finish the story without telling them what had actually happened to Murphy, or to the kid who played with him just moments before the attack.

Why had he let them talk him into this? He should have known better.

"That's all the stories I can tell you." Michael stood, spilling popcorn all over the floor. "That's it."

No more war stories, no more thinking about it, no more letting the junk in his past hijack his future. Period. He'd probably already wrecked his chances with Stephanie, if he'd ever had any. Maybe the only thing that mattered now was that his mom needed more help than he—or anyone else—had been giving.

"Hey!" Abby disapproved, but she had no idea what she was asking.

Michael didn't stop until he reached the bathroom door at the end of the hall, where he stood with his back to his sisters, trying to fend off the tsunami of emotion that had suddenly crashed on the shore of his soul.

"I'm sorry, you guys." He fought to keep his voice steady. Had he really been wallowing in the past all this time? "Take the popcorn to bed with you, if you want."

"But Michael…," Abby whined.

"Just…don't worry about the thunder, okay?" He used his baby-sitter voice. "It's going away now." He wiped the back of his hand across his face so they wouldn't notice the beads of sweat on his forehead.

Instead of returning directly to their room, Abby stopped behind him and Olivia tugged at his shirt.

"I have to use the bathroom," Olivia announced. He stepped away from the door, and she shut it in their faces. Abby held a handful of popcorn, nibbled on a couple of pieces, and looked up at him curiously.

"Are you okay?" she asked. " 'Cause all of a sudden, you're acting really weird."

He looked away as she continued her interrogation.

"You're not scared of the thunder, are you?"

"Listen, I'm just tired, okay? I really shouldn't have let you girls get out of bed in the first place."

He could hear the water in the bathroom running…and running.

"Hey, Livvy!" He pounded on the door. "Are you done in there or what?"

"I'm supposed to brush my teeth after drinking soda," came her little voice, "because soft drinks can cause bacteria which can lead to tooth decay."

"Who told you all that? Okay, just hurry it up, huh?" He steered Abby down the hallway by her shoulders, back to their room. "And no more getting up."

He waited in the doorway until Olivia came out of the bathroom. She grabbed his hand as she slipped by.

"Do you like Stephanie?" she asked in her most innocent voice.

Michael groaned and tickled her under the arm. "Not as much as I like you, little sister. Head to bed."

She squirmed away and Abby took the baton.

"But that means you like her, Michael. You just won't tell us. Why won't you tell us?"

Oh wow. If it was obvious to these two...

"Look, even if I did like her, I'm an ex-military gearhead, and she's a nice birdwatching girl who doesn't have anything in common with ex-military gearheads. Okay? The princess and the toad. And they all lived unhappily ever after, the end."

The girls stared at him.

"You're not a toad, Michael," Olivia assured him. "I think you're more like a lizard."

The two girls dissolved into giggles, and Michael roared and chased them into their beds, then turned off the bedside lamp.

"That's it!" he told them. "I'm going to strangle you two if you don't—"

"You never prayed with us," Olivia interrupted, and he sighed at yet one more delay tactic. But what could he say?

"All right, Livvy. Your idea—you pray. Keep it short."

"Can I get a drink of water?" asked Abby.

"No!" He wasn't going to fall for that one. "You're in bed now, and you're going to stay there. Pee in a bucket if you have to, but—"

"Don't say that, Michael," Olivia chirped at him, and he could hear their mother's voice in hers, just enough to shut him up. "I'm going to pray now. Are you folding your hands and closing your eyes?"

"Just pray," he told her, "before I turn out the light and close the door."

She talked to God in her clear, tiny voice. By this time, the thunder didn't rattle the windows much, and their room was lit only by the occasional blink of far-off lightning. Olivia prayed for Stephanie and the hurt birds in the back of Mr. Mooney's shop, for Aunt Sydney, for Mom and Dad out camping, and that He would protect them from the thunderstorm.

"And dear God," she finished, "please help Michael not to be scared of the lightning, or whatever he's scared of. In Jesus' name, amen."

Michael closed his eyes. He would have to plead the Fifth if they asked him anything else.

"Okay," he told them, standing. "Now go to sleep. Mom and Dad will be back tomorrow."

"Michael?" Olivia again.

He paused. "What?"

"I want you to have this."

He squinted into the darkness and saw his younger sister pull something off the wall. She padded over to the door and held it out to him. A feather softly stroked his hand. Her dreamcatcher.

"Why would you give this to me?" he asked. "Aunt Sydney gave it to you."

"It doesn't work. I still have bad dreams. Maybe it will work for you."

"It won't work for him, either," Abby said. "It's just a bunch of feathers and beads. It's pagan hooey."

"Where did you hear that?" asked Michael.

"That's what Mom called it. She didn't like it, but Dad let Livvy keep it."

"And now I'm giving it to you," concluded Olivia.

"A dreamcatcher that doesn't work." Michael took it from her, hoping he hadn't hurt her feelings. "Thanks, Liv. That was nice of you."

"I think maybe you need it more than we do," she replied, slipping back into bed. His eight-year-old sister, the psychologist.

He closed the door behind him and stood quietly in the hall, trying to forget what Olivia had prayed.

"Or whatever he's scared of." And what was that, exactly?

"Michael?" Abby called from the other side of the door.

"Yeah?"

"I don't care what happened in the war. You're still our hero."

He was glad the door was closed, so they couldn't see the tears in his eyes.

"Are you still there, Michael?"

"Still here, Abs. But go to sleep now. I'm serious."

Michael shuffled back to the living room, stumbling over the popcorn bowl. He should never have let them get up, never should have let them talk him into telling the story. At least he hadn't finished it. He could imagine what his sisters would have told their parents the next day.

So the thunderstorm kept us awake, and Michael told us a bunch of cool stories about roadside bombs and how his friends got killed, plus there was a little kid playing soccer right in the middle of the road, and...

Another flash of lightning lit the jagged profile of Bernard Peak, reminding him the storm wasn't quite over like he'd told the girls. Mom and Dad were still out there, but he knew they'd be fine. He closed his eyes but couldn't forget the flash of gunfire or the soccer ball at his feet that no one would ever reclaim.

Here's the hero who couldn't do a thing to help his friends, he thought, *or anybody else, for that matter. Here's the hero who's so tied up in his past that he's letting it sink his future.*

Stupid story.

thirty-one

— ❧ —

How did it get so late so soon? It's night before it's afternoon.
December is here before it's June. My goodness how the time
has flewn. How did it get so late so soon?

DR. SEUSS

Here, let me help you with that." Will grabbed the other end of the canoe Michael was wrestling up onto the dock. "Don't need to do everything yourself."

Michael just grunted and heaved on the canoe as if Will wasn't there, and they lifted it into place on the rack they'd built. The old boats didn't leak anymore, but not too many people would be renting canoes after Labor Day.

"Thanks," Michael mumbled.

"You okay?" Will looked at his son, not really expecting an answer. Michael broke his foot in the eighth grade and didn't say anything for three days. He'd nearly killed himself at Boy Scout snow camp, because he didn't tell anyone his long johns were soaking wet from the ice. "The girls said you were a little, I don't know…down the other night."

"The other night?"

"Yeah. When you were baby-sitting. Night of the big thunderstorm?" He tried to sound nonchalant. "I think Abby used the term 'stressed out.' "

"I don't know why she'd say that."

"I don't either."

"Look, Dad, I'm the one who should be asking you." Michael glanced up at the house, where Stephanie was helping Merit cut a bouquet of roses off the bush, the last of the season. "You—and especially Mom."

Will followed his son's gaze as they walked back to the snack bar.

"I appreciate that, Mike. Really. But we thought you might want to tell us a little more about what you went through."

"By 'we,' you mean you and Mom?" Michael held the door open.

"You know what I mean. When you got back from the Middle East, we thought we'd let you come back at your own pace. Get your wings back when you were comfortable."

"Like I'm an injured bird or something? one of Mr. Mooney's charity cases?"

"It's just an expression, okay?" Will said, holding on to his temper. "You've hardly said a word about what you did over there. Maybe it would be good to talk to somebody."

"I don't think so. You guys have other things to worry about." Michael shook his head and turned away. He picked up a brush and a bucket and started cleaning the counter.

Is this how he plans to cope?

"Come on, Mike," Will said. "You can't just pretend nothing ever happened."

Michael shrugged and kept scrubbing. "I learned from the master."

"What's that supposed to mean?"

"I mean you're great at just plugging along at everyday life, pretending like Mom's not even sick. Especially after all the reporters got bored and left. Mom's not so bad at it herself."

"We're not talking about Mom right now, Mike. Look at me. We're talking about you, about what happened to you."

Michael spun back to face his father, brush in hand. "So if we just talk and talk about my problems, everything that happened to me is going to be all better?"

"I just thought—"

"Yeah, well, I don't know about your life, but my life never seems to work that way."

"My son, the philosopher."

"Not me." He huffed. "I'm not the one with the problem. Mom's the one who's being voted off the island, and you just stand here like you can't do anything about it. Or you won't."

"Wait a minute. I—"

"Wait? That's just it—the waiting. Why are you always waiting? Why don't you *do* something?"

Will couldn't look at his son's pleading eyes. He had no good answers. "I explained everything to you. You know why we can't."

"Yeah, but if it were my wife, I would do something, instead of just sitting around and… Aw, forget it."

Michael threw his brush down, stepped over the bucket, and headed for the door. He must have exhausted his quota of words for the day. Will hadn't heard his son say that much to him all at once in a long time.

He watched Michael leave, slamming the door. Then he kicked the bucket so hard that soapy water sloshed all over the floor.

"Do something?" Will yelled, throwing a roll of paper towels at the mess before falling to his knees. "Sure, I'll do something. I'll work on my to-do list while my wife gets sicker and sicker. I'll scrape paint and fix docks and…"

He leaned his forehead against the floor in surrender. "And I'll pray, I guess."

Water soaked through his jeans, but it didn't matter. He scrubbed the floor, adding his own tears to the suds.

"This is where You wanted me anyway. Right, God? On my knees."

He knew the answer.

He mopped once-dusty corners as he prayed, using his shirt sleeves to attack a grimy spot, scrubbing and scrubbing until paper towels and his knuckles shredded. He almost didn't hear the door open, and he didn't turn to see who had stepped inside.

"Sorry," he snapped, "we're closed."

"Oh dear. Will?"

He peeked over his shoulder. His wife stood in the doorway, breathing hard and holding an armload of white roses. These days her face seemed pale enough to match. He scrambled to his feet, tossing the shredded paper towels aside and tucking his shirttail back in.

"I was just, uh…the floor needed cleaning."

"You wouldn't rather use a mop?"

"Right. Next time. I just kind of got going and, uh…"

She cradled the cut flowers from their yard, and their soft, heady fragrance drifted into the room. She never took her eyes off his face. "Will, are you—"

"Here," he interrupted as he stepped forward, nearly tripping over the bucket. "Let me put those in some water for you."

Merit paused for a moment before surrendering her flowers.

"Can I do anything?" he asked, fumbling the roses into a vase.

Merit was still trying to catch her breath, but she crossed her arms and looked him straight in the eye. "As a matter of fact, you could get those dead mice out of the refrigerator. Feeding that poor hurt hawk is one thing, but if I open that door one more time to see those horrible little eyes bulging out at me from inside that plastic bag, I'm going to—"

"Say no more." He held up his hand. "I'll have Michael take care of it."

❧

"You sure you don't mind?" Stephanie asked as they pulled up in front of the Mercantile in the Land Rover. "We could do this later."

Michael shook his head. He was happy to do anything to get away from his dad just now.

"No problem, really," he told her. "Mom wanted them out of the fridge, and I really didn't want to clean the bathrooms this afternoon anyway."

"You'd rather help deliver a bunch of dead mice to help feed a hungry kestrel."

"Better than cleaning a bathroom."

The jingle bells announced their arrival, while Mr. Mooney rang up a couple of hunters wearing green camouflage coveralls and orange hats. Michael wondered if they wanted to hide or be seen. And it reminded him…

"Ah, lunch!" Mr. Mooney said, spotting their package. "Kevin's going to love you for it."

"I've got four of them this time." Michael held up the Ziploc baggie. "Couple big ones too."

"Here you go, Kevin." Stephanie approached the perch in the corner of the back room. While Michael watched, she carefully slipped on a leather glove and fed their injured bird of prey.

"How much longer before he's good to go?" Michael asked. "What's it been, now—since April?"

"Something like that." Stephanie stepped back as the little kestrel daintily tore the mouse into bite-sized strips. "We won't know how strong that wing is until we give him a real flight test. I guess it depends on if he's healed or not. And if he's imprinted on us."

"We don't want that, right?"

"Right. No good getting him too comfy with people if he has to make his own way in the wild."

Michael wondered if there was a real-life application there. "So what should I do to offend him and keep him ticked off at us?"

"Just be yourself."

"Thanks a lot." He wished she didn't have a point.

Stephanie moved with liquid grace around the bird, part crocodile hunter, part runway model. Michael couldn't keep his eyes off her. Neither could Kevin the kestrel, but for entirely different reasons.

"Hello?" Stephanie broke into his thoughts, and he realized she held her hand outstretched toward him. "Hand me another one, please?"

"Oh, right. Sorry." Michael passed along another rodent treat and imagined for a moment how Jessica Frazer would have handled this. The thought made him chuckle. His ex-girlfriend would have freaked at the first sign of a dead mouse, not to mention feeding one to a bird of prey with sharp talons and a beak that could rip things into shreds.

Between Jessica and Stephanie, there was no comparison. He wasn't sure when he'd figured that out, but today it was obvious.

"What's so funny?" Stephanie asked, but he waved an excuse.

"Nothing."

He'd never seen a girl handle a wild bird quite like this. Someone who wasn't worried about breaking a fingernail.

At the same time, he wondered about imprinting. Would the same idea they'd applied to rehabilitating Kevin the kestrel now apply to him? How comfy could he get here in Kokanee Cove? Would he just have to fly away again, the way he'd done before?

"Michael?" Stephanie's voice brought him back to reality once more.

"Here." He shook his head, cleared his thoughts.

"You sure?" Her voice changed as she fed the bird another mouse, which Kevin accepted with a wary bob of his head and a soft screech. "You look like you're on another planet."

The front door bells jingled, and Michael peeked out to see the hunters leaving. The hunters in camouflage. The memories hit him full force in the gut, despite the promise he'd made to himself about leaving it all behind.

Stephanie looked at him like he was coming down with a fever. "Are you okay, Michael?"

He turned away and started for the door to the front room, but she held him back by the sleeve.

"Michael, what is going on with—"

"Nothing, okay?" He pulled free but stopped trying to escape. "I've just been thinking." He leaned one hand against the door, unable to move.

"Is it the thing with your mom?" Her voice softened and she looked at him with those big eyes, tender and a little afraid. Prettier than he'd realized at first.

For one crazy moment, he thought maybe she would understand, the way no one else could. Maybe if he told his story, just this once, he could really and truly bury this thing. For good.

"I'm sorry." Stephanie turned back to the bird. "It's really none of my business."

Maybe not, but he knew he had to tell her. *What a way to kill a relationship before it's even begun.*

"All right, you want to hear the story?" he asked. "You want to know what's wrong with me?"

She turned back with questioning eyes. "I'm not trying to be nosy, Michael. I'll listen, but you don't have to—"

"When you hear it, you'll probably go screaming out the door."

"That's a silly thing to say." She smiled at him as she wiped her hands on a paper towel. "Just tell me. You know I won't scream…too loudly."

He wanted to believe her. Maybe he did.

She crossed her arms. "I'm just kidding," she said. "But really, it's okay. Whatever it is, you know God is in—"

"Sometimes I wonder, Steph." He shook his head slowly. "You don't know me. You don't know what I did."

He had to say that, had to offer his disclaimer and an easy way out. But he also knew it was too late to turn back. Who else could he tell? Not his dad and certainly not his mom or the girls.

Stephanie waited, lips pressed tightly together, like she was holding her breath. Like she understood.

"So we're on escort." He blurted out the story as fast as he could. He needed to get it over with, this obsession, this splinter in his soul. "Convoy from Samarra to Mosul. On our way through this town, Bayji. Not a very friendly place, especially since the highway narrows into the marketplace, and a lot of bad guys hung out there. Anyway, there's a bunch of women crossing the highway, so we slow down, right?"

He took another breath and tried to keep the emotion from creeping into his voice, tried to stop his lip from quivering. Stephanie just stared at him with those wide, beautiful eyes of hers. The kestrel fluttered his wings and continued eating.

"And then this kid comes out of nowhere with a flat, old soccer ball, kicks it right at us. Twelve, maybe thirteen years old. The ball rolls under the tire of our Humvee, right? What are we supposed to do? Run over it? So Williams gets out and reaches down, and that's when all hell breaks loose." He paused and swallowed. "I'm sorry."

For saying "all hell breaks loose" to a pastor's daughter or for crying in front of her? He wasn't sure. But he had to finish.

"And this kid is right in the middle of it all. I mean, bullets flying, everybody's screaming—Arabic, English, it's crazy. Williams gets hit in the hand, so there's blood everywhere. We're returning fire. I can't tell who's who."

"Did you…?" she managed, though it was only half a question. Michael could tell her hands were shaking.

"I don't know. That's the part that really gets me. *I don't know what I shot, or who, or how.* I try to remember, but it's just bits and pieces, and they're scrambled. All I know for sure is that the kid didn't walk away. Everybody said he was part of the ambush, a way to make us stop and get out. I don't know. I just see him lying there…"

He couldn't go on, couldn't escape the fractured nightmare that had played and replayed in his mind. So he hung his head and sobbed like a little boy, no older than the one who had been gunned down in the dusty streets of Bayji. By the insurgents? By accident? He would never know. He cried like the mother who came out only minutes later to gather the body of her son.

"I'm so sorry, Michael." Stephanie rested a soft hand on his shoulder, exactly like Merit would have done. "But you know it wasn't your fault, don't you?"

"Wasn't it?" He snapped his head up. This part he knew. "I shouldn't have let Williams get out. We should never have stopped. I could have kept it from happening. That was my job!"

"No. It doesn't help to say that." That sounded like something Merit would have said too. She held up a finger to quiet him. "You can't say that."

"But I could have," he argued, out of breath and wanting more than anything to be wrong. "I could have."

"You couldn't. Don't you see? It wasn't your fault. Nothing was your fault. You were doing your job and it was hard. And you can't bring that little boy back to life by blaming yourself for something you had no power to change."

He buried his face in her soft shoulder and let her hold him. She was right. He couldn't do anything about what had happened. Couldn't change it. He'd tried, but he couldn't.

He couldn't change what was going to happen to his mom, either.

thirty-two

———— ❧ ————

The woods are lovely, dark and deep,
But I have promises to keep,
And miles to go before I sleep,
And miles to go before I sleep.
ROBERT FROST, in "Stopping by Woods on a Snowy Evening"

Stephanie paused for a moment, first to catch her breath and shift the package in her arms, then to watch the woods fill up with snow. It brought to mind the words of her favorite Robert Frost poem, the one she had memorized in fifth grade. The lines seemed to fit this afternoon, especially since it was also the darkest day of the year.

Dark in more ways than one. She'd been to funerals before—her Grandma Holmqvist had died a couple of years ago, and that had been sad enough. Grandma hadn't been a churchgoer and never claimed Jesus as her Savior, so what did the preacher have to say? She made people laugh, she cooked a good meal, and she was a tough old Swede, stubborn to the end. That, it seemed, had been a legacy far more bitter than sweet.

But it had been over in less than an hour, and this funeral in Kokanee Cove—if that's what it was—seemed to be stretching over nine months. Why would God choose to do it this way?

"Do you have something else in mind here?"

She spoke into the snow, almost expecting God to answer with specifics about how He would heal Merit. It would be the "I told you so" ending to the way nearly every newspaper, radio, and TV news station in the country had trashed the Sullivans the past several months. God could do this. The question was, would He?

Stephanie sighed, suddenly wishing the snow would melt and songbirds would return to the mountains today. Then this funeral would either be over or put aside—just like this dark day that had never quite seen sun.

The good news was that after today, every day got a little longer, a little brighter. It might still seem like the dead of winter, but tomorrow would bring a few more seconds of sunlight. And then the next day a few more, and the next...

"Right, God?"

When Stephanie stopped again to listen, she heard only the soft patter of falling snow—though perhaps she imagined the sound more than actually heard it, like the soundtrack on an old movie that added an extra clip-clop of horseshoes or echoing footsteps. As Mr. Frost would have said had he been along for the walk, the woods seemed lovely, dark, and deep.

"And miles to go before I sleep," Stephanie quoted. It was actually only a few hundred yards, but that didn't have the same ring to it.

Her boots crunched this unusual, first-of-season snow as she made her own trail down the road to the resort. The pungent aroma of wood smoke— one of her favorite smells—met her just before she sighted the pale orb of the porch light.

The cabin could use some preholiday cheer, and it was up to her to provide it. She thought about simply leaving her gift on the porch and going home but decided that would be rude. This required follow-up, and Michael Sullivan would need a little push.

Michael Sullivan.

She swallowed hard, trying unsuccessfully to put away the confused swirl of emotion that his name conjured and fool herself about the real reason she had walked all this way. It didn't work, but she couldn't turn back now.

She stepped onto the porch, stomped the snow off her boots, and knocked on the door.

Michael appeared and stared at her as if Frosty the Snowperson had just shown up.

She nearly swallowed her tongue. "Ho ho?" she said in a halfhearted greeting. Maybe she should have left the package anonymously, after all. "Um... I'm helping with deliveries this year, and this one's for you. I mean, all of you."

She held it out, waiting for him to say something. Her heart stopped beating.

"Oh!" He blinked and seemed to focus on her. "Wow, Stephanie, you weren't supposed to work, right? I wasn't expecting you today."

"Obviously. But maybe..."

"I'm sorry." He stepped aside. "Come on in. Is it cold out there?"

"Not too bad. My nose fell off back there in the woods. I gave up looking for it."

He stared at her with a puzzled expression for a moment before grinning. "Sorry. I'm a little slow. I'm getting over a cold, so my mind is kind of...you know. Blah."

"Oh, I'm sorry. I know the feeling."

"I'm fine now. So it's cold?"

Stephanie shrugged. "Just cold enough for snow, I guess. It's probably snowing a lot more up the hill in Athol and Coeur d'Alene."

The conversation seemed doomed to silly jokes and extended weather reports. Except for that one time in Mr. Mooney's store, Michael never said anything serious.

But that wasn't why she'd come.

"Aren't you going to open the package?" she asked, pointing to the brightly wrapped box.

"You mean I don't have to wait for Christmas?" Michael grinned but didn't wait for her answer before tearing off the bow and silver paper.

"No. It's a pre-Christmas thing. Uh, for all of you."

"Right. You said that."

"Uh-huh. Anyway, I noticed that you guys could use a little Christmas spirit around here."

"Whoa." He held up the unwrapped boxes of white outdoor lights. "Maybe you're right."

"Come on," she said, tugging on his sleeve. "We're going to put them up."

"We are?"

"You had something better to do?"

"Well, I was going to rebuild that old forty-horse Evinrude that's sitting in the boathouse."

"You can do that later." She pushed him toward the front door, and he grabbed a coat on the way.

"Guess I don't have a choice," he said, smiling.

For the next hour, they worked together in the snow, stringing lights around trees and along the porch. They didn't say much, but that was okay.

Finally, Stephanie balanced on the far end of the porch railing to hang the last couple of lights at the end of the gutter.

"How's that?" she called over her shoulder.

A snowball hit her back with a thud. She jumped down to face her attacker.

"Oh, so that's the game, is it?" She giggled and strained her eyes but couldn't see him in the near dusk, even though the snowfall had lightened to a thin saltshaker drizzle.

Then a movement caught her eye—just around the corner of the house, stepping out from behind the overgrown lilac bushes. *Watch this, Michael Sullivan.* She quickly packed the hardest snowball she could, hauled back like she'd seen major league pitchers do, and let it fly.

The snowball flew in a tight arc and connected perfectly with the top of her target's head just as he stepped into the clear.

"Yeow!" Will clutched his head in surprise and fell to one knee.

"Oh my goodness!" Stephanie froze in horror then bolted forward to help him up. "I am so sorry. I thought you were Michael...I mean...I didn't mean...oh..."

Will rubbed his head, wiggled his face a bit, and looked over past her. "This girl has an arm, Mike. Sign her up for the team."

Michael. Stephanie turned to see her intended victim standing behind her. He must have been hiding behind one of the big cedars in the front yard. He covered his mouth with a gloved hand, his shoulders shaking, then doubled over laughing. Will looked at his son, then at Stephanie, and joined in himself. But Stephanie just couldn't bring herself to laugh.

"Well, I'm glad *somebody* thinks it's funny," she told them. "I'm embarrassed."

Michael pointed at her. "You should have seen your face when you—when you realized." He dissolved into laughter again.

"All right." Will pulled himself together. "Let's go inside for something hot to drink. Maybe your mother wants something too."

"I should go," Stephanie told them, but Michael shook his head and grabbed her arm. She didn't pull away.

"Hey, come on," he said. "Don't you want to see how the lights look?"

She did. They gave Will the honor of plugging them in.

"You guys do good work." He beamed as he admired the lights. They twinkled through the snow and outlined the cabin in warmth. "I wasn't going to put anything up this year, you know."

"It was her idea." Michael pointed his thumb at Stephanie.

"He did most of the work." She shrugged. "I mainly supervised."

"You've got to stop doing that modesty thing," Michael said.

"Me? I thought you were the one who—"

"All right." Will rubbed his head again, then nodded toward the front door. "Why don't you two stop arguing about who's the most modest and come in. Maybe Stephanie can stay for dinner."

That hadn't been part of her plan. She looked at Michael, who nodded toward the door as well. Stephanie moved forward.

The lights flickered once and went out. Not just the Christmas lights but the whole house's.

"Uh-oh." Michael made his way around the porch and pointed across the water. "Everybody else has power."

That didn't stop them from going inside and heating up a large bowl of homemade minestrone soup on the top of the wood stove by candlelight, which Abby and Olivia thought was totally cool. Merit chatted with Stephanie from her place on the couch while the men—and the girls—set the table, sliced bread, tossed salad, and ladled steaming soup into six bowls.

"I'm sorry we're not having a chance to enjoy your lights, Stephanie." Merit pulled a comforter over her shoulders. Her face looked drawn, her voice sounded strained, but she glowed in the candlelight. "That was sweet of you to think of us."

"I just thought we needed a little extra light around here, this time of year."

That was as good an explanation as any, though Stephanie knew it missed the mark, like her snowball, by a wide margin.

"Yeah," added Mr. Sullivan, "and you should see how well she throws."

Merit didn't get the joke, but Michael started laughing again. He helped his mother rise and find her place at the table, just as the lights flickered and came back on.

"Ah, there we go," Mr. Sullivan said, turning to scan the house. The refrigerator kicked back on and the microwave beeped.

Michael stood and switched off all the inside lights again, one by one. He joined them back at the table with a smile.

"I just thought the candlelight was nice, this once," he explained. He looked at his mom, as if he were the one hurting.

"Me too," agreed Abby.

Their soft white lights flickered outside, and through the window Stephanie could see a small fir tree she had decorated, flocked with fresh snow and glowing with fallen stars. She took Merit's ice cold hand in her right and Michael's firm, warm hand in her left, and Mr. Sullivan bowed his head to ask God's blessing.

Despite the warmth, she shivered as she gave thanks, wondering what kind of bittersweet gift she'd just been handed.

thirty-three

———— ❦ ————

*Have you ever been hurt and the place tries to heal a bit, and
you just pull the scar off of it over and over again.*
ROSA PARKS

Another blanket?" Will held a comforter toward her, and Merit nodded
for him to drape it over her shoulders on top of the two she already
wore.

"Thanks." She set her steaming mug of tea on the end table and gestured
at the snow-kissed windowpane and the dark woods beyond. "What do you
think?"

"I think I might have a look at the furnace when—"

"No, no. I mean about them."

Will looked out the window and saw Michael and Stephanie walking
into the trees. He turned with a questioning look on his face. "They're fine,
Merit. It's *us* I wonder about."

She reached for his hand, but he crossed his arms and remained standing.

"It's like you walk around with a black cloud over your head, honey," she
told him. "Please don't—"

He sighed and paced in front of the window. "I see you getting weaker
every day. I see you hurting. How am I not supposed to worry about that?"

"I know, Will. But we just can't be like this."

"Like we have a choice."

"We *do*. I have this feeling it's going to be okay."

Will whispered something under his breath.

"What's that?" she asked, but he shook his head.

"You don't want to know."

"Will, please don't do this. We have to be working together, not against—"

"Yeah, it's a little late for that." He slammed a hand against the wall, swiping a lampshade in the process. "A little late for everything."

"Will!"

The lamp toppled, taking her mug with it and sending a shower of hot tea onto the oval rug at their feet. He hardly noticed; his forehead rested against the wall. Merit didn't move to pick up the mess until he caught his breath again.

"I'm sorry, Merit," he said. "I don't have enough faith to cover this family. I never have."

"How much do you need?"

"I don't know, but…" He looked at her with teary eyes and took her hands in his. "Maybe not as much as I thought."

❧

"You didn't have to do this," Stephanie told Michael as they retraced her earlier steps, back toward the parsonage. He lit the way with a powerful flashlight. They passed the giant grandfather fir that towered over the road, and it seemed to lean more than usual. Maybe the springs that dotted this hillside had started to undermine its roots.

"It's okay." Michael didn't seem to notice things like old, leaning trees. He didn't seem to notice a lot of things, actually. "It's the gentlemanly thing to do, right? Your folks would be upset if I didn't walk you home."

"Maybe. But they're used to me wandering around."

They walked in silence until Michael slipped his gloved hand into hers. She glanced his way, but he kept his gaze straight ahead. Now and again he opened his mouth to say something, then bit his lip. She could barely see his pinched face in the reflected light from his flashlight.

"Just say it," she told him.

He stopped under a grove of firs close to town, where the snow hadn't yet piled up. She wasn't sure if she should expect a kiss or a speech, but she was prepared for either.

"Look," he began, "I'm really glad you came over the way you did. My dad and mom were, too."

"Well, you needed lights, right?"

"Yeah, we sure did." He smiled. "Thanks. I don't think you know what you did for us." He paused. "I really care about you, Stephanie. You make me laugh, and you help me see things better."

"That sounds like a good thing." She smiled.

"I know, but…"

"But what?" *But.* She hated that word.

"But our timing just isn't good." He fumbled for more words before continuing. "You know how everything's really…I don't know, up in the air at my house, with my mom sick."

"I know." Of course she did. "But what does that have to do with…"

She nearly said something she might have regretted. She'd already been forward enough, coming to the house with the lights.

Michael sighed, his breath hovering like fog. "It's just that—" He wrestled with the words. "I go into that house, and all I can think about is my mom dying in a few months."

"She's not going to die," Stephanie blurted, finding she didn't regret the words. She had doubted before, but not anymore, and it almost surprised her.

By the way he raised his eyebrows, it surprised Michael too.

"Oh, so you know these things, huh?" he asked.

She felt the slap of his words and didn't know if she should duck or reply.

Michael continued, "Look, I didn't mean it that way. I don't want to argue with you. Especially not about this. But see, what I'm trying to say is…my dad is a wreck. Like, a total zombie sometimes. Maybe you didn't see it when you were there, but when it's just us, oh, wow."

"I know it must hurt. I still don't understand what you're saying, though."

"I'm saying you have no idea what's going on in our house these days. But it just tears me apart inside, and it's like this huge pain is the only thing I have room for right now."

This sounded worse with each word.

"I care about you, Stephanie, but then it all comes crashing back at me, and it's not fair for me to get you tangled in our mess. Not right now. I feel like I'd be dragging you into a pit of quicksand or something. Do you know what I'm trying to say?"

"I know." She bit her lip and fought back tears. She couldn't start bawling now, but his words had cut deeply. Yes, she understood, but she had to find out—

"Michael, do you ever think about—I mean, do you ever pray for God to heal your mom?"

He bent his head back and stared at the dark, starless sky. "As if."

Her jaw dropped, but she resisted the temptation to fire back a reply too quickly. She carefully measured out her words. "What do you mean 'as if'? Don't you believe God could heal your mom?"

"Sure, in theory, but... No. Look, I'm sorry. It's easy for you to say. You're the preacher's daughter."

"So I've been told. And that's supposed to make me more spiritual?"

"Well, it helps, doesn't it? I mean, it kind of comes with the territory."

"Michael, you know my family. My dad's just a regular person, like everyone else. But that's not the point here, is it?"

"Are you going to tell me the point?"

"The point is, you can't tell me you haven't prayed for your mother."

"I didn't say I didn't, did I?"

"Well, why are you—"

"You started it." He sighed. "But I don't think you get it."

"Yes I do, Michael." She realized where this was going. "This isn't about you and me. This is about you and God."

"Oh come on. I've done all the right things. I've prayed—"

"And we pray and we pray and He doesn't ever seem to answer. Isn't that what you were going to say? You've prayed?"

"Yeah, but—"

"Sometimes I don't understand it, either. But I believe God is going to heal your mom. I wasn't sure before, but now I am. He's going to do it, Michael. A lot of people around here believe that."

"Well, that's great."

"Don't be sarcastic. Besides, people don't automatically die from cancer anymore. There are treatments. Survivors."

"I know that. But this is different."

"It's *not* different. Can't you imagine what kind of a story that would be? what kind of a testimony?"

"This isn't a story for the six o'clock news, Steph." His voice flattened and became uglier than she'd heard it before, like he was talking to someone else. "This is my mom and she's sick. She hurts. I see it every day. I'm sorry, but I just can't think about anything else right now."

He held the flashlight out to her. "Tell your parents hi for me," he mumbled.

And he turned and walked back down the trail, leaving her holding the flashlight.

"Michael!" she called. "Wait!"

But he just kept walking, disappearing into the night.

❧

Only the flickering light of a candle on the windowsill pushed back the darkness. It reached its fingers toward Merit, who sat on the couch with her three youngest children—one of whom she had not yet met face to face but still knew just as intimately.

"And if it's a girl?" Abby snuggled as close as she could get, helping Merit sit up a little straighter. At the moment Merit felt like a mommy sandwich, and it suited her just fine. "What are we going to name her if she's a girl?"

"Well…" Merit tried not to sound as spent as she felt. "Your father and I haven't decided on a girl name yet. He keeps saying it's going to be a boy."

"I don't think so," Abby said. "But Mom, I have a question."

"Mmm-hmm?" Merit could hardly keep her eyes open, but the girls wouldn't notice in the darkness.

"Do you think Michael really likes Stephanie?"

"What makes you ask that?"

"He always acts really weird around her. Like he laughs goofy."

"But they fight a lot too," added Olivia.

"I hadn't noticed." Merit smiled, but the effort drained her.

"That's because you're always sleep—" Olivia began, but Abby reached over and poked her shoulder.

"Livvy! Dad said we weren't supposed to say that sort of thing."

"But it's true. And I can say anything I want as long as it's true."

"No, you can't. You're going to make her worried, and then it's going to be all your fault if…if…"

Abby couldn't finish her scolding, and it was just as well. Merit rested her hands on theirs, one on each side.

"You know what?" she told them, her voice barely above a whisper. "You two are going to make wonderful big sisters, if you can stop bickering long enough. You need to promise me you'll be nicer to each other, whenever I'm not around to watch your little brother."

"You'll be here, Mom."

"No, I just meant—"

"You're always going to be here. You're not going anywhere." Abby sounded grown-up when she said it, so sure of herself. Maybe she knew something the rest of them did not. Something even the doctors didn't know.

"We'll be good big sisters anyway," Olivia replied. "We'll teach her to play Barbies, and how to swim, and—"

"Oh!" Merit winced at the unexpected kick to her kidney, and her daughters both asked what was wrong.

"Nothing, nothing." She held her breath and tried to relax, but junior wasn't done yet. Funny how this happened more and more lately. She remembered the girls kicking before they were born. But this one! Merit took her daughters' hands and placed them on her widened stomach. At the five-month-plus mark she didn't think she looked too bad.

"Here—feel the baby kicking?" she asked, waiting for another movement. "There!"

"Yeah!" Olivia responded. "I feel it." She bent over as if to kiss the baby, only she had something to say. "Don't you kick Mommy so hard," she whispered. "I know you want to come out and play with us, but you have to wait a little more. How much longer, Mommy?"

"Just a few more months." She rested her own hand on her baby and thought she felt a knee or an elbow. "Right, little guy? It won't be long now. I know you're ready, but we have to be patient."

"And then we'll all be together," said Abby, "and everything will be great."

Merit didn't want her daughters to see the tears in her eyes, so she turned her face away.

She saw Will standing in the kitchen, a piece of firewood in his hand, watching. Someone stomped onto the side porch—Michael, most likely—and the door swung open. A blast of cold air followed their son into the house.

"Close the door!" hollered Will.

The silent whirlwind tramped down the hall and slammed another door behind him.

Just a few months, yes, and everything will be great.

thirty-four

———— ❧ ————

Many waters cannot quench love, neither can the floods drown it.
SOLOMON'S SONG 8:7

Michael looked up from his workbench when he heard the soft knock at the shop door, and he knew without turning who was there.

Stephanie was the only one who knocked. Will hollered, and the girls just pushed in. Merit hadn't been to his door at all. And despite their awkward truce the past few months, he didn't mind her visit.

"Come on in!" he told her, putting down the carburetor from the Evinrude he'd been working on. Those old sixties outboard motors were always getting clogged.

"Sorry to bother you." She stood just inside the boathouse door, dripping, her dark hair matted to her face. He tried not to stare. He saw her every day, and yet he didn't remember her being this beautiful.

"Whoa," he managed. "Is it still raining that hard?"

"Just like it has for the past week." She stepped closer and pulled a paper plate out from under her windbreaker, then set it on the workbench next to his motor. "You've been holed up in here the whole time and haven't even noticed, huh?"

"Guess not." He studied the plate, which held a small mound of homemade cookies covered in plastic wrap. "What's this?"

"Oh. My mom made cookies yesterday, and she thought I should bring some to work with me to share." She paused. "So I am."

She'd been friendly lately—so had he. That didn't fix what he'd broken in December—what he'd broken and didn't know how to mend.

Michael picked up a rag and wiped his hands mostly clean before pulling back the wrap and picking up one of the cookies. They looked very good, especially to someone who had forgotten to eat lunch two hours ago.

"Well, tell your mom thanks from all of us here on staff at the Kokanee Cove Resort. That would be me." He smiled weakly and stuffed the cookie into his mouth. It mostly fit. She stood watching him for a moment, awkward and dripping, before heading for the door.

"No, wait," he mumbled between mouthfuls. "You don't have to run off."

She stopped.

"Uh…" She looked over her shoulder. "I need to get back to the store. A few people have come by for books this morning. One guy even checked out that Dr. Dobson book on parenting."

"Great. But there's nobody there now."

"How do you know? You haven't looked out the window for weeks."

"Only when you walk by."

Perfect foot placement, squarely in his mouth. She didn't answer.

"Look, I'm sorry," he said. "I didn't mean…" His voice trailed off, and all they could hear was the gentle patter of rain on the tin roof.

"It's okay," she whispered.

But it wasn't, not like it had been. He had to fix it. He took a deep breath. "All right, I've been thinking about this ever since that talk we had last December—"

"What talk?"

She was going to make him spell it out. Served him right.

"About how I couldn't handle a relationship just then, and our timing was off, and all that."

"Oh, that," she said, as if it hadn't been hanging between them for several weeks.

"Yeah, that. And I think you were right about how the problem was between me and God."

"Really?"

"Yeah. I don't know why you're bringing me cookies today. You have every right to be upset at me."

Stephanie turned, parked her hands on her hips, and cocked her head to the side. "Michael, I don't know what you want, but I'm not mad at you and I never was." She paused. "Well, maybe a little. But not now."

"I was a total jerk."

She giggled, shielding her mouth with her hand. "You said it, not me."

"No, really. I don't know why it takes me so long to apologize, but I am sorry." He picked up the carburetor to give his hands something to do. "And I want you to know that I've been praying for my mom. I don't want you to think I don't believe or anything."

"I never thought that. But you do make me guess at a lot of things. Why are you so mysterious?"

"Well, it's just hard to talk about, you know? This is the hardest thing I've ever been through."

"Harder than..." Her voice trailed off, but he knew what she meant.

"Harder than my combat stories? Yeah. I wouldn't have thought so, but yeah. And the worst part is that it's not even me who's hurting."

"I know." Her eyes could have melted him into a puddle on the floor.

"All she can do is sit up in bed or lie on the couch, and I know she's in a lot of pain. It's all over her face. And I want to fix things, but I can't..." His voice got husky and he cleared his throat.

She took a step toward him. "We're all still praying, Michael, especially now that the baby's so close. You know we are, right?"

"You mean the people at your church? Yeah, I know. My dad talks with your dad all the time. They go out in your dad's boat and freeze their tails off on the lake."

She laughed, and it warmed Michael more than the space heater he'd plugged in beneath his workbench. Why hadn't he told her this weeks ago?

"You should come on Sunday, Michael. We're having an Easter sunrise service."

She would be there, which made it an offer he couldn't refuse.

"Is it Easter already? I thought Easter was always in April."

She rolled her eyes. "Goodness. You have been shut away from the world out here, haven't you? It's early this year."

"Oh. I never did know how they figured it out each year. Is it just something the Pope decides?"

"Nothing like that. It's the first Sunday after the first full moon on or after the vernal equinox."

He looked at her and wrinkled his nose. "You want to run that by me again?"

She did, adding that the vernal equinox was when the amount of sunlight equaled the amount of darkness.

"Didn't they teach you that in school?" she asked.

"I went to public school, remember, not homeschool. I'm functionally illiterate."

"No you're not." She moved toward the door. "But listen, you really ought to come. I know your mom's not up to it, but you can stop working for one day, can't you?"

He nodded.

"I know your dad appreciates all the help," she said, "but you need to have a life too."

"A life. That's ironic."

She turned red and opened the door.

"I didn't mean anything by it," she said. "I'm sorry." She surveyed the drizzle through the door, her hand on the doorknob. "By the way, I lied."

She slipped out into the cool drizzle.

Michael hurried after her, sliding on the dock outside the boathouse. He didn't notice the rain.

"Stephanie, wait!" He had to run to catch up with her by the gas pumps. The clouds opened up, dumping solid sheets of rain on them, obliterating the line between sky and lake. For a moment, Michael wondered if the docks would stay afloat under the load.

But then he forgot the rain, because when he caught her, he managed to grab her hand and twirl her around on the dock like a dance partner. He wasn't sure who was more surprised, but he didn't give her a chance to react.

He kissed her. And she kissed back.

He pulled away and brushed a strand of wet hair out of her face. "You said you lied about something," he said. "What did you lie about?"

She didn't look repentant, like she'd sinned. She just smiled up at him as the cold rain dripped down her face. Then she surprised him with a kiss of her own.

"My mom didn't bake the cookies," she told him. "I did."

He laughed, the first time he'd laughed in months. "Is that all?"

"I just thought it would sound, you know…"

"Yeah, I know." He did. "But about this Sunday—"

He didn't have a chance to finish the sentence, because they heard a mighty crash, like a rifle shot, only louder. It rumbled like thunder, only it clearly wasn't thunder.

"What's that?" Stephanie turned to face the explosion of noise, and Michael's first reaction was to grab her around the shoulders. If someone had dropped a bomb on the navy base or something had blown up…

He stopped to think and realized he'd heard about these kinds of things in California, when it rained too much and hillsides collapsed in giant mudslides, burying homes and roads and towns. Was this the same thing?

The thundering lasted only five, maybe six, seconds, tapering to the sound of the pouring rain and the occasional crack of another crushed tree branch. He wondered if Abby and Olivia had heard the sound down in town at church over the din of their practicing for the Easter musical.

He grabbed Stephanie's hand, and they ran to the house, where Michael's dad met them on his way out, wearing an old jogging suit and a worried look on his face.

"How's Mom?" Michael asked.

"Not so good," he told them, looking toward town in the direction of the noise. "And now all the power's out again. Trees must've taken the line down, which means they're probably blocking the road too."

At the moment Michael could care less about power lines or roadblocks. "What do you mean 'not so good'?" he asked.

Michael's dad looked as if he didn't want to answer. He crossed his arms and stared in the direction of the downed tree.

"It's my fault!" He stomped his foot. "I should have gotten her out of here before instead of waiting. She's going into labor. And now if the road's blocked, we might have to load her on a boat to get her out of here."

"A boat?" Michael gulped. "You mean like...the one with the engine I just took apart?"

"You've got to be kidding me. Our only usable boat doesn't have a running motor? You didn't tell me about—"

"I didn't think we'd need it for a while." Now was not the time for another of their father-son arguments. "And besides, you asked me to recondition that one before we got too far into the season."

"I did?" His father gripped his forehead and paced in tight circles. "But..."

"Maybe the road isn't blocked the way you think," Stephanie suggested.

"Maybe not," replied Michael. "Let's go see."

Stephanie shook her head. "I'll see how Merit is doing while you guys figure it out. We shouldn't leave her alone."

"Right." Michael nodded. Anything would be better than standing in the rain, fearing the worst but not really knowing what they were up against. Without waiting for his father, he trotted down the driveway to see what had happened. "I'll be right back," he called.

Five minutes later, Michael stood in front of the massive tree trunk stretched across the road, his hands on his hips, wondering what would have happened if anyone had been driving by here a few minutes earlier. An unfortunate power pole bent low over the accident, humbled and bowing to the sheer might of the massive old fir. Somewhere in the tangled mess, a disabled power line lay flattened under the branches like a trampled snake, no match for the tree's girth.

"Wow." Michael's dad came huffing up behind him, his sneakers squeaking in the rain. "I knew it was big, but it looks even bigger laid on its side. How wide do you think it is?"

"I don't know. Six feet across maybe? We could almost cut a tunnel through this thing."

"Right now I wish we could."

Michael could see only mangled fir branches and angry raw mud oozing from the high side of the road—even when he stood on his tiptoes. The ancient roots had not been able to hold on any longer in the rain-soaked hillside, and lashing winds had provided the necessary push. The oddest part was the precision with which this roadblock had been laid, giving them no room to maneuver around it—not even with the Land Rover.

They both hopped back as another tree snapped and crashed next to the grandfather tree. This one tumbled harmlessly off to the side.

"Well." Michael's dad had obviously seen enough. "One thing's for sure: we're not getting through this roadway anytime soon."

They ran back to the house, trying to figure out a way to get Merit to the hospital and keep her comfortable in the meantime.

"If we have to row her out," mumbled Will, "that's what we'll do."

Michael couldn't quite imagine that, but right now he couldn't imagine much of anything in this surreal storm. He nearly slipped as they returned to the yard.

"Mr. Sullivan!" Stephanie looked desperate as she leaned out the front door. "I don't know too much about these kinds of things, but I don't think we have much time."

thirty-five

———— ❧ ————

I've read the last page of the Bible. It's all going to turn out all right.

BILLY GRAHAM

Oh, Lord…" Will whispered the start of another desperate prayer for his wife, for her life, for Michael and Stephanie. The silent words tumbled from his heart like they'd never done before. He wondered if he could feel closer to God when Merit needed his full attention. He dabbed at Merit's forehead with a damp washcloth and left the prayer for later.

Even though Stephanie wasn't a trained midwife, he could tell she was right.

They didn't have much time.

Merit groaned, shuddering at another contraction. Her forehead glistened with the effort. The sheets were soaked with sweat.

"When was the last one?" he asked, trying to hold his panic in check.

Stephanie glanced at her watch. Her other hand held Merit, who squeezed the life out of it.

"Um, I'm not sure. Two or three minutes, I think."

"You think?" Will snapped. "You've been standing here, haven't you? The doctor's going to ask, and we're going to need to know."

"Will, honey, please." Merit panted, her eyes shut with the exertion. "It's okay. Not her fault."

He took a deep breath, wishing he could breathe for his wife. "I'm sorry. It's just…I should have taken you to the hospital a long time ago, as soon as—"

"Stop, stop." Merit held up a trembling hand. "It is the way it is, and God is in control. Not her fault, not your fault. It's going to be fine."

"No, it's *not*!" he yelled, wishing he could put his fist through the wall. "You can say that, but…"

He heard himself for the first time. Heard his words echoing off the walls, the steady pounding of rain, the beating of his heart. He might have screamed if he'd thought it would do any good or if he thought anyone would listen to him.

God, he silently prayed, *she really thinks it's going to be fine. Does she know something I don't?*

At the moment it seemed entirely plausible, because he couldn't remember feeling more helpless in his life than he did right now standing watch over his struggling wife.

"This is like a bad episode of *Little House on the Prairie,*" observed Michael from the doorway, where he'd been hovering since coming inside.

"What?" Stephanie squinted at him. "That was totally random."

"No, really." Maybe he thought he was adding to the conversation or maybe he was just changing the subject, pulling them away from his father's awkward outburst. "The people in that show were always having babies in log cabins. Somebody rides off to get the doctor, but before the doctor comes, the lady has the baby anyway, but they boil some water and it turns out fine. I mean, the baby usually looks about six months old, but—"

"I can't believe you're talking about a TV show right now," said Stephanie, turning back to Merit. Will would have added his own version of "shut up, Michael" but Stephanie seemed to have it covered.

"No, it wasn't about the TV. I was just…I don't know." Michael shrugged. "It just seems like we ought to do more than mop her forehead."

"You're right, Michael. We ought to be. But I can't deliver a baby, if that's what you're saying. Don't even start to think that."

"No, no, no. I'm just…oh, forget it. I'm just freaked out."

"Don't be." Stephanie sighed. "Right now your mom doesn't need freaked out people around. Why don't you go…boil your water or something."

"Sorry. Here's another reason they need to get cell phone coverage out here."

"Coverage…" Will pressed his hand to his forehead. "Coverage! Michael, I can't believe we've just been sitting here!"

"Me neither. I think I'm going to paddle a canoe to town and get some help."

"Not yet. The radio, down in the store. See if you can raise someone and get George over here in a big, fast boat. Have him arrange for an ambulance to wait at the city dock."

"George?" Michael repeated. "Who's George?"

"Paramedic," snapped Stephanie. "And your dad's right. You need to call for help. Now."

"Emergency channel sixteen! What am I, brain dead?" Michael bolted out the door and down the hill.

Stephanie glanced across the bed at Will. "Was he really in the army?" she asked.

"Air Force." Will shook his head. "And yeah, I know what you mean. Sometimes I wonder myself."

They watched Merit breathe.

"Listen," Will said to break the silence. "I didn't mean to yell at you a minute ago."

"You don't need to apologize. We'll—we'll get through this."

For a moment, Will almost believed her, the same way he believed Merit when she told him something would work out. Hadn't Merit always been right before? Hadn't she always been the one with enough faith for both of them? Will nodded and moved to the window.

Merit cried out louder than before. "Will! Don't you dare leave me!"

"I'm not going anywhere." He returned to the bed and held her hand as she shuddered and moaned.

"Neither am I, Mrs. Sullivan." Stephanie mopped Merit's brow with a washcloth.

"How many times have I told you?" Merit arched her back and gritted her teeth in pain. "It's…Merit!"

"I'm sorry…Merit." Stephanie smiled sheepishly. "Is there anything you need us to get you?"

"Drugs." Merit groaned again, then forced the shadow of a smile to her chapped lips. "Really strong drugs." She waited a beat before saying, "Kidding. Just…just be here with me, both of you. Pray. That's all I need."

Will looked out the window after the next contraction and thought about carrying Merit down to the docks and paddling her to safety himself. But the early spring storm had intensified, and the rain lashed against their windows with ferocity.

"What's that noise?" Merit looked toward the window, and Will hoped it wouldn't blow in on them. A small stream of rainwater had already found its way through a small crack in the ceiling.

"I'll get it." Stephanie disappeared into the kitchen and returned a moment later with a small pot, which she placed in the corner to catch the drips. Merit focused on the drips, staring at the ceiling.

Will leaned over to whisper in her ear. "How are you doing, honey?"

She answered by biting her lip until it started bleeding. Her chest rose and fell, and her nostrils flared as she gasped for air.

"Maybe you should try some of that Lamaze breathing," he told her, "like we did with Abby."

"That was Olivia," she corrected, her eyes squeezed shut. "Didn't work then; wouldn't work now."

"Are you sure? Because—"

"Will!" she interrupted. "Just be quiet and hold my hand. That's the best thing you can do right now."

"Right." He hadn't let go.

"Somebody's coming," announced Stephanie, looking out the rain-splattered window.

"Michael?" he asked.

"No, it's a couple of boats. The fireboat maybe. I see a flashing light."

"That was quick." Will hadn't checked his watch, but Michael couldn't have been gone more than a few minutes. How had George come so soon?

Less than a minute later, the town paramedic burst through the front door, followed by...

"Sydney?"

Aunt Sydney had no time for pleasantries. She tossed her rain-soaked slicker on the chair and brushed her brother-in-law aside.

"She insisted on riding over with me," explained George, mopping his head with a towel. He unsnapped the top of his paramedic's case and set it on the chair next to the bed. Will and Stephanie backed out of the way.

"You guys made it here awful quick." Will stayed as close to Merit as he could, but he could no longer reach her hand. "Did Michael get you on the radio?"

"Not until we were already halfway here," George said as he snapped a stethoscope into his ears.

"So you were already coming?" Will asked.

George nodded. "We didn't know how far the rockslide went and were worried it had hit you guys too. Came over to check. Glad it didn't."

"So you didn't know—"

"No idea." George shook his head and took Merit's pulse. "Merit, you're a couple weeks early, aren't you?"

She nodded weakly.

"Need me to help get her back to the boat?" Will asked. "We should get her to an ambulance quick, right?"

George shook his head. "Wish we could do that, Dad, but we don't want to deliver your baby out on the icy cold and rainy lake—or on the highway."

"What?" Will felt lightheaded and thought he might need to sit down. "You're not going to keep her here, like some kind of... *Little House on the Prairie* episode."

"No choice, Will."

"No, no. Absolutely not." Will waved off the idea like a swarm of mosquitoes. "We could lose both of them."

"I don't think you get it, my friend. This baby's coming right now, whether we're ready or not." The paramedic looked at Will, while Merit fought her way through another contraction. "Can you handle this without passing out on me, Will?"

Will looked at his wife and then through the window at the fireboat with its blinking blue light.

All my fault. I should never have waited.

"Will?"

He nodded weakly and took his wife's hand.

She looked up at him. "The pain is killing me, Will!"

Oh Lord! He tried to keep his eyes from filling with tears, tried to keep his focus. She'd never said anything like that before. Never sounded that desperate.

"No one's..." He gulped and looked for the fire in his wife's eyes that would tell him she was still the same Merit. It was there—a few degrees dimmer, but there. "No one's dying here."

"Okay," she answered, taking a ragged breath, "but I'll kill you if you faint on me."

"Quit it," said Sydney, interrupting with a schoolmarm's gruff tone. "And nobody's going to faint. But if he does, we'll be fine." She straightened out Merit's sheets.

"Thanks a lot, Sydney," Will said. "I appreciate your coming, but you don't need to—"

"Now Merit," she said, ignoring him, "you listen to me while George gets his equipment ready. I know a natural breathing cycle that's going to filter out *all* the negative energy and release the pain if you let it. It's a yoga technique. I think it's going to do the trick for you too."

Merit looked up at her husband and managed a wink before the next wave of contractions rolled over her, and she closed her eyes.

thirty-six

———— ❧ ————

Do not abandon yourselves to despair. We are the Easter people and hallelujah is our song.

POPE JOHN PAUL II

Will wiped the sweat from his brow and checked his watch. Nearly 4:00 a.m.

"How are we doing, Chief?" he asked.

George looked up at him but didn't smile. "Well, I'm not an obstetrician, but as far as I can tell, your daughter's fine."

Will grinned, watching his daughter. Ten fingers, ten toes. Eyes like her daddy's, head of beautiful chocolate brown hair like her mother's, and a set of lungs like her two older sisters—combined.

Aunt Sydney had charmed the tiny newborn into submission after the initial squall. Or perhaps the little girl had charmed her aunt, as Sydney rocked her and gently sang a few verses of Bob Dylan's "Blowin' in the Wind." Will wasn't sure about Mr. Dylan's theology, but if nothing else, his youngest daughter would be properly introduced to the greatest hits of the sixties.

"But your wife's really weak," George continued. "We lucked out with the delivery, but I don't know what to do with somebody in her condition. She should have been admitted to a hospital a month ago."

"I know." Will wiped his hands dry on a fresh towel. "I let her talk me into staying here, which I never should have done. Can we get her out of here soon?"

George nodded as he snapped his case together. "As soon as we get her ferried over in the fireboat, I'm sending her to Coeur d'Alene in the ambulance."

"At least the storm's let up." Will gazed out the window at the nearly full moon peeking through scattered clouds. Its glow reflected into a million slivers of pale blue light on top of the gentle waves lapping at the lakeshore. Out of habit, he almost called Merit to the window, it was so beautiful.

"That's in our favor. If you can get her ready to go..." The paramedic snapped open a little notebook, checked his watch, and made a few notes. "Guess I'm the delivering physician of record. What was it, about 3:00 a.m.?"

"Three-oh-four," Sydney told him, still holding the baby but gazing at the paramedic with an odd smile. "And you did an unbelievable job."

Will's eyelids drooped with exhaustion, but he couldn't miss the look she gave the man. George wasn't married, was he?

"Er, thanks," George replied, still scribbling in his notebook. "So...Baby Sullivan. Three hours, four minutes into the new day. Easter day, as a matter of fact."

"Resurrection Sunday." Will dropped to his knees by the side of Merit's bed. Like the ancient tree that had trapped them at the resort, the weight of this time pressed fully on Will's shoulders and on his heart. He knelt by his sleeping wife, buried his face in the quilt, and sobbed quietly.

"I'm sorry," he whispered, first to his wife but then to God. "I didn't even believe You could do this."

What had he believed? Not enough, it seemed. But now he prayed with the unusual but entirely distinct impression that God was listening.

"I can't tell You that I like any of it, but if Merit says it's okay, then what can I say different? It's all up to You now, God. Now she can get treatment. Now You can do Your thing. Please do Your thing. If anybody deserves it, it's Merit."

He wasn't sure how long he knelt there, praying in a way he'd never prayed before, a way he had rarely been called to pray outside the comforting confines of a written script in the approved Book of Worship. When he had finally emptied his heart and lifted his head, George was gone, leaving Will alone to pack a few things for his wife.

"What does she need?" He looked at Sydney and the baby, still sleeping in the corner. They needed to take the baby in for a checkup too, but he knew she would come home again. Unable to imagine what that would be like, he pulled open the curtains and stared at the disappearing stars as they glittered on the lake, anticipating the dawn. An owl fluttered noiselessly by. Down on the water, a procession of lights that were not stars drew nearer, red lights and white, early morning fishermen headed out to catch the big one.

But so many? And on Easter morning? He squinted as the parade grew closer.

"What's that?" he asked himself.

"Who are you talking to, honey?"

Merit's raspy voice brought him back. He hurried to her bedside.

"You just relax," he told her. "I'm not talking to anybody."

"Hmm." She nodded weakly, her eyes barely open. "Where's the baby?"

"She's sleeping with Aunt Sydney." He checked again to make sure. "She's fine."

"Is she?"

"She's beautiful, Merit. Looks just like her mother."

"I'd like to hold her when she wakes."

"If you can pry her from your sister's arms."

A light knock by the door announced that George had returned.

"Ready to go?" he asked, quietly enough not to wake anyone still sleeping.

Will waved back at him. "I'm just getting a few things together for Merit."

Merit reached up and clutched his hand. "I want to stay here, Will. I want to stay home."

"Absolutely not. We're taking you to town in the fireboat in a few minutes, and then they're going to take you and the baby to the hospital. We should have done it a long time ago. This time you don't have a choice."

"I was afraid you would say that." All the usual fight had drained from her voice, and he knew she wouldn't argue with him anymore.

"It's not even a question anymore, Merit."

She nodded and started to close her eyes, then snapped them back open. "What's that noise?"

Will hadn't heard anything, but when he listened for a moment, he realized she was right.

"Sounds like singing."

Will stepped out on the front porch to check and nearly collided head-on with Pastor Bud, just ahead of Abby and Olivia.

"Daddy! " Olivia cried as she and her sister clutched their father.

"There you are!" The pastor had traded his usual jeans and fishing cap for a proper Sunday morning pair of tan slacks and a knit pullover sweater. "I hope you don't mind."

"Uh…" Will held on to his girls and watched the growing crowd on his lawn, unsure he could have objected even if he'd wanted to.

About fifty people, not counting kids, had gathered like Easter carolers on the lawn, facing the porch and many holding hands. At least another fifty were making their way up the hill from the docks. All joined in softly with the words to the Easter hymn Will had heard so often growing up:

Christ the Lord is risen today, alleluia!

"We didn't want to wake anybody," explained Pastor Bud, as his congregation sang on, "but we heard you were on your way to the hospital. We figured if Merit couldn't make it to this Easter sunrise service, well, we'd just bring the sunrise service to Merit. Before she leaves, that is."

Stephanie accompanied the song with her guitar, warming the background. Michael stood next to her, holding a sheet of music.

Raise your joys and triumphs high, alleluia!

"Did those two contact you on the radio?" Will asked.

Bud smiled and nodded. Though it was a touching gesture, Will knew it would have to be a short service.

Where, oh death, is now thy sting? Alleluia!

Will didn't like those words and their reminder of what lay just ahead. But he let himself sing along and felt the words move him—or maybe it was just exhausted emotion after the longest night of his life. Longer still for Merit.

Where's thy victory, boasting grave? Alleluia!

Will had never believed in sappy Kodak moments, when background music would rise to the occasion, but a spotlight from the fireboat broke through the mist just then, sending golden beams of light to flood their service.

Ours the cross, the grave, the skies! Allelu...

The singing faltered at that point, as if the choir conductor had waved his baton for them to halt.

"Mom!" Michael dropped his music and rushed past Will.

Merit held on to the doorpost for support, wrapped in her terry cloth robe and wavering. Will joined his son to catch her before she collapsed.

"What in the world are you doing out here?" Will grabbed his wife around the shoulders and held her tightly, while Michael held her from the other side.

"Please," she begged them. "Please just let me be here for a minute."

"You're going right back to bed until the boat comes," replied Will. "This is crazy."

"Then I'm crazy." The tears flowed down her cheeks and she raised her voice. "I'm crazy for coming to this lake. Crazy for wanting our family to be together again. Crazy for not letting them kill our daughter. If that's crazy..."

The congregation stood listening to Merit's sermon, silent except for the twittering of birds behind them, as the spotlight dappled the yard.

"Honey, you are not crazy." Will held her but made no move to steer her back to the bedroom. George had returned and stood with his folding stretcher at the edge of the crowd, but he just listened as well.

"You've never been crazy. Maybe the rest of us were—or I was. But you..." Will wasn't sure he could finish saying what weighed on his heart. He took a ragged breath. "You've shown me what really matters in life. And I know God must have… He *does* have a reason for all this, whether I understand it or not. Whether He chooses to heal you…or not."

He felt a soft nudge at his elbow—Sydney. How long had she been standing there, holding the child? His daughter fidgeted and squirmed, and Sydney handed her to him. Michael helped his mother while Will stepped forward to address the crowd. He had an introduction to make.

"You people have been amazing," he told them, "the way you've supported us through all this. The way you've prayed for Merit and this little girl, even through all the attention, the kind none of us ever wanted." He held up his daughter's head so they could see her from the lawn. "And now here she is. We, ah, don't have a name yet. But I want to introduce you to…"

Merit's hoarse whisper caught his attention, and he turned to hear her better.

"Her name is Colleen Sydney Sullivan."

That was his wife—making the announcement in a way that headed off argument. He'd never imagined Merit would want to name the baby after his mother. Or after her sister.

"Oh my Lord…" Sydney breathed, shedding her own tears. "I've never had anyone named after me before."

He slipped his arm around her and repeated the name so everyone could hear. "Colleen Sydney Sullivan, born on Resurrection Sunday, and it seems like we ought to keep singing, doesn't it?"

Pastor Bud nodded at Stephanie, whose cheeks were streaked with tears. She gamely picked up where they had left off, and Michael added his own strong voice.

Hail, the Lord of earth and heaven. Alleluia!

Merit sagged against her son. George took his cue and moved in with the stretcher, which they unfolded on the front porch.

Praise to Thee by both be given. Alleluia!

Aunt Sydney took the baby as Will helped lower Merit to the stretcher, and, though she didn't know the words to the hymn, she joined in at each *Alleluia*. And so, it seemed, did her namesake.

Thee we greet triumphant now. Alleluia!

As they picked her up, Merit looked at her sister and blew a soft kiss, then looked up at Stephanie as they passed by, holding out her hand and brushing her fingertips against the younger woman's elbow. People sang without her accompaniment, as Stephanie leaned down and kissed Merit on the cheek, and they exchanged words that Will couldn't hear.

Hail the resurrection, thou. Alleluia!

"Oh, Lord Jesus…" Will whispered his own prayer as he followed the stretcher and the woman he loved more than life itself, his hero.

Michael followed too, holding a corner of the stretcher, stumbling, not bothering to fight the tears anymore. The girls came running as well, yelling for the boat to wait. Merit reached up her hands and held them in her embrace.

"You girls behave yourselves," she whispered, her hoarse voice nearly drowned by the low rumbling of the fireboat's engine. They sobbed and tried to hold on to their mother.

Merit looked up at Michael with a weak smile. "I want you to give that book we have about heaven to your aunt Sydney. Will you do that for me?"

Michael swallowed and nodded.

"And if I don't see you again for a while," she continued, "you be sure to take care of your dad. Promise?"

Michael gripped her hand as they lifted her stretcher over the side of the boat. "You're going to be okay, Mom," he said, barely choking out the words. "Your faith, remember?"

"It's not about my faith anymore. Mine's like it always was." She looked at him with a sad smile and kissed his hand before letting go. "Now it's about yours."

She waved at her children as Will and the others settled her into the back of the fireboat and George let go of the lines.

thirty-seven

———— ❧ ————

*God made the world round so we would never be able to see
too far down the road.*

ISAK DINESEN

If Stephanie didn't know better, she might think nothing had changed in
Kokanee Cove during the past several weeks. From where they stood on
Blackwell Point, she and Michael could see the mailboat plowing through
gentle waves on its way to Lakeview, like always. If she bothered to count, she
might have tallied a dozen fishing boats within sight and nearly as many sailboats. A warm wind carried across the waters and rose against the bluff, ruf-
fling her hair in the gentle May sun. In the woods behind them, a warbler
sang cheerily, probably trying to impress his mate.

Had anything changed? Maybe she should wonder if anything had not.

"I remember once I was sitting here on the bench praying." Stephanie
had probably already told the story, but Michael didn't seem to mind hearing
it again. "Your mom startled me when she walked up. I think she liked the
view up here."

"How could she not?" Michael bobbed little Colleen in his arms like a
pro, turned in a circle, and finally rested his gaze on Stephanie.

"What?" she asked.

"Nothing. I mean, I was curious about something, but it's probably none
of my business. You never said, so I never asked."

"You're not making any sense, you know."

"Yeah, I know. Sorry."

"Don't apologize. Just ask."

"All right." He sighed. "But you don't have to answer if you don't want to."

"Would you cut it out? You're driving me crazy."

The thought of marrying Michael had flashed across her mind, but they'd never talked about it openly. But the way he was acting now—he wasn't going to ask an *important* question, was he?

No, of course not. They'd known each other less than a year and had never discussed the matter, unless one counted his roundabout hints and her vague what ifs.

But why was he acting so strangely?

"All right," he said. "I've been wondering ever since the morning Syd was born, when we carried Mom out on that stretcher, she whispered something to you. What did she say?"

"Oh." She breathed a sigh of relief. She wouldn't have minded his asking the other question, but she was glad she didn't have to deal with it yet.

"I understand if it's a private thing," he said. "I was just curious."

"It's okay. She just said to take care of her hero son for her."

He chuckled, as if it meant something to him this time.

"She knew, Michael."

"That she wasn't going to make it?" He stared at the lake. "She always said she would! Or that we would…"

That they would stay together. He didn't have to say it.

"Yeah," she said. "I think that's what she meant."

"What do you think, Syd?" Michael wiped his eye and held his little sister close. He crouched by the large bag, close enough to see but not too close. He had a right to hide, to change the subject. Ever since his mom had died a month ago, they'd had enough tears to last a long, long time.

"Careful," Stephanie warned them. "I wouldn't get too close with her."

One never knew with wild birds. She reached into the bag with gloved hands and carefully pulled out the young kestrel.

"How long's it been?" Michael asked.

Since she'd rescued this beautiful bird? Since they'd met? Or since his mother's funeral? She looked up at him and tried to answer with her eyes.

Long enough? Not nearly long enough? Kevin the kestrel struggled against his wraps, and she turned her attention back to the task at hand.

"Too long," she finally answered. "We should have let him go a couple of months ago. But with everything else...you know."

"Yeah, I know."

"Okay, then, let's do this." She held the talons between her fingers, well away from her chest, and squeezed the bird's wings hard enough to hold it still. After months of slow rehabilitation, this kestrel's time had come. He sensed freedom—of course he did—and jerked his head from side to side, even under the sock that kept him in the dark and relatively calm. "Can you yank the blind when I say?"

Michael nodded and reached for the tip of the sock. At her nod, he pulled it off the way a mother pulls a bandage off a child's elbow, then stepped back, sheltering little Sydney from the flapping wings with his arms. Sydney the angel—the perfectly healthy angel—gave a little startled yelp but did not cry.

"See ya, Kevin," said Michael.

"Fly!" Stephanie released the bird and it flapped into the sky. That cold day when she discovered him injured in the snow must have faded from his memory. All he'd needed was time. Now it was his time to fly.

And he did, gathering height and circling as if in thanks, but not looking back or down. Kevin the kestrel took his rightful place in the thermals off the bluff, riding the warm air higher and higher, until they could hardly hear his lonely screech echoing against the side of the mountain.

"You think he'll find his family again?" Michael wondered as they craned their necks to watch the bird circle out of sight. "Hope he knows how to blend back in."

A lot of questions today. Not many answers.

Stephanie gathered the hood and the burlap bag, then smiled and nodded. She slipped her arm into Michael's, and they made their way back down the path to the resort.

"I think he will," she said. "Kestrels have a sense about those things, don't they?"

"Yeah," Michael agreed. "I even prayed for the little guy."

"You've been praying a lot more lately. I didn't think tough Air Force guys did that sort of thing." Bringing up the Air Force was sure to get a reaction, one way or another.

"You know better." He chuckled, then slipped back to serious. "Just like I prayed for her…and Mom."

He looked at his infant sister with a gentleness in his eyes, and for a moment, Stephanie thought he looked more like a father than a big brother. She could imagine her own father holding her in much the same way.

A dad? In a way it suited him, but Stephanie wouldn't tell him so. Not yet. She held on to his arm and let him talk as they continued down the path. Will needed some help with the docks this morning.

"What do you think happened to the miracle everyone was praying for, Steph?"

The question didn't surprise her. She'd wondered herself over the past month, more than she cared to admit to her parents, perhaps more than she cared to admit to herself. But she *had* wondered. After all the prayer meetings, all the people on their knees, all the well-meaning Christians who had written to say they believed God would provide a miracle… It had sounded so encouraging at the time.

"Your mom's healing, you mean?"

She was stalling and she knew he could tell, but he nodded as if he understood.

"I'm not yelling at God anymore, I guess," he said.

"Did you ever?"

"Are you kidding? All the time. Especially when I was on duty. I would tell Him exactly what I wanted Him to do, and then when it didn't happen, I gave Him all kinds of grief."

"I know it hasn't been easy."

"No. I wore my game face a lot. My combat face."

She studied him, wondering. He had the nicest smile, when he did smile. And those eyes... "That face—do you still wear it?"

He bent his head and touched his sister's nose with his own, Eskimo-style. Then he shook his head slowly. "Not since she was born, not anymore. But I still wonder."

She let him talk.

"I mean, everybody in the church was praying for a miracle, weren't they? You were convinced."

She nodded.

"It just seemed like a logical deal," he said. "A no-brainer. Like God would get my mom through the pregnancy, and then she would get some kind of reward. He wouldn't let her die. Wouldn't that have been perfect for all the talk show attack dogs and the magazines and the newspaper columnists?" He raised a hand, as if framing a tabloid headline. " 'Lunatic Idaho Woman Healed!' You were right. That would have been perfect."

The headline faded in a moment of silence as Michael dropped his hand and his gaze.

"If God had asked me," he whispered, "I would have voted for that kind of ending."

"Me too, Michael," Stephanie said without hesitation. "Your mother was special."

As soon as she'd said it, she realized how trite her words sounded. And while the sentiment seemed to satisfy him, it still didn't answer his question.

"Yeah, but I still don't know what happened to that miracle we were supposed to get."

Stephanie didn't mind the question except that she wasn't close to finding an answer, either. Why did everyone always think she was a theologian?

"I guess..." she answered, not knowing what she would say, "I guess you're holding the miracle in your arms."

thirty-eight

———— ❧ ————

Isaac brought her into the tent of his mother Sarah, and he
married Rebekah. So she became his wife, and he loved her;
and Isaac was comforted after his mother's death.

GENESIS 24:67, NIV

A hh!" Will jerked his hand away from the gas pump as fuel spilled over the back end of a fishing boat. He grabbed a rag out of his back pocket and wiped up the spill, thankful the owner had stepped into the store to buy some drinks. He replaced the cap on the blue and white Bayliner.

"Better start paying more attention," he lectured himself.

But he couldn't turn it on, just like that. Half the time, he felt like he was a zombie, hardly awake, hardly alive. Was this what life would be like from now on, without Merit?

He hurried back to the counter, rang up a candy bar and a six-pack of Coke for the man, and gave him change for a twenty.

"Free gas?" The out-of-towner grinned at him from under a thick mustache. "I mean, if you don't want me to pay for it…"

"Right! Sorry, hold on." Will trotted back out to the gas pumps to check the total, then hurried back in. By that time, two other customers had lined up to buy chips, Popsicles, and a map of the lake. He tried not to appear overly morose, and finally the bell on the door tinkled as they left.

Merit hung that bell. Will let himself tear up, then swiped a handkerchief across his face. The strong smell of gasoline nearly made him gag.

"Whew!" He reeked like a gas pump, so he tossed the handkerchief into a nearby trash bucket.

Watch it ignite, he thought. *Or me.*

It was nice to be busy, but busy and klutzy at the same time didn't work well, even after reading all those how-to books. Maybe he should just lock the door, hang up the Gone Fishing sign, and crawl back into bed. But even the sign reminded him of Merit, who used to hang it in her kitchen.

Besides that, Merit had planted all the flowers by the front porch. Should he tear them out?

Merit had painted the wall in their bedroom hunter green. Should he paint over it?

And Merit's perfume still scented his pillow, faintly but distinctly. Should he turn out the lights, pull the covers over his head, and cry all over again?

He couldn't get away from Merit's ghost—even if he'd wanted to. Instead, he rolled in his pity like a dog in the grass.

One thing he knew: it wasn't like it always was anymore, and it would never be again. He'd done plenty of wallowing since they'd buried Merit, but still the casseroles came every couple of days like clockwork, as if the women of the church were going to feed him and Michael and the girls for the rest of their lives. He supposed they should enjoy the lasagna and tuna helper while they could. He was certain it was all very tasty, and if he'd been at all hungry, he might have eaten some instead of dumping his portions down the garbage disposal.

Which he still needed to fix.

His choice of an on-the-job dinner wouldn't meet with anyone's approval. But what was wrong with a package of past-date peanut butter cookies and a large helping of dip-style corn chips, washed down with Diet Dr Pepper?

"Are you eating that junk food again?" Stephanie pushed in through the glass door, little Sydney riding snugly on her arm. "That's where your son learned it."

Michael followed right on their heels.

Will tried to sweep the peanut butter cookies off the counter, but she'd already seen them and pointed to the evidence.

"How was your walk?" he asked.

Stephanie wouldn't be distracted. "Fine. But you'd better not let any of the church ladies see you eating that stuff. Don't they bring you enough food?"

"More than enough," he mumbled, brushing at crumbs. "Be sure to tell them thanks again for me."

"Maybe you should tell them yourself."

"Well, I do, when they bring it."

"No, I mean at church. I know we're not Lutherans, but you still need to give us a try. Michael likes our services."

"Yeah, Dad," Michael agreed. "It's not what you think. You'd like it."

Mike had extra incentive, and Will didn't blame him. Merit had thought a lot of Stephanie too, because she brought a bit of sunshine with her wherever she went—like now. She handed Sydney to him while she checked the cash register.

"Should we surprise them at church?" he asked Sydney in a soft voice, walking around the store with her in his arms and recognizing without a doubt his wife's sparkling blue eyes. He nearly had to look away. But his precious, costly little girl smiled up at him, and for the first time he knew—he really knew.

"Your momma did the right thing, sweetheart." It was a whisper between just the two of them, a covenant. "Someday I'll tell you all about her."

When he looked back at Mike and Steph, the answer seemed obvious.

"Maybe this next Sunday." He meant it this time, though he wasn't quite ready to admit out loud that he needed something more, something like Merit always used to have. Everybody knew she'd been the one to believe and accept, even when things looked bad or when God seemed to have other plans.

But he couldn't piggyback on her faith anymore. Wouldn't want to anyway. And he was tired of running on empty.

"Is your dad preaching, Stephanie?" Obvious question, but it kept the conversation going without sounding too needy.

"Every Sunday morning, if we can get him back from fishing in time."

Will smiled. "Yeah, I see him head out early these days."

Michael walked around the store, nose upturned, sniffing the air. "You smell that, Dad?" he asked.

"Gas rag." Will pointed his thumb toward the trash can, and Michael followed the odor.

"Whoa, better get rid of that thing. Don't want to set the place on fire. You know, spontaneous combustion." He crossed his arms and turned toward his dad. "Smells like you managed to spill gas all over yourself too. Better let Steph take the baby for now, and maybe I should handle the pump this afternoon."

"Be my guest."

They walked out together while Stephanie set Sydney in a crib behind the counter, as Merit might have done. She walked the trash can out the door, waved it in their direction, and set it down on the dock. Michael waved back that he would take care of it.

"Think she might be a keeper?" Will asked as they passed a Fish and Game poster on fish species in Lake Pend Oreille.

It was a dumb question, but Michael flashed him a quick, shy smile as they walked down the dock toward the boathouse, the kind he wore when he scored a basket and glanced up at his parents in the bleachers. Just a flash of teeth and a little Michael Sullivan sparkle of the eyes, nothing more. Will hadn't seen that smile, though, since Michael had returned from the Middle East.

"A keeper? Now you're talking like an Idaho guy, Dad."

"Think so?"

A pair of noisy Canada geese fluttered just ahead of Jake Halliday's J24, sails snapping to attention before an afternoon breeze. Jake never used his outboard, saying there was no challenge in it. The geese didn't seem to care one way or the other.

"Yeah, I guess you are." Michael stopped for a moment and looked back at the store. "But, Dad?"

Will knew what his son was going to ask, but he waited just to be sure.

"How did you know you were going to marry Mom?"

That explained the look back toward the store, the way Mike and Stephanie held hands, their long walks in the woods. He smiled a little inside. Mike couldn't do much better.

"I almost didn't," he answered, "on account of her crazy family."

"No kidding? You mean like Aunt Sydney–crazy, or another kind of crazy? How come you haven't told me this story before?"

"Never seemed like the right time. But her parents were even worse."

"I heard a few things, but…"

"They were the original hippies, your mom liked to say. Hippies before there were hippies…"

He couldn't help smiling as he retold the story and they continued to the boathouse. As they talked, he tried not to see Merit in Michael's eyes or in the gentle way his lips turned up in a smile. Tried not to, but did.

And for the first time in his life, he realized he'd forgotten his son was adopted.

His heart still ached just as much as it had last month, just as much as it did when Merit made her decision months before that, but when he rested a hand on Michael's shoulder, the heartache softened just a bit. And when he had finished his story, they stood watching the sailboats cross paths out in the bay, listening to the rustle of sails as they flew across the blue water, and the shrieks of Abby and Olivia as they chased each other down the docks.

"Your mom really loved this place."

"I know she did. She loved a lot."

Will didn't mean to look back at the store window, but when he did, he caught Stephanie watching them, holding little Sydney in her arms. The little Sydney Merit had only been able to hold a precious few times before…

Michael was right. Merit did love a lot.

"Glad you're back, Mike," he told his son, mussing his hair. "Glad *I'm* back too."

Michael didn't duck the way he did when he was a kid. He let his father muss all he wanted.

"So am I, Dad. So am I."

acknowledgments

This story was inspired by the true-life news account of Rita Fedrizzi, a forty-one-year-old Italian woman who found out she had cancer at the same time she learned she was pregnant with her third child. When I read a newspaper article about her some years back, I immediately tore it out and saved it for my story idea file.

And sure enough, Fedrizzi's courage provided the basis for Merit Sullivan's dilemma in this story, though their situations weren't entirely the same. Characters in this novel do, however, mention Fedrizzi by name, and I have tried to honor her example.

I am also indebted to the people of Bayview, Idaho—who may recognize portions of their town in the fictional location of Kokanee Cove. Remember, though, that this is fiction, so as an author I've enjoyed the freedom to mix and match real settings with, well…what I've made up. What is *not* made up is the rugged beauty and warm heart of this part of the country.

As always, I could not have written this story or anything else without the love and support of my wife, Ronda. I could go on, but you get the idea.

For God's glory,
Robert Elmer

More rich stories of love, faith and sacrifice by Robert Elmer.

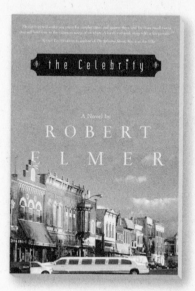

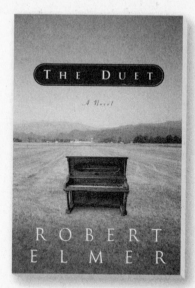

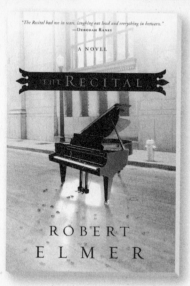

To learn more about WaterBrook Press and view
our catalog of products, log on to our Web site:
www.waterbrookpress.com

WATERBROOK
PRESS